DARKNESS EMBRACED

A ROSSO LUSSURIA VAMPIRE NOVEL

What Reviewers Say About Winter Pennington

"Pennington's novel is a fascinating look at the werewolf and vampire cultures. *Witch Wolf* is a rollicking story told with a wry sense of humor. It's an engaging read that leaves the reader asking for more."—*Just About Write*

"[Witch Wolf] is a nice mix of urban fantasy with police procedural/murder mystery. If Pam is your favorite vampire on *True Blood*, you're going to love Lenorre."—*Rainbow Reviews*

Raven Mask is…"an engrossing read involving vampires, werewolves, and some very hot, kinky sex and excitement!" —*Just About Write*

"I really enjoyed the story and the characters were wonderfully written. I'll definitely be picking up the second in this series!" —*Bibliophilic Book Blog*

Visit us at www.boldstrokesbooks.com

By the Author

Witch Wolf

Raven Mask

Darkness Embraced

DARKNESS EMBRACED

A ROSSO LUSSURIA VAMPIRE NOVEL

by

Winter Pennington

2011

ISBN 10: 1-60282-221-2
ISBN 13: 978-1-60282-221-4

This Trade Paperback Original Is Published By
Bold Strokes Books, Inc.
P.O. Box 249
Valley Falls, NY 12185

First Edition: May 2011

CREDITS

EDITORS: VICTORIA OLDHAM AND CINDY CRESAP
PRODUCTION DESIGN: SUSAN RAMUNDO
COVER DESIGN BY SHERI (GRAPHICARTIST2020@HOTMAIL.COM)

Acknowledgments

I debated not writing acknowledgements for this book. How many people really want to read an author gushing on and on about people they don't even know? I thought to myself, "Who should I acknowledge?" And then it occurred to me. I was looking at it the wrong way. Instead of, "Who should I acknowledge?" it's more like, "Okay, who might want to hunt me down if I don't acknowledge them?"

So here are the people that aided me during the process of writing this book:

My parents, Rebecca, Calvin, Desiree, Dee, Tiffany Pennington, Radclyffe, and my editor, Victoria…a very big thank you goes out to you.

You can take me off your naughty list now. Though I'm sure after reading this book, you might be tempted to put me back on it.

Dedication

To those beautiful souls, you know who you are.

PROLOGUE

England, 1810

Life and death placed a wager and my body was their playing ground.

Sleep would not come.

Having been bedridden for too many days to keep track of, I grew restless. It was not a restlessness of the body, for my body was sore and weary from fighting the long battle.

I was wasting away, pale and bird-thin, with Death's kiss lingering like half moons beneath my lashes.

She would take me slowly, this merciless lover.

I needed to feel the cool night air against my skin. The room was stuffy, suffused with warmth from the glow of a bedside lantern. Having a room of my own had at first been a pleasant respite. Now, the walls silently mocked me like the bars of a prison. They confined me. The solitude was a painful reminder of my failing health.

The others would not come near me unless they had to.

I forced myself out of the bed, fighting the cutting betrayal of my body. I slipped my feet into a pair of slippers and retrieved the thick woolen cloak from the armoire, sluggishly settling it about my shoulders. Ironic, that I would take such a precaution given my condition.

Most certainly, if I was caught leaving the cage of my bedroom, let alone the manor house, I would experience the verbal chastisement of my aunt, who made a fairly convincing warden.

I no longer cared.

The condemnation of death has a way of teaching one about such things.

The opinion of my aunt and her household were of little importance to me. If it was the last time I would see the light of the full moon high above, so be it. I wanted it.

I grabbed the lantern from the bedside table and set about making my way through the house. It wasn't so difficult to do. I'd been a housemaid in my aunt's care long enough that I knew the place.

The bolt on the door slid with a quiet click.

The night air pierced my lungs like a blade, sharp and cramping. I headed in the direction of the woods, a place I often went to be alone with my thoughts. Each step of the way, my body protested from weeks of inactivity and abuse. My ribcage felt eternally bruised, beaten by the persistent fits of coughing that had plagued me for weeks.

Each day, the coughing grew worse. Each day, the invisible vice around my chest tightened.

Inevitably, the illness would consume me as it had my father. With every second that passed, the weight of Death's hand grew heavier.

I clutched the cloak to my body, following the spill of lamplight with slow and careful steps.

I was nearly to the woods when the sound of hoofbeats carried like quiet thunder through the night. A handful of riders burst from the woods on horses as fast as hellions.

I stood there dumbly, too scared and weak to run. The lantern trembled in my grasp. One rider rode forward on his mount, and the lamp's glow illuminated his pale face and sharp features. He set heels to his horse and the lantern slipped from my fingers. Reality came crashing down a little too late.

Strong hands gripped my waist, tearing the ground from under me.

❖

The sound of heavy iron clanking startled me awake. With it came cries of alarm and desperate sobs. Somewhere in the room a woman murmured a frantic prayer.

I dare say none of the noise quite compared to the roll of nausea that turned my stomach. I moved, only to find that my hands had been inconveniently bound behind my back. I managed to sit up, leaning back against a corner of the cell when a spill of light flooded the room, blinding and painful.

I forced myself to breathe past the pain. I'd spent weeks feeling as if my lungs were being cut out of me. A little headache was not so much compared to that. When the light was no longer blinding, I recognized the tall man with the sharp, hawk-like features. His long brown hair shimmered like polished wood in the low light. He pointed at two girls huddled in a corner of the cell and two men, one with red hair, the other black, swept past him.

The girls tried to hold on to each other when the men pulled them apart. They screamed, sending the subsiding pain in my skull back to piercing. If my hands had not been bound, I would have covered my ears. As it was, I huddled in the corner, wincing, and praying for them to make the girls quiet. Perhaps it was crude and selfish, but in that moment, all I wanted was for the pain to stop.

The girls were taken from the cell. Their screams ended, though the quiet sobbing and frantic prayers did not. A man crawled out from an opposite corner of the cell, beseeching the man with the hawk's nose with his upturned face.

"Please, sir," he begged in a raw voice, "I have a family."

Hawk-nose ignored him, turning his attention toward the door. I followed his somber expression.

A woman appeared in the doorway in a gown of exquisite white silk, striding into the room like a bright beacon, casting a glorious light into the dark hell of my prison. Her hair tumbled to her hips in waves like those of a black sea.

"This is all?" she asked in a voice that was languorous and sweet.

"Sì," hawk-nose said. "We seek your permission to hunt again on the morrow."

She spared a cold glance out over the cell, completely overlooking me where I huddled on the floor.

"You have it," she said.

The man that had begged hawk-nose hobbled forward on his knees. His blond hair was dirty and stubble showed at his chin.

"Please, great lady, I have a family to provide for," his words sped up, "mouths to feed. Please, great lady, whatever you do, spare me."

She turned her attention to him, giving me the marvelous view of her frosty profile.

"As do I," she replied in a voice as cold and unmoving as winter.

He continued to beg. She turned, ignoring him as much as hawk-nose had. Her fine silks trailed across the stone floor.

I inhaled and a fit of coughing seized me. Something thick threatened to block my airway. I bent at the waist, unable to stop the wracking cough. The pain blossomed behind my ribs, spreading out across my torso like angry claws.

I held my breath, trying to control the cough when at last it won.

I didn't need to see my face to know that bloody sputum had trickled out across my lower lip. I could taste the metallic tinge of blood in my mouth.

Short of breath and dizzy, I willed myself not to fight the pain. The more I fought it, the more it hurt.

I felt the brush of cloth against my mouth and jerked away, shoving myself against the wall.

The eyes that met mine were not one solid blue. They were the blue of a midnight sky flecked with shards like a bright summer day.

"Severiano." Her voice carried through the cell, making me shudder, making my pulse leap frantically beneath my skin. She touched my cheek, and I fought not to flinch. When I didn't, when I had no more room in which to huddle, she brought the dark cloth up and wiped the rest of the blood from my lips.

I frowned, not understanding that small act of compassion.

"This girl is sick," she said. "Have the Cacciatori become such lazy hunters as to prey upon the weak and unwell?"

Hawk-nose gave a small bow at her side. "We did not know that she was sick, Padrona, only that she did not run. We did not think anything strange of it."

She folded her slim fingers around the black handkerchief. Her other hand rose to cup my chin with cool fingers. I shivered.

"Is it true?" she whispered, eyeing me intently. "You did not run from the Cacciatori?"

I made no reply.

She leaned back on her heels. "What is your name?"

"Epiphany," I whispered.

"Epiphany," she said as if tasting it. She tilted her head. "Severiano."

"Sì, Padrona?"

Her fingers tickled down my cheek.

"Bring her to me…unharmed." With that, she stood in all her white glory and left.

I swallowed, feeling as if I would choke on my pulse.

❖

Hawk-nose went to the door, speaking in a language I did not understand. When he returned and clutched my arm to drag me to my feet, I didn't fight him. The dark-haired man that had helped take the two girls stood by the door. Hawk-nose shoved me in his direction, and I stumbled, tripping over my own feet and falling.

Someone caught me.

"She said unharmed, Severiano," the man said.

I really was unwell, for he had moved fast enough that the wave of nausea threatened to return. I swayed on my feet, held upright only by the man's arm around my waist.

I was going to be sick.

"I know that, Dominique."

"Then learn how to follow orders," said Dominique, keeping me from toppling over. "Are you all right?" he asked me.

"Does it matter if I'm not?" I retorted, rather boldly given the situation.

The world swayed and he cradled me in against his bulky chest.

I met his blue-gray gaze. "I'm already dying," I said. "If you think you can scare me more than the death I face, you're wrong."

"You're not dead yet, piccolo," he said, carrying me out of the room. "If you want to keep it that way, keep your mouth shut and do as you're told. There are things far worse than death in the Sotto."

"Sotto?" I asked, eyeing the stone walls illuminated by torchlight. "That is this place? The place Hawk-nose has brought me?"

"Hawk-nose?" he asked.

"Uh, you know, the man with the nose," I said, gesturing at my face.

His laugh rumbled against my body.

"Our Queen may like you very much, piccolo."

"Queen?" I asked, thinking furiously as he turned down a hallway. "The woman in the cell was your Queen?"

"Yes."

"Who are you?"

He stopped. "If the Queen of the Rosso Lussuria has chosen you, you will know."

"Chosen me for what?"

"You will see."

"You are vague," I said, teeth chattering with cold. "Has anyone ever told you that?"

"And you're very brave for a girl that has been taken from her world and brought into ours."

I forced myself to smile weakly. "I've had some time to become fairly well acquainted with the idea of my death."

"Not yet, you haven't," he said cryptically.

"Dominique." A voice as thick as syrup rumbled through the hall. I noticed the way he greeted the other man as if he knew him well. Dominique turned on his heel. When he turned, my stomach turned as well. I groaned, cursing my fragile body.

"Dante," Dominique said.

"A bath has been prepared for her, at the Queen's request."

Dante wore a black tunic that looked a little outdated for our age. I frowned, thinking on it. In fact, neither of them appeared to be Victorian gentlemen. A lock of hair fell over the side of Dante's face, obscuring it from view.

Dominique nodded and started following him.

"I have legs," I protested. "I can walk."

"I'll not have you cracking your skull for the sake of your pride, piccolo," Dominique said.

"Who gives a wounded animal a bath before they put it out of its misery?" I asked.

Out of the corner of my vision, I saw Dante glance back at us.

"How am I to die, then?" I continued rambling. "In much the same manner as those two girls the both of you dragged from the cell, I imagine."

"Has she been babbling the whole time?" Dante asked.

"She's feverish," Dominique said, moving toward him. "Untie her hands."

"You think that's a good idea?" Dante asked.

"She is sick. She does not care."

I felt his fingers plucking at the knot, tugging it free.

Once I could move my arms, the pain in my shoulder blades multiplied. Dominique steadied his arm around me, holding me out from his body enough to draw the cloak off his back.

"Here," he said draping it over me and settling me back in against his chest.

"Thank you," I murmured closing my eyes against the dull throb in my head.

I felt his legs working as he walked. I was focusing on the rhythm of his steps when the exhaustion pulled me under.

❖

"Epiphany," a woman's voice spoke my name.

I tried to think past the cloudiness in my head.

Candle flame sent a dancing light throughout the room. A sea of black velvet stretched above me. My head finally made sense of what I saw, a black canopy. I sat up with my heart pounding in my ears.

A hand touched my shoulder, guiding me back to the mound of pillows. "You are in no immediate danger," she said.

I thought it had all been a strange fever dream. I met her striking and binary colored eyes.

"Where am I?"

"In my bedchamber," she answered, propping her elbow on the pillows beside me and resting her jaw on her hand.

"May I ask why?"

"You fell asleep," she said. "Dominique, my guard, brought you here."

"For how long?" I asked. She was the most beautiful woman I had ever seen. Her brows were dark against her pale skin, dark and arching. Her lips were fleshy and sensuous, made for kissing and tracing with fingertips.

The thought sent my nerves to tingling.

"You slept for a few hours," she said, calmly watching me.

I covered my mouth with the back of my hand and sat up, coughing against the tickle in my lungs.

I groaned as the tickle turned into that damned bruising pain. When I drew my hand away, there was blood on my skin.

I tried to take another deep breath and winced.

"Epiphany," she said. I took the kerchief she offered.

"Why are you being kind to me?" I asked.

She shrugged as much as her position would allow. "Why not?"

"I watched a man beg you for his life and you treated him as if he did not matter." I set about wiping the blood off my hand. "Yet, here I sit, not begging for my life, and you show me compassion. Why?"

"How old are you?" she asked.

"Twenty-four years of age," I said. "Why?"

"You are young," she said, reaching out and brushing a damp lock of hair out of my face. "Too young, I think, to feel death's touch so soon." Her fingers brushed the curve of my ear. A strange feeling fluttered at the bottom of my stomach. "Sleep," she said. "We will speak more after you have rested."

I closed my eyes. "You have not told me your name."

"Renata." Her breath tickled my lips and I looked up. She smiled, inches from my face, holding the length of her body above mine.

"Renata," I whispered, "you do realize that my body is being taken by the consumption?"

The low laugh she gave was like silk and velvet. Her eyes sparkled. "Ah well," she said in a silky tone, "you've not yet been consumed."

Before I could speak, her hand slipped to the back of my neck. She pressed that sensuous mouth against mine.

I had been kissed before, when I was much younger. I had been kissed by a girl before too. When I was a child, my friend Abbey and I had been playing blind man's bluff in the parlor of my father's estate. I'd gotten exceptionally good at catching her whilst wearing a blindfold. Abbey had a bad habit of giggling. Once, when we were nine, I caught her and she caught my face in her hands and kissed me, slipping her wriggling tongue inside my mouth.

Thankfully, none of my father's house ladies were in proximity of the parlor, or both Abbey and I would've endured a thorough scolding.

This was so very different. Her lips parted against mine. Unthinkingly compliant, I opened to her. My hands trembled slightly at her shoulders.

Her tongue slipped past my lips, spilling slowly into my mouth.

It was nothing like the way Abbey had kissed me.

Renata kissed me as if she meant to drink my soul from my body. If I had any thoughts, her mouth erased them. I found myself returning the kiss, as if it were natural, as if I'd done it more than once. I felt the tips of her canine teeth gliding across my tongue and paid no heed of them.

Her kiss superimposed the tide of pain, masking it with pleasure.

When she broke it, I was panting, mind boggled. My body no longer felt real.

She licked her lips and smiled, revealing small, pointy canines.

"What are you?" I breathed.

"Your salvation, if you agree. I'll return on the morrow's eve."

"Agree to what?" I asked, but she had disappeared, leaving me with a fierce ache that burned between my legs.

In time, I slept.

True to her word, she returned the following evening wearing a gown of black velvet that laced between her breasts. Long sleeves trailed from her wrists, offering glimpses of blue taffeta nearly identical to the midnight blue in her eyes. Again, I was reminded that she seemed not to embrace the modern and ridiculous fashion of crinoline and corsets.

"If you are a queen," I said, watching her light several candles around the room, "where is your crown?"

"I've no need of a crown," she said idly.

"That's a rather odd thing for a queen to say."

She sat on the edge of the bed. "Power rests within," she said, "not atop one's head."

"You are not like the others who are afraid to come near and catch my disease."

"I am not like the others who can catch your disease," she said in a manner of matter-of-fact tone.

"How is that?" I asked.

She stood, changing the subject. "Do you feel well enough to bathe?"

I remembered Dominique's words. *If she has chosen you.* A part of me wanted to question her until she relented, but a greater part of me knew intuitively she would not relent until she chose to do so.

A bath was drawn and an attendant summoned. The attendant was a girl that appeared to be some two or three years younger than I was. She was gentle and quiet, with hair the color of dark honey. She kept her triangular face lowered while helping me into the tub. The water was warm and the waves of steam felt terribly good to my aching lungs.

I placed a hand on the edge of the tub, sitting upright while she poured rosewater in my hair and attempted to scour my unruly curls with some vigor.

She rubbed oil into my skin, and although it smelled better than lye, it was unfamiliar and I recognized only the mild smell of mint.

"What is that?" I asked.

"It will help you breathe," she said and I recognized the French accent to her words.

It cleared my nasal passages but set my throat to itching. Once the oil was washed from my skin, I felt cleaner and more alert than I had in a long while. I toweled off with a bath sheet while the girl procured clean garb, holding open a white flax-linen chemise that she slipped over my head. The nightgown was in pitiful condition, soiled with sweat and dirt. In the low candlelight, my skin was visible beneath the white folds of the chemise.

"It does not leave much to the imagination, does it?" I asked, looking at her.

Her eyes flicked briefly to mine before she moved behind me, using the bath sheet to wring the excess water out of my hair.

"It fits well enough," she said.

True, it did fit.

"What is your name?" I asked.

"Justine."

The weight of damp hair fell against my back.

"Why am I here?"

There was a long pause filled with silence. Finally, she said, "That is not for me to say."

I emerged from the bath to find the room beyond warm and heated by a brazier. Renata sat on the edge of the bed, gazing off into the distance. When I entered, she turned her head slowly to look at me.

That one look made me stop.

"You wish to know why you are here," she said, rising. She stopped in front of me, close enough that I had to tilt my head back to look up at her. She was a good head taller than I. "If you were offered a second chance at life, would you take it?"

It was a strange question, and I did not comprehend why she asked it. I only knew by her visage and the tone of her voice that she was not jesting.

"There is no cure for what ails me, lady."

"Ah," she said, lips curving, "but there is."

One moment I was gazing into the blue fragments of her eyes. The next I was falling into them, drowning in waves that crashed in my mind and thrummed against my skin.

Ensorcelled by her, rationality left me. A carnal hunger sang through my veins, kindling a fire between my legs.

I knew the kind of aching fervor that had nothing to do with illness and everything to do with want and need and the dire urgency to feel her bare skin against mine.

I pressed myself against her, molding the lines of our bodies. Her lips found mine, parting. Our tongues touched and I fed at her mouth. Her hands branded my skin, resting at the base of my spine. A flood of strange longing spilled from betwixt my legs, dampening my thighs.

She drew away, breaking the kiss, breaking her spell.

I cried out, falling to my knees on the rough floor.

A great void nipped at the edges of my being.

I was crying and shaking and did not know why.

"Epiphany," she said, her voice rendering a spark in the void. I raised my chin to look at her.

"Do you begin to understand?" she asked.

"What are you?" The question spilled from my mouth in a breath.

Her eyes glistened with amusement. "I am the one mortals pray their Gods will keep them safe from."

Her words made me think past the void. "And when they pray, whose side are you on?"

She smiled. "Neither."

"There are stories," I said, "stories of demon-women who crawl into one's bed at night."

"Shall I crawl into your bed, Epiphany?" She closed the distance between us, touching my hair. "Would you have me climb atop your body and show you pleasure such as you have never known, such as no mortal lover can give you?" I turned my face into her hand, unable to resist the call of her skin. She traced my bottom lip with her thumb.

"What have you done to me?"

"This." She trailed her hand down my throat, causing my eyelashes to flutter. I leaned my head back, arching into her touch. Her hand continued its steady descent, sweeping across my breast. My nipples stiffened like tiny dart tips against the chemise. "This is your own doing. I no longer hold you in thrall, and yet"—she caught my nipple between her fingers, sending a shock of pleasure and shame through me—"you sway at my touch."

She jerked the chemise out from under my knees, raising it. Her fingers traced the dampness at my thighs, and without thinking, I opened to her.

Those fingers slid across the lips between my legs and I gasped.

"You are a virgin, no?"

Whatever she was, it did not matter. She parted me, brushing those fingers against the source of pleasure between my legs. Her fingers circled me, sweet and slow, summoning waves of honey and ecstasy from my withering body.

I cried, albeit silently, joy and sorrow spilling down my cheeks. "Yes."

She drew her hand away and the void returned, threatening to crush my heart.

"Epiphany," she said, lightly touching my shoulders and coaxing me to her, "come here."

I went as she pulled me into her lap, arms encircling me. She stood and I wrapped my legs around her waist, feeling the fall of her silken hair against my face.

"What are you doing?" I whispered, knowing full well we were moving toward the bed.

Her reply, when it came, was a whisper. "Making you mine."

God help me, I wanted her to.

Chapter One

America, Present Day

The air hit my lungs like inhaled fire. No amount of practice or centuries of experience could stop this. It felt like I was dying, but I wasn't. I was waking. Although my body protested, I knew in my mind that I couldn't die.

I was already dead.

I tried to think past what felt like a blowtorch being held against the inside of my chest.

It was always like this at first.

Then, the hunger, that damned gut-wrenching hunger hit like a fist. I doubled over as it sang through my veins like barbed wire. My hands clawed unwittingly at the silken sheets.

Death, it was always death, baying at my heels like some ghostly hound.

The intensity of the pain was mind numbing.

A voice called from deep within my chamber, "Good evening, Epiphany."

I turned toward the voice, gazing at the black and leather clad figure that stood stoically at the end of my bed. Vasco often dressed like he was about to attend one of those human BDSM play parties. His long hair was braided neatly in what must've been a hundred little serpentine braids. There were threads of silver tinsel twined intricately throughout each braid. I knew that if there had been any light in the room it would've reflected off each thread, making him look like some gothic fallen angel with a twisted halo.

"Vasco," I said, voice strained as I waited for the pain to neutralize. "What are you doing in my room?"

He spread his arms out fluidly, like some bird of prey ready to take its flight. "Our Mistress calls and I obey."

"Put the chivalry back in its little lace box." If I had been human, my breath would've steadied as the pain began to mellow. As it was, my head was clearing.

I got out of the large four-poster bed. The silk sheets and silk gown I wore helped give my body an added graceful slide.

Vasco strode to the corner of the room. His knee-high boots were silent against the carpeted floor. A light sprang to life between his fingers as he lit the only oil lamp. I preferred the dark but didn't complain. The mirror behind it sent a flickering flame dancing throughout the entirety of the room. The pain in the center of my body had subsided, but not by much. Instead of the sharp pain it had been, it was now becoming a dull and persistent ache.

I watched as he leaned his tall frame against the wall, crossing his legs at the ankles. He was waiting for me.

"Vasco…" I let the suspicion cloud my tone. "What's going on?"

"Tonight is the night, colombina."

I gave him a sullen look.

"Are you ever going to stop calling me that?" I asked. "A dove I am not."

His lips broke into a wide grin. The grin was wide enough to show the elongated canines curtained behind his lips. Vasco was probably the least dangerous of the Elders, at least toward me. He was also the most androgynous Elder in our clan. In the years that I had been with them, I had heard but a few that were brave enough to call him childish names behind his back. In all honesty, I think most of the male Elders envied him, for Vasco was comfortable with not only his femininity, but with his sexuality.

"You're a dove of peace to my soul, colombina. You need to ready yourself," he told me.

"I'll dress once you tell me what's going on."

He sighed and let his arms fall down to the sides of his body.

"How she forgets this night is coming is a mystery to me," he said talking to the ceiling.

"What night?" I was about ready to throw one of the pillows at him if he didn't start talking. Why some of the other vampires made it a habit to be so vague all the time I'd never understand.

His azure gaze held mine. "Your challenge, Epiphany, your test."

"Oh. After two hundred years the mind forgets," I murmured kneading my temples with the tips of my fingers.

"Ah," he said, "but you knew this night would arrive."

"Did you tell her that I have no desire to become an Elder?"

His shoulders rose in a shrug. "Unfortunately for you, colombina, it does not matter what you desire or do not desire. Our Queen has given you the gift of immortality. Thus, you are obliged to stand amongst her ranks."

"As a henchman," I said, "and only that if I pass her tests. She will not allow us to strike out on our own."

He pushed off the wall, quick in the way that vampires are quick. One minute they're there, the next they're not. I took a subconscious step back.

I hated it when he did that, when he used his speed against me. It was always a reminder. Granted, it was a very subtle reminder that there were others that were stronger and faster than me. I knew why he did it. I knew that Vasco put me in my place for a reason. It wasn't cruelty. It wasn't necessarily even a power play. He never told me why. He didn't have to tell me. I just knew.

Vasco wanted to see me stand on my own two feet. When the rest of the Rosso Lussuria was either cruel or cold to me, Vasco had become my friend and in some respects a mentor. Just like any good friend and mentor, he wanted to see me succeed. Then again, the random thought that it was a lot like a mother bird shoving the baby out of the nest before it's ready also occurred to me.

There were times when you either sank or soared.

"You know what happens to a vampire that breaks the binds of clan," he said.

"They are declared Il Deboli," I whispered. The Weak. Being declared Il Deboli meant that any other clan within the territory could slaughter another vampire in our modern world caught without a clan's aid. It took extreme measures in vampire society to keep the peace. We were a selfish lot, an arrogant lot, and most vampires left to their own devices had a tendency to go on some major power trips. There was nothing that would bruise a thousand-year-old vampire's pride more than having to share territory with Il Deboli. This was why the society was carefully established. Only the strongest and most powerful of us held a throne within each clan.

Therefore, if the need arose, each clan had a leader that could knock any naughty little vampires silly. Beneath the throne sat the Elders, which Vasco was among. The Elders were the voice of the clan as a whole. Underlings did not have much of a voice. We served those more powerful.

Ultimately, true power rested with the Queen. Yet, the Elders were granted courtly privileges that we were not. Underlings were to be unobtrusive, to go about tasks quietly, carefully keeping our eyes averted. The only time Underlings would raise their gaze was when they were directly spoken to. To do so when you were not spoken to was to challenge another.

"Sì," he said and the sadness in his tone made my heart ache.

One of Vasco's powers was that he was a master at projecting his emotions onto another.

Unfortunately for me, I was a master at absorbing those emotions like a sponge. Empathy, they called it, the ability to read and sense the emotions of another. If I had not already come into my power before I turned two hundred, I would not be offered the chance to become an Elder. Powers were a finicky thing; some vampires gained them and some did not. Yet, among the Rosso Lussuria, a vampire had to have power in order to protect herself. If you did not, you were automatically at the mercy of someone who was more powerful. For nearly a hundred and fifty years, Vasco's friendship had given me a measure of protection from the Elders.

I shook my head, as if that one small gesture would shake off the emotions he'd projected.

"I don't know if I can do this, Vasco."

"Do what, bellezza?"

"You know," I said softly.

How could he not know? He, like every other vampire in the Rosso Lussuria, knew what I had once been. He, more than anyone, knew what such a trial would cost me.

"Her?" he asked.

I dipped my head.

He reclined against the wooden bedpost with a look of sympathy.

"You cannot keep avoiding her," he said. "It has been a hundred and fifty years, Epiphany. You are in the full bloom of your powers. It is your right to take a seat among us Elders." Things were serious when he used my name and not one of the many nicknames by which he called me.

"I know how long it's been, Vasco. I am not unaware of the time that has passed or of my power."

"I do not understand why you would hold on to memories that will only hinder you."

I swallowed past the knot that tightened my throat. He didn't understand, not completely. He knew full well what I had become when our Queen cast me from her bed. He had seen the wreckage of me, then. It had been one hundred and fifty years, and still, I feared facing her. Even with Vasco's protection, I'd deliberately avoided her. She was our Queen and my Siren vampire. But she had been so much more to me.

Once, she had been everything.

It was rare that Underlings were forced to attend open court. So for years I had succeeded in avoiding Renata. When I did see her, a place inside me that I thought numb and empty ached beyond all reason, beyond thought. If she spoke to me, I kept my words short and politic and tried not to reveal how much merely a look from her sent my limbs to trembling.

I did not want to see her. I did not want to stand before her in open court and see the place where I once knelt by her throne.

Even now, the memories were crippling. If only I did not enjoy the rush of pain so damnably much. Well and so, Renata had cast me aside like a broken toy that no longer entertained. I was no longer her plaything, no longer the Queen's pet...

"Epiphany," Vasco said calling me back from the dark place of my emotions. "You must do this for yourself."

"Get out," I said. "Let me dress."

"I do not desire you, colombina. You may dress in front of me." He sat on the side of my bed with a small flourish, making himself at home.

My brows went up. "We are not one another's type, Vasco. I know this." I paused and added, "Yet, I also know that you want an excuse to see what is in my closet."

Vasco's eyes widened. I think he tried for a look of innocence, but all he managed to do was show off the brilliant blue of his irises. The Gods themselves must have personally declared that his eyes would be the blue of the clearest ocean. Poseidon, perhaps.

"Pity, pity." He pouted a little too pretentiously. "I do look dashing in women's clothing."

The corner of my mouth twitched from the effort it took not to laugh. There was more than one reason Vasco and I got along.

"Damn you," I said, laughing, "get out."

He made it very difficult to succumb to a dark and brooding mood.

I blinked and he was suddenly on his feet. "It wouldn't hurt to dress to kill."

This time, there was something almost vicious in his smile.

Was it vicious or vindictive? I couldn't tell. Maybe it was both.

"Thank you, Vasco." I nodded in the direction of the door.

He gave a sweeping bow. "I will await you in the hall."

I stood there for several moments, feeling the pangs of hunger, feeling the dread unraveling like some great basilisk in the pit of my stomach.

I relaxed, putting my forehead against the closet door. Vasco had said I'd known this night would come, and I had. I knew that one night she would call me to stand before her. I knew that this night would come, that I would be forced to either conquer the challenges ahead of me or be conquered by them. I would fail and remain an Underling for eternity, or I would rise above and possibly, just possibly, get a little respect from the rest of the clan. The newest vampires, most of whom were Americanized like me, were condemned to be someone's dog for two hundred years, even if they came into their powers early. Those were the rules. Thankfully, being "undead" for two hundred years taught one a measure of patience.

The question I would be forced to answer was: In the past two hundred years, had I gained enough power to overcome whatever challenges lay ahead? Was empathy a power strong enough? I should have been happy. I should have felt eager to jump at the chance to prove myself, to become something greater than what I'd been for the past two hundred years, but that dread began flicking its little forked tongue in my ear.

If I became an Elder, I would sit with her again. Mayhap, not so close as I once had. I would not kneel like a loyal bitch beside her throne.

I would have a small throne of my own, but I would always have to see her.

So be it.

In all the years that Vasco had sheltered and protected me from the cruelty of the other Elders, he could not save me from this. Two hundred years as an Underling, as being treated as a common vampiric whelp, and I feared I was starting to believe it.

I wrapped my palm around the doorknob. If I could run away, far away…would I?

I searched inside myself for the answer.

No.

If there was one truth to my damned existence it was that being someone's bitch for two hundred years was getting old. One cannot constantly live in the fear of potentialities. There comes a time when you realize it is not so much fear that you have to conquer, but the self from which it springs.

CHAPTER TWO

Having experienced my own death, you would think I wouldn't be afraid of anything. Yet, there are certain emotions and instincts that are not so easily erased from the mind, immortal or no.

I wore red, red like freshly spilled blood. There was a long strand of white lace that crisscrossed up the front of my torso, tied securely, holding the dress closed. Vasco was just outside my door, leaning against the stone walls of the hallway as if it was all oh-so-boring to him. A smirk crooked the corner of his mouth.

I held my arms out with my palms up and did a little turn. "Well?"

"Hmm," he murmured, "you're going to wear a dress?"

I pulled the skirt of the dress up to reveal the white leggings tucked into my knee-high boots. "I am wearing pants underneath, Vasco."

"Ah, well," he said, "that makes it a bit more practical."

The look in his face changed.

I tilted my head. "What? What's the look for?"

"Colombina, I have to check you."

"Check me for what?"

"Weapons."

I laughed. "Oh. Good grief! Where in the world would I hide a weapon in this dress?"

He shrugged. "It's mandatory. Turn, face the wall, legs spread…"

Vasco's mouth erupted in a fierce grin.

"I bet that's the first time you've ever said that to a woman."

I did what he asked. I turned, faced the wall, and placed my feet evenly spaced. "Get it over with."

Vasco glided forward. He didn't take his time about it. If I had been a male, and a pretty male at that, his hands might've lingered. Fortunately, they didn't. It wasn't personal. Vasco might not have liked women, but I did and I didn't like men touching me just as much as Vasco didn't like having to touch a woman. We were on the same page in that book. His hands trailed the curves of my torso, down my legs, sweeping inside my skirt.

His hands were between my knees when I knew he'd felt my body tense in discomfort.

"Colombina, be thankful that it is I doing this and not one of the others…"

I rolled my neck, forcing myself to relax as his hands continued their upward sweep. "I am thankful."

He did a series of quick pats near my inner thighs. I was grateful it was Vasco. I didn't trust one of the other Elders to touch me. Who knew what kind of liberties they'd try to take? It's a shame sometimes that we try to be so civil. There were a few Elders that I wouldn't mind driving a sword through.

I felt more than saw Vasco stand. "Turn."

"Wondrous," I said, turning. He was going to pat down my front.

I felt his hands gliding over my stomach, a second before I realized his hands were hovering above my breasts. It appeared as though he wasn't sure what to do.

I started laughing.

"They don't bite, Vasco."

I leaned forward, wiggled a little to get the material to give, and then held my breasts up. I didn't flash him, just showed him that there was nothing hiding in my cleavage. "See, no dagger. No shotgun. No wooden stakes." It was my turn to grin. "Call me skeptical, but I don't think an AK Forty-seven would fit in there."

"Epiphany, you are being cruel and have been reading too much for your own good." He crossed his arms defensively over his chest.

"Perhaps I have been reading too much," I said, "but I am not being cruel. I just think it's amusing, is all. You should be thankful that I'm not a lover of men, or one of the female Elders that wouldn't hesitate to try and take liberties."

"They would not dare," he said in voice gone cold and dark. His tone was cold enough to drain the heat out of the sun.

I went still.

"I'm sorry," I said. "I shouldn't have teased you."

"No, you should not have. I am just thankful I do not have to touch them." He actually shuddered.

"If I hadn't teased you, you would've forced yourself to check and make sure I wasn't hiding anything. Which is why I did what I did. Sorry, Vasco, but neither one of us wants you to feel me up."

"For that," he said jokingly, "I might praise some form of Divinity."

I made a little "hmph" noise in my throat. Vasco didn't really believe in anything, to my knowledge. I wasn't sure what I believed. Oh, I believed in some form of Divinity, in some kind of Divine. The Big Bang theory really didn't explain how I was capable of dying every single dawn and waking the following night.

He turned and looked down the torch lit hallway as if someone were talking to him from the other end of it. I knew there was no one there. It was just Vasco and I.

"We need to go."

"Vasco," I said trying to disguise the uncertainty in my voice with blankness, "what are the challenges?"

His hand lifted as he thoughtfully touched one of his tiny braids. "Epiphany, I cannot tell you. Our Queen has not given me permission."

"Do you think I will succeed?"

He shook his head. "I do not know." His hand touched my shoulder. "I wish that I could offer you some words of comfort, colombina, I really do."

I crossed my arms over my chest. "I know."

I started walking down the hallway. I didn't have to look back over my shoulder to know that Vasco was there. I may not succeed, but one thing was sure. I needed to feed, and soon. We walked in silence, following the lit torches that led to the banquet hall. A spill of lamplight, much brighter than the torches, flooded out from the double doors that were held open by one of the lesser vampires. His long blond hair hid his face from our view. I bowed my head in acknowledgement as Vasco and I entered the room and found a seat among the tables.

It was a large room, with several rectangular tables in the area closest to the doors. The cloth on the table was black. I did not know if the black was chosen because it gave the room a dreary feel, or because blood doesn't show very much. There were wine glasses placed neatly at the end of black placemats.

Renata was not here. Thankfully, she did not feed with the rest of the clan. Vasco chose a seat and I followed. I felt the Elders watching from their segregated table. He had chosen a spot away from everyone else. No doubt, the Elders were not happy with his decision. I sat beside him. There was a small flamed heater built into the table, as there was no electricity within the Sotto. Running electricity underground wasn't a good way to stay unnoticed by the humans that surrounded you above ground.

The nearest city was Bolivar. Though most of us had not seen it. We stuck to wooded areas, living in underground tunnels and chambers that were made centuries ago by mortal slaves.

When the beginning of our kind spread out across America, they saw it necessary to establish kingdoms where we could live in secrecy but at the same time find sustenance. It was necessary for us to reside where mortals could not find us. This was why we executed Il Deboli. Their non-allegiance and solitary ways often ended up drawing attention to our world and existence. It was a measure of precaution for the sake of our kind.

Why did we not live openly? There were a few vampires throughout our history that had been brave enough to step out of the shadows. Those that did so were met with resistance and persecution. In England, before the rise of modern medicine, some humans considered the consumption to be a form of vampirism and persecuted those that were only ill. That was a bit of irony. The humans waged their holy wars and hunted any vampire brave or foolish enough to attempt life above ground, as well as innocents, until the belief in our existence faded entirely and we became nothing more than the whisperings of folklore.

Even now, in this modern day, too many humans were quick to hate and condemn that which they feared and did not understand. I did not have to be an active participant in their society to perceive as much.

For a couple of years after I was made, we had stayed in the Sotto in Devonshire. It wasn't until Renata decided to relocate the entirety of the Rosso Lussuria that we made the long and troublesome journey to America.

Vasco smiled and reached across the table for the earthenware pitcher that was set off to the side of the heater. "The elixir of life," he said, "still fresh from the Donatore's veins."

"It seems to grow richer with the centuries. Perhaps we are feeding the Donatore better?" The taste was ruby gold in my mouth, and I could see Vasco thinking the same thing as we sipped in silence.

"Perhaps. Or maybe the humans are healthier before they come below." Vasco shrugged, clearly unconcerned with how our dinner came to be.

The Donatore were humans that lived among the Rosso Lussuria, though they had their own separate quarters and were rarely seen.

The Rosso Lussuria and Donatore had an agreement dating back thousands of years. They were willing victims, consenting to feed our kind in exchange for certain powers of their own. There was a way to prolong mortality, to give the humans a taste of our strength and heightened senses without actually killing them and bringing them over. Humans afraid of death, or humans who craved power, were the ones who stayed with us.

A drop of vampire's blood to a human was a powerful thing. It made the Donatore stronger, faster, immune to illness and disease, and harder to kill than other humans. They were not as gifted as true vampires, but with each month that their contract was fulfilled and their duties served, a drop of our blood was given in exchange for theirs. If one of the Donatore were to break the agreement, he would be condemning himself to death, for without our blood, most of them were old enough that their youth would fade and they would die quickly. I, who had once been the Queen's pet, knew this, for I had seen both parties extract their payment.

The Donatore were not our only blood source. Each clan had an elite group of hunters respectively known as the Cacciatori. It was not only their fellow mortals that humans should fear when wandering unaccompanied during the night. Many years ago, parents told their children stories of our kind. Though the stories might vary, from depicting the Cacciatori as a roving hoard of demons to depicting them as the dark and magical figures of the Wild Hunt, the stories had been used for centuries as a warning. Yet, as warnings often go, some were unheeded.

It was the Cacciatori that had taken me from the human world. The Cacciatori were the only vampires granted permission to venture outside of the Sotto. The humans they kidnapped were either slaughtered or given the chance to become Donatore. For safety reasons, the humans being considered Donatore were not offered an ultimatum between death or service. Given a choice between the two, the human would choose service out of the possibility of life and might turn against the Rosso Lussuria at some point or another—it was purely survival instinct to choose life. They were not informed that if they refused to serve, they would die.

But, neither were they made vampires. It was exceptionally rare for the Donatore to be brought over, as it was for a human to be brought over when taken from the human world. We thought of it as population control. Fewer vampires meant less competition for power and fewer to feed.

Vasco set about pouring us both another glass. When the crimson liquid met the brim of the glass, he handed it to me. My nostrils flared slightly.

The blood was rich, like something velvety on my tongue. I wasn't aware that I'd swooned into Vasco until I felt his arm drape across my shoulders. I watched him for a moment and drained my glass. It would take a few glasses until the thirst was quenched, until the hunger was satiated.

I'd lost count of how many glasses I'd had. By the time Dante approached, I was still basking in the glow of having fed, gazing languidly at the room. He stopped in front of our table, crossing his arms over his chest. It occurred to me that the gesture wasn't meant to be one of intimidation, but as Renata's personal guard, intimidation was his forte.

"Epiphany," he said, voice deep like something thick and sticky. His dyed red hair was cut short in the back and longer in the front. A fall of red side-swept bangs veiled his right eye in shadow. If it were me, I would've either grown the hair out so that it could've been tied back or lost the bangs. The bangs would ruin his peripheral vision if he was not careful in a fight. He wore a leather vest over a white frilly shirt with a bunch of lace at the neck and wrists. The shirt should've made him look softer, but the leather seriously clashed with it. His black leather pants had silver studs tracing the outline of his legs. At six foot five, Dante was the kind of guy that could snap me in half. I didn't hate Dante, not like I despised a few of the Elders. I didn't know Dante enough to hate him, but he was Renata's bodyguard, and that alone made me wary of him.

"Epiphany?" he said again, this time with a questioning tone to his voice.

"What is it, Dante?"

"The Queen would like to see you." He'd called her Queen instead of Mistress, which meant he was trying to be formal.

"Then," Vasco said as he stood, "we will follow you."

Dante shook his head. "She wishes to see Epiphany alone."

"Well, damn," I said casting a glance at Vasco.

Vasco gave me a sympathetic look. He knew I wouldn't want to pay Renata a visit. It wasn't just that I was scared of her. No, I had other, more complicated reasons.

CHAPTER THREE

D ante might as well have been leading me into the inferno. The hate I kept trying to convince myself to feel was swept aside in a tide of nervousness and fear. I kept my arms crossed over my chest, trying to feel secure in myself and failing. I was too nervous. After fifty years of love and passion, the past one hundred and fifty seemed void and meaningless.

I followed Dante to a door at the back of the banquet hall. He held it open for me, and I entered the narrow room beyond. The small room led to one of the many winding hallways within the Sotto. Yet, it'd been years since I'd been in this area. The torches flickered as we passed to emerge into a long, narrow hall with two heavy double doors at the end of it.

Have mercy. If I didn't think Dante would pick me up and haul me over his shoulder kicking and screaming into that room, I might've tried to slip away. Worse yet, I didn't know what kind of reaction Renata would have. She was the Queen. I couldn't exactly refuse to meet with her.

Dante placed three solid knocks on the door before opening it.

He held it open and waited. I didn't move to step through the doorway.

"Enter, Epiphany," he prompted me in that deep voice.

If he was trying to scare me, he was failing. There wasn't anything in that moment that scared me more than stepping into that room. Dante was downright adorable compared to Renata, or maybe that's just how I felt.

I stepped into the room.

"Epiphany," her voice was so sweet, so soft, and so hauntingly melodic. It brought back too many memories, memories of her words in my ear, of her mouth sliding hot across my skin.

I hated her for it.

I went to my knees. "Mistress."

It is strange to say that for a vampire of her age Renata rarely liked to be called Queen. In open court with all of the clan assembled, she did. Which is why, unless we were all being formal, most of us just called her Mistress. Though some of the Elders made a habit of calling her Padrona, the Italian equivalent.

The soft glow of candlelight sent shadows dancing across the floor. I kept my eyes lowered, watching as the edge of her shadow drew near. I felt her touch on the back of my neck and shivered.

"It has been too long," she said.

Unsure what to say, I was silent.

"Epiphany," she said, "look at me."

I raised my head obediently.

I knew what I would see, knew what she wanted me to remember.

Her beauty made my heart ache. Her hair tumbled to her waist, rich and black, except when the light caught her tresses…

I shut my eyes to block out the sight of her, remembering the candlelight flickering on her hair, picking up the dim midnight blue highlights.

"Renata," I whispered. "What do you want?"

"To see you."

"Why?"

"Is it your place to question me, Epiphany?" Unlike Vasco, Renata had years of practice to perfect the English language.

I bowed my head again. "No."

"No. Come here, Epiphany."

I didn't want to go to her. She moved to sit on the edge of her bed, watching me with a remarkable intensity. It wasn't just her eyes that were fascinating. It was the force of her personality burning in them that called to me.

She put a hand out and I took it. Her skin was warm as she twined her tapered fingers with mine.

"It bothers you to touch me?"

I averted my eyes, not because I had to, but because it hurt too much to look at her. The memories sang through me, piercing my insides like sharp and invisible thorns. "It reminds me."

I could tell she was smiling when she said, "Of something that transpired a hundred and fifty years ago."

"I know."

"And yet"—she trailed her other hand down the side of my body—"it feels as if it were just yesterday."

It wasn't unusual for Renata to tease me, but this time there was something different in it. She'd never actually touched me after sending me away. There were looks and words, but it was always so subtle. Other times that I'd been in her presence, there had always been someone with us, whether it was Dante or Dominique or an Elder.

Now, we were alone. For the first time in over a century, it was just her and me.

The realization unnerved me.

"Renata," I said trying to pull my hand away from hers.

She didn't like that. Her fingers dug roughly into my skin as her other arm hooked my back. She held me closer.

"Renata," I said again trying to move back while she barely even broke a sweat holding me captive. She was older and was my Siren, which meant she was stronger.

"Stop," I pleaded, vainly trying to wriggle free.

She laughed. "Oh, you do play the captive well, Epiphany. I'd nearly forgotten how well." She gave another fierce jerk and I lost my balance. My hands caught her shoulders as she pulled me down into her lap. I used the grip I had on her shoulders to try to hold myself away from her.

She smiled brightly, her eyes lit with humor like the moon lending its light to the darkened sky.

"Epiphany," she said grabbing a handful of my gown and inching it upward.

My heart was pounding. One of the side effects of being well fed was that my heart was about to beat its way out of my chest like some trapped and angry bird. That bird was currently hitting my ribcage. I gave up trying to hide the panic.

Renata licked her pale lips, eyeing the tiny drum in my neck.

Distantly, I heard the whimper that fell from my mouth. It sounded weak and pathetic, but I didn't care…that look on her face.

It had been so long since she'd looked at me like that, since I'd felt the line of her heat so close.

I shut my eyes, digging nails in where my hands clutched her shoulders.

Renata gave a little satisfied moan that ended with a laugh.

"Surely"—I pushed on her shoulders—"this isn't a part of your test."

"If it is?" Renata asked, pinning me to her with that one long arm. "Do you think you are strong enough to resist or evade me, Epiphany?"

Her hand swept between my legs, caressing the inside of my thigh with a touch as soft as a feather's brush.

"Answer me, Epiphany." Her breath was warm against the side of my neck.

I couldn't move. I froze. If I moved, it wouldn't be away from her. If I moved, I would've offered my neck to her. She was my creator, my Queen, and had once been my lover. It was an intimate thing, the sharing of blood between vampires, and I had spent too many years knowing the joy of her mind and body to be able to forget it.

"No."

She laid a gentle kiss upon the pulse in my throat.

The muscles in my body clenched tight as I battled a century's worth of memories.

"You couldn't, could you?" She squeezed my thigh over the leggings, whispering in my ear, "So tense…more tightly strung than an archer's bow."

"Why are you doing this?"

Renata's distracting hand moved to my hip, her thumb playing over the jagged bone. "I have missed you."

"You should've thought of that before you cast me out." I glared at her, at her damned beautiful face.

For a moment, I thought I had startled her, that I'd shocked her by having the courage to say such a thing. It wasn't courage. In part, it was stupidity, but mostly, it was anger. The anger tainted everything, all my qualms, all my worries. Any other emotions I had were suddenly paper thrown in a fire.

Her eyes darkened, and my anger was eclipsed by fear. If the anger had been fire in my veins, the fear was ice.

Renata grabbed a handful of my long hair and pulled until she exposed the long line of my neck. "Your blood," she whispered, and her fingertip traced the vein in my throat, causing my heart to beat faster against my skin, "is mine. You may have grown bold, but you are not bold enough to challenge me, Epiphany."

"I am not challenging you."

She touched my cheek and I flinched, looking away from her. Her thumb slid across my lower lip. "So much anger. I never knew that casting you from my bed would breed such resentment."

I felt it then, beyond the tides of my anger, a small wisp of remorse went through her. I never understood why she'd cast me out. I still didn't understand it.

"What did you think it was going to breed in me? Did you think I'd come groveling at your feet, begging for your touch, begging for one more night with you?"

"Yes."

I laughed then, bitter and sour. "You've always known me so well."

The room reeled in my vision. My back hit the mattress. Renata used her lower body and hands at my wrists to pin me to the bed.

I didn't fight her. If I fought her, she'd only overpower me.

She smiled softly, almost sweetly. "I know you better than you think I do, Epiphany. I can break your anger. You may show it to me, but I know what lurks beneath it."

"And what is there, Renata?"

"Love," she said in a silky voice. "You still love me."

"No."

"Yes."

"No," I tried again.

"Your anger is only a mask."

She bent at the waist, bringing our faces closer together, her hair an onyx canopy.

"Epiphany," she whispered against my cheek. "Do you miss me?"

Her lips brushed my cheek, seeking my mouth. I turned my head and forced myself to stare at the stone wall. "I don't understand."

"What is there to understand?" She tried to catch my mouth and again I turned my face away from her. Her fingers dug roughly into my jaw. "Look at me."

This time I refused, gazing fixedly at the stone wall. "You may be Queen, but you can't rape me. That is against our laws."

"Rape?" She said dryly. "Epiphany, you are fooling yourself. It wouldn't be rape, cara mia." Her hand slid down the front of my dress. I shuddered both at her touch and at hearing those words from her, words that were once spoken so deliciously. "Beyond this mask of protective anger, I know you are willing."

She started pulling up my dress.

"It would be," I said, watching her with a look that was probably more hungry and scared than angry and defiant. "As I have not given you consent."

"I am your Queen," she said, "your Siren. I do not need your consent."

"Now you are the one fooling yourself."

The skirt of the dress was bunched up over my hips. The tips of her fingers slipped beneath the waistband of the leggings. "Oh no, Epiphany." Her fingers played under the tops of my undergarments. I tried to find that anger that had been such great aid earlier, and couldn't.

I didn't want to fight her. It was true. In some part of myself, I was willing, more willing than I wanted to admit. Every facet in me ached for her.

So many years, and the true battle was against my own feelings.

Her fingers dipped lower, low enough that I pressed myself into her touch.

"You may lie to yourself," she whispered, "but not to me, Epiphany. You may never lie to me."

She lowered her mouth and traced the line of my waist with her lips and tongue.

A sound close to a whimper escaped me.

I watched as her mouth opened, and knew what she intended to do before she bowed her head.

Her fangs pierced the skin of my stomach and I cried out at the fiery pain and pleasure. Her power fell over me like a warm cloak. I was cold, so cold, and only her touch could keep me warm. My blood filled her mouth and I writhed for her, writhed as her hands moved up my torso. She locked her mouth around the wound and sucked. I was floating, aware only of her mouth on my stomach, of my blood rushing out and into her, of her jaw working at me, of her tongue like velvet against my skin.

It had been a long time, too long. My heart ached for her, ached for this sharing. I wanted more. I wanted so much more. I wanted her to tear my clothes off, to take my will, to bend me to hers as of old.

In that moment, I would've done anything she asked.

Distantly, I heard the loud clatter of the door hitting the wall on the other side of the room, but I wasn't really aware of it. No, what I was aware of was the woman lying between my legs, of her tongue lapping at the two circular wounds she'd created. Her hands held my waist, and I was small enough that her nails tickled my back. The wounds were beginning to heal. I didn't want them to heal.

She drove her fangs into me again and my hands clawed at the sheets.

"Epiphany! My Queen! What are you doing?"

Was that Vasco?

Did I care?

It felt like something hit me. If I were human, I was certain the breath would've been knocked out of me. My body struggled to process what had just happened. I looked down at Renata and felt anger. No, not anger…rage. I didn't think. I acted. I grabbed a handful of her velvety hair and pulled.

I screamed as her fangs tore my skin.

"Epiphany!" It was Vasco. I heard him speaking in fast Italian. What he was saying, I couldn't translate for the death of me.

Anger. Fear. Panic. Vasco was panicking. I was feeling his panic as my own.

He grabbed my face and turned me to look at him. "Bellezza," he said. "Colombina…look at me."

"Look at me," Renata said and I couldn't help myself. I turned to look at her.

"Colombina," Vasco said in a gentle voice. I started to turn to look at him and Renata said my name.

Sharing blood had called to my power and they were playing tug-of-war with me, casting their emotions at my empathy.

Vasco's power pulsed against mine, like he was water and I the sponge. He showed me gentleness and protection, but when I turned to look at Renata she showed me passion and lust.

It was the latter my body craved.

"Vasco," I said and felt his hopefulness. "Let go of me."

His hope crumbled in my mind.

"No, colombina." He seemed so sad. Why did I have to make him so sad? Why was I so determined not to let him protect me? Vasco always protected me.

I grabbed his hands and screamed like a cat coming out of water. I thrust him away from me.

"Do not touch me!"

"I will touch you," Renata said, licking my blood off her lips. She started moving toward me. Yes, I wanted her to touch me.

"Epiphany!" Vasco yelled at me. "Fight her, damn you!"

I shook my head. "No, I don't want to."

Renata was getting closer. I reached out my hand, chest rising and falling in anticipation.

"Do not let her make you weak!"

Weak? I licked my lips, tilting my head. Did my desire make me weak?

"Am I weak?"

"No, my darling," Renata said. "You are mine."

Then Vasco did something.

An image of Renata and me lying in bed. Her nude body spooned mine. Her breath warm against my neck as she stroked my hair.

"It is not always weak to succumb," she whispered in my ear. "I enjoy you this way, Epiphany. I love that you trust me." Her fingers slipped between my legs as she began to part me.

Trust. She had broken my trust.

I tried to scream when I came back to myself, but I couldn't breathe. I was drowning. I pushed up off the bed, moving clumsily to the far side of the room. I probably looked as unstable and dizzy as I felt, but it did not matter. What mattered was that I got away from the two of them.

Vasco and Renata stared at me. Their power pushed at me and this time I pushed back.

"Stop it," I said. "Both of you."

Vasco's pupils returned to a normal size as he withdrew his power.

Renata's eyes were still swimming, like echoing waves calling me home. Somewhere in the back of my mind I could've sworn I heard the ocean roaring. "Epiphany." She moved to the edge of the bed and offered her hand. "Come back to me."

I took a step forward and stopped myself.

"No." I shook my head, hands trembling. "No, stop this."

I felt her power shift, like an invisible wave threatening to take me under. For the first time, I stood my ground, bracing myself against the tsunami of her power.

Her power receded, going back to the ocean from whence it came. I knew, without a doubt, that she could've forced me. Why she didn't, why she did not use that power to break my will, I did not understand.

"She would have failed had you not interfered." Her words were scalding as she turned to Vasco.

"No," he said, "She would not have, my Queen."

"She was already giving herself to me," Renata said. "You had no right."

It seemed a thousand thoughts flitted through Vasco's eyes. "This was a part of your test for her?"

Renata gave a very slow nod.

Vasco cursed and then asked, "Why?"

She gave me a considering look. "I wanted to taste her power. To see how strong she has grown."

If lying was a piece of candy, I was sucking on a really big piece of it.

"That's not all," I said.

Renata gave me a satisfied smile. It reminded me of the way she used to smile, like a cat teasing its helpless prey. "No," she said, "not all."

"What do you mean?" Vasco asked.

"It wasn't just to see how strong I've grown," I said, but my attention was all for Renata. "I felt your remorse. You meant what you said earlier." I didn't repeat her words, not in front of Vasco.

She considered me for a long while. "Did I?"

"Yes."

She turned to Vasco and a flicker of anger went through me again.

"Renata," I said and this time my voice was firm.

The look she gave me wasn't very friendly. "You have grown bold, Epiphany," she said. "But I am still your Siren and you will not talk to me in such a way."

"I hate you."

My words were like a spear that I wrapped my power around and threw at her.

Pain. As if my heart would burst. Fear.

I stumbled as Renata pushed me out too fast. She had so much more experience that it seemed all it took was a flick of her wrist.

"Do not try to read my emotions." Her eyes narrowed, darkening again.

She cared. There was some part of her that cared. I had not expected that. I'd expected her to get angry or to feel hurt, but not pain, not fear of what I thought of her.

I searched her for an answer. Renata turned away from me, as if she did not want me to find words written in the expression of her features.

"Why did you cast me out?" I asked.

"Because you no longer held my interest," she said and her words were empty.

"That's a lie. I don't have to be in your head to know that is a lie."

We stared at one another, until Vasco said, "If you were trying to challenge her, my lady, why didn't you pick someone that Epiphany would actually fight?"

"You loved me," she said and her voice wasn't empty this time. "You couldn't fight that."

"You set her up to fail," Vasco said, surprised. "You don't want her to become an Elder."

"I did not set her up to fail."

I laughed, but it wasn't a funny laugh. It was the kind of laugh you give when everything was going horribly wrong and there was nothing you could do about it. "No, you didn't," I said. "You set me up to stroke your ego. I won't fight you, Renata." I took a step closer to her, this time of my own will. "You've always liked that I didn't fight you."

"You fought me earlier."

I moved forward again, and this time I realized that the stone floor was cold beneath my feet. At some point during our little power play, I'd lost my leggings and boots.

"It's kind of pointless to fight you, Renata. Don't you think?"
"Why?"

"You are my Queen and my Siren. You were my lover."

"Once," she said.

"More than once," I said.

She gave a sly smile, eyes lit with remembrance. "True."

I felt the heat rise to my cheeks.

Her lips curved even more, noticing my blush. "That is why you do not want to fight me? Because of love?"

I started to smile and stopped myself. It wasn't her power; it was just the ridiculous effect she had on me. "Am I supposed to want to fight my Siren, my Queen?" I asked, very carefully avoiding answering her last question.

She sighed almost wistfully. "It is such a waste." She looked me up and down.

"You're the one that threw it away."

"I had my reasons."

"I'd love to hear them."

"No."

"Suit yourself."

The look she gave me was too complex to decipher. At last, she said, "You have changed, Epiphany."

"Is that a good thing or a bad thing?"

"I am not sure yet. I do believe that some of Vasco's confidence has rubbed off on you."

I smiled at that. "Well, he had plenty to spare."

She gave Vasco a displeased glance. "She is no longer the aching, trembling thing I once knew. You have inspired change in my Epiphany, Vasco."

"No, my Queen," Vasco said. "I have helped Epiphany bring herself into the light. This is the real Epiphany." He motioned at me with his wrist like a magician unveiling his assistant. "Do you not like what you see?"

Renata looked at me again and I fought the urge to fidget. "I have always liked what I see. I would not have brought her over and made her mine had I not," she said, "but I am not so certain this newfound confidence and boldness is beneficial to her. It makes her more difficult to bend to my will."

"Then stop trying to bend me."

"And what would I accomplish by doing that?"

"I'd be happier with you."

She laughed. "Happier with me? That does not matter to me, Epiphany."

"In some part of you, it does."

She wasn't angry this time, just thoughtful. "I told you to stay out of my mind."

"I can't help it," I said. "I feel you as if you are a part of me."

Renata nervously licked her lips.

My mouth hung open for a moment, words caught on the tip of my tongue as I stared at her. "*That's* why you cast me out," I said, the shock and disbelief making my words a whisper. "You saw my power. It wasn't because I am or was weak. It was because you were afraid of what I would see in you?"

She shook her head. "I do not know what you are talking about, Epiphany."

"I do," Vasco said, moving around the side of the bed like some deadly panther. "You cast Epiphany out because you didn't want her power letting her get too close to you. I knew you had the potential to be cruel, Renata. I never realized you were scared."

She seemed unexpectedly tired, as if the years were catching up with her. She rubbed her temples, much as I had done earlier. It was a strange gesture for her. "I never claimed to be cruel, Vasco."

"No," he said.

"You could've fooled me," I said without thinking.

"Once, you would have never spoken to me that way," Renata said.

"What do you want me to say?"

"I do not want you to say anything. I am merely pointing out a fact."

"Does my newfound confidence bother you?"

She seemed to consider it. "I am both proud and disappointed to see that you are stepping into your own."

I hadn't expected her to be that honest with me.

"But," she continued, "I worry for you."

"Why?"

"I do not believe you have the power to reinforce this newfound boldness."

"Do you speak truth, my lady?" Vasco asked.

"I do."

"You do not think that Epiphany will pass the other challenges?"

"No." She gave a soft shake of her head, tresses slithering around her like a cloak. "Which is why I needed to test her power myself."

"If she could break your hold she could break the others," Vasco murmured.

"Precisely."

"And I failed at that," I added.

"Quite dreadfully," she said with a little smirk.

I held her gaze, resisting the urge to go to her, to feel her arms around me. "Vasco has a point."

"What point is that?"

"You said you knew I wouldn't want to fight you."

"I thought that might be the case," she said tilting her head. "I was not certain."

"So now," I said, "I am beginning to think this entire thing is a manipulative ploy in order to deflate my confidence so that I do indeed fail. Yet, what you gain by my failing I cannot fathom."

"She has been spending entirely too much time with you, Vasco."

Vasco gave a slight bow. "I enjoy her time, my lady."

"You would," she said and there was some spitefulness in it. Spitefulness or jealousy, I wasn't sure.

"What does that mean?" I cut Vasco off before he could say anything.

The look she gave me was long and hard. I realized in that moment that she didn't like that Vasco and I spent so much time together.

I actually laughed. "You're jealous? You cast me out and now you're actually jealous that I found one person among the Rosso Lussuria to call friend?"

"I told you to stay out of my head, Epiphany. I will not ask you again."

"I'm not in your head, Renata. I'm in your heart. There's a big difference."

She closed her eyes and I wondered if she were counting to ten.

"You were never this frustrating to deal with."

"Everything changed when you cast me out."

"You act as if I completely deserted you, Epiphany."

"Didn't you?"

"Vasco," she said, "tell her."

He put his fist over his heart and bowed. "You made me swear an oath never to tell her."

She waved it away. "You are free of your oath. Now tell her."

"Tell me what?" I stepped forward, resting my weight on the pad of my foot.

"Epiphany," Vasco said, "she did not desert you."

I stared at him, uncomprehending.

CHAPTER FOUR

"Did you not think to question your friendship?" Renata asked.

"No. Why would I? Vasco has shown me kindness. I do not question that."

"He showed you kindness because I appointed him as your protector," she said. "I did not throw you to the wolves as you are so quick to accuse me of."

I wasn't sure I believed it. Vasco stood and didn't bother to say anything in his defense. "It's true, isn't it?" I asked in a voice that was almost a whisper.

"Colombina." He spread his arms out. "It is true."

I shook my head. "No," I said, "I don't believe you. You're both lying. I don't know why, but you're lying."

He moved forward as if to touch me. I whirled away from him before he even got close.

His eyes widened. "Colombina…"

I put my hands over my face. "No. How can it be true?" I glared at him. "You are telling me that this friendship…all of these years have been a lie? You've only pretended at someone else's command? At her command?"

"We are friends." His voice was soft as he reached out toward me again.

"Stop trying to touch me!"

He spread his hands again, but this time he was trying to make a point of harmlessness. "Look inside of me."

I stubbornly shook my head. "No."

He was quick, so very quick. His hands dug into my upper arms as he shook me. "Look!"

His power hit me and there was nothing subtle about it. Vasco didn't pour his emotions down my throat. He simply opened himself up and my power sucked it in like some great black hole.

Candles sent a dance of light and shadows across the room. I was kneeling on the familiar stone floor of Renata's bedroom. She regarded me from where she sat in the corner of her room, displeasure rendering her beauty even colder.

She said my name, only it wasn't my name.

It was Vasco's.

"My Queen." I bowed my head.

She bid me to stand and I rose, waiting.

"I have a task of great importance for you, Vasco. A task I am unwilling to place in the hands of any other but you."

"What is your will, my lady?" The words flowed smoothly, in spite of the niggling sense of unease I felt. I was afraid of what she would ask, but I was her creature. Whatever she asked, I would do.

"Epiphany," she murmured, features taking on a thoughtful expression as she traced the carved wooden arm of the chair. "Watch her. Protect her. See to it she does not fall prey to the Elders."

The unease left in a whoosh of air. "It will be done."

The vision changed, and I was suddenly in the banquet hall, leaning against the far wall. I saw myself, and knew for certain these were Vasco's memories I was viewing, not mine.

It is a strange thing, seeing yourself from the perspective of another. Vasco's thoughts clouded mine, making it hard to differentiate between the two. I knew this; he had known I had been Renata's pet. He had known I had been cast out, though he too did not understand why. He saw my vulnerability and felt, not pity, but compassion.

I watched and remembered, though I did not want to.

I moved as inconspicuously as I could through the tables, careful to keep my distance from the others. The dress I wore in his memories was modest, solid black, but the black brought out the paleness of my skin and the pale gray of my eyes. I have always been small, but the way I held myself made me appear even smaller, as if I was trying very hard not to be noticed.

I had been.

I felt Vasco raise his glass to his lips, watching and wondering.

The vision changed. My boots were silent against the stone floor. I walked down one of the lesser hallways that led to the library. It was odd seeing the Sotto from Vasco's height. There was a startled gasp and I turned on my heel, heading quickly in the direction of the sound. Someone groaned and I started running. I hit the bend at the end of the hallway.

"What's it like no longer being the Queen's favorite little bitch?" Lucrezia's voice sent a shiver of disgust through me.

"Lucrezia!" I said harshly. She turned, long auburn hair framing a round face with wide pale green eyes that were not quite sane. I agreed with Vasco's thoughts. I didn't think she was quite sane either.

"Vasco!" she said, surprised. "How nice of you to join us…"

Epiphany, my body in the vision, made another small noise of discomfort. I felt Vasco's emotions in that moment. He wanted to protect me, not because he was ordered to, but because what Lucrezia was doing was wrong.

Lucrezia kept my body pinned against the wall.

Her wrist twisted and there was another disturbing sound. I didn't want to think of the woman pinned to the wall as myself. It was both a blessing and a curse that I was reviewing the memory from Vasco's perspective. A blessing because I didn't want to remember that bitch touching me. It was a curse because I saw that when Renata cast me out, I had lost the will to live, to survive. It was there in my flickering eyelids, in the set of my mouth, the slack submission of body. It was a pitiful sight, and Vasco wanted to save me from it.

Lucrezia's cheek rubbed cat-like against the back of my mahogany hair as she cooed at Vasco, "Want to play?"

"Let her go."

"No, thank you." She smiled so sweetly and traced the lobe of my ear with her tongue. "Are you sure you don't want to play, Vasco? She's up for grabs now." She made a pleased noise low in her throat. "And so very tasty."

I grabbed the hilt at the back of my neck. My sword sang free of its sheath. "I will not ask you again, Lucrezia."

"Oh." She widened her eyes in a pretentious fashion that was undeniably Lucrezia. "Looks like our friend has brought a toy."

She moved and that was all it took to set Vasco over the edge. I knew from my own memories and personal experience that there were cuts high up between my shoulder blades, cuts Lucrezia dealt me.

From Vasco's memory, it was not so obvious.

The tip of my sword dug into the delicate skin beneath her jaw and I used it to push her back, following as she kept back stepping. "I'm stronger than you, Lucrezia. You don't want to play this game or any game with me."

She hissed at me around the blade digging into her chin. "You should have told me you'd claimed the woman as your bitch, Vasco! I didn't think she was quite your type."

I gave the sword a little push and a drop of crimson blood slithered down the steel. "Touch her again and I'll cut your heart out and feed it to you."

I withdrew my sword, wiping the blood on my tunic, and turned toward the girl…

I was suddenly on the floor staring up at Renata's ceiling.

"Epiphany." It was Vasco's voice. He touched my cheek lightly. "Epiphany?"

"I'm not quite sure, yet," I managed to say.

He helped me sit up, propping my back against his torso. "You wouldn't let me guide your vision," he said, as if he were in my thoughts and felt my confusion. "If you had let me guide it and didn't try to take control, you wouldn't feel like this."

How did I feel? I felt unreal and confused. I blinked. "Vasco…"

"Si?"

"Don't you ever do that to me again. For future reference, I'd rather stay in my own body."

His lips spread into a grin. "So I noticed."

I heard movement and turned to look at Renata. She knelt beside me, touching my forehead with nimble fingers. "I did not know you could project memories, Vasco."

"I cannot, my lady."

She gave him a questioning look. "Her?"

He nodded. "It seems Epiphany's powers of empathy only want to absorb. Her power doesn't care whether it is thoughts, emotions, or memories that it is absorbing."

Renata made a little, "Hmm," sound as her fingers tickled lightly down my neck.

"He didn't protect me just for you," I whispered, watching her.

"So I noticed."

Had she seen the memory?

Her hands found my shoulders and she started pulling me away from Vasco. His grip tightened around me for a second, I think, afraid of what she would do. I didn't have the energy or the will to fight either one of them. Renata gave him a look of warning and he let me go.

Her hands moved at my back.

"Turn around," she whispered the words against my hair and I shuddered.

I moved to my knees and turned. Renata opened the back of the dress and pushed it down off my shoulders. She exposed my back, touching the scar there. The knife Lucrezia had used had been silver, and though my body had healed, it had left two light pink scars like an angry X between my shoulder blades. One thing Vasco hadn't witnessed was that before he'd arrived, Lucrezia had told me she was going to carve the target on my back. She'd stayed true to her word.

The rage was a bitter and hateful thing in my mouth as Renata's fingers traced my scarred flesh. It wasn't my rage. It was hers. The muscles in my back twitched and jumped, as if my skin remembered the blow.

"Renata," I whispered.

It was like something hot sliding down my spine. I said her name again, through clenched teeth.

I turned and caught her wrists in my hands.

Vasco hissed and I knew it wasn't at Renata. He'd never seen the scar. I let go of her wrists.

"I thought," he said, swallowed, and tried again, "I didn't know she'd maimed you."

"I know," I said. "You were too late. You saved me, Vasco, but you were too late. The knife was silver."

Renata looked at him in one of those very slow movements. Her anger brought forth the blue topaz color in her eyes. "You never reported to me that she had been abused."

I wasn't looking at him as he repeated himself, "I did not know Lucrezia had maimed her."

"I am not maimed," I said, "only scarred."

Renata touched my cheek and I flinched.

I will kill her.

I gazed up at her and said, "I won't stop you."

I thought I saw a small flicker of surprise flit across her features.

"It seems you are right, Vasco. Epiphany's power seeks and it finds."

"Si," he said.

"It's never been like this," I said.

"I know. I believe that Renata not only tasted your power, but has, ah, given it a boost of sorts."

"With practice would I be able to read a person's thoughts whenever I wanted to?" I asked.

"I am not sure, colombina. Our powers are polar opposites. Where yours absorbs, I project."

I nodded; it was something I already knew.

"Some." Renata brought my attention back to her.

There was something in her demeanor that made me ask, "How do you know?"

She smiled ruefully. "It seems you have gained a power more similar to my own."

Renata explained while deftly tying the lace at the back of my gown. "Telepathy was one of the first powers I gained," she said. "I had no idea your empathy would be so similar."

"You can read minds?"

"Better than you can," she said, but there wasn't any arrogance in her tone. "I have had years of practice to read the thoughts of others and to project onto them what I wish them to feel."

I peered at her over my shoulder. I licked lips that were dry. "Have you read mine?"

"What do you think?"

That was unnerving.

I pushed the hair out of my face. "What will the challenges be like?"

"Difficult," she said. "I cannot make it any other way."

"What are they?"

"You will see."

"Why can't you tell me?"

She touched my brow. "It would be unfair and it would displease the Elders."

"You are their Queen."

"Even a queen has rules to abide by." Her fingers traced the line of my jaw. She stood in a fluid motion, her velvet skirts like dark water. My eyes followed the line of her body, the paleness of her shoulders beyond the sheer sleeves.

"There is a way to avoid all of this," she murmured thoughtfully.

"How?"

"Come back to me."

Her words pierced me.

The proposition was sweet, so sweet, and bitter. Why did a part of me enjoy that bitterness?

I lightly shook my head. "No," I said, "you cast me aside. I am not your pet anymore, nor do I wish to be. I will not voluntarily remain an Underling merely to be cast aside again."

"You do not realize what I risk by asking you to return to me."

"Oh?" I said snidely, "Pray tell, what great risk are you taking?"

"You think I simply tossed you aside, but your selfishness blinds you, Epiphany."

"I don't understand."

"No," she said, "you do not."

"Then tell me."

"I do not comprehend it myself, my Queen," Vasco said smoothly.

Renata moved fast, burying her hand deep within the tresses of my hair. She pulled my head back. Her lips were dangerously close to my cheek as she said, "Have you not wondered why Lucrezia wanted to torment you?"

"I thought she was a sadistic psychopath."

"There are those Elders that believe I played favorites."

"You are still their Queen," I said. "Our Queen. To harm you is a death sentence."

"A queen is not invincible," she said, hand traveling down the back of my neck, "just as neither you nor Vasco are invincible."

Her hand slid distractingly across my shoulder, fingers light and tickling. She touched my cheek again, and this time I turned my head so that my lips brushed her palm.

"You are our creator," I said against her skin. "You are more powerful."

Her thumb traced the line of my brow and I shuddered. It wasn't a sexual gesture, but the sensuality in the way she touched me brought goose bumps to my flesh.

I felt the loss of her.

I had felt it since the day she cast me out.

"Creator. Queen. Siren. I am but one vampire."

There was a wary knowledge in her eyes that made the breath catch in my throat, not from arousal, but fear.

"What haven't you told me?"

She looked away, withdrawing her hand. "I have told you nothing that is not of your concern."

I moved with her as she stood, catching her wrist. "Renata."

"Epiphany," she said, but she wasn't looking at me. Her voice was soft. "Release me."

I didn't and she said my name again.

"Bellezza," Vasco warned.

I shook my head. "No. I have spent the last two hundred years obeying orders. I have spent the last two hundred years huddling beneath the mantle of someone else's power, afraid that if I did not, someone would break me to their will."

Renata gave me a considering look. "I broke your will once."

I smiled sadly. "No, I gave you my will. There is a difference between what one freely offers and what is taken by force. I have huddled like a child for too long. I have been afraid to test my limits, afraid to embrace my abilities, afraid that they would not be enough. My greatest folly is that I have underestimated myself. I see that now."

She looked at me as if I'd sprouted a second head, not a disgusting one, but one that made her curious. "Are you sure this is not your doing, Vasco?"

"Quite sure, my lady."

"If you want me," I said to her, "then you will have to accept me as an Elder."

"There is a fine line between confidence and arrogance, Epiphany. Tread lightly."

"At times, one must test that line."

"Be wary that the line does not break," she said, "for if it does I will not have you at all."

"Are you saying that these challenges might kill me?"

"The challenges? No. The challengers? Yes."

Vasco was suddenly beside me. "That is not legal," he said. "A vampire that does such a thing forfeits their life."

"It is easy to forfeit that which you do not care about."

He opened his mouth, then closed it, opened it again. "You would let them slay Epiphany?"

"No," she said and touched my hair. "My punishment for such a crime would be swift, but I may not punish someone if I am unable to prove just cause."

"Are you saying they could make it look like an accident?"

"Of sorts, yes. There are fates far worse than death."

"Tell her," he said. "She needs to know. You need to prepare her. If there's one thing I've learned with Epiphany, it is that keeping her ignorant will not protect her, Renata."

She gave Vasco an unfriendly look. I shuddered where her hand had stopped in my hair. "Lucrezia will be among the Elders challenging you."

A knot of fear wrapped itself within my throat. I swallowed past it. "She will try to kill me?"

"After what I have seen of Vasco's memory," she said, "I would not put it past her."

"I thought you were going to kill her?" I asked.

She wound a piece of my hair around her fingers. "You will find with your power that what a person thinks and what they do are two different and often contradictory things. A thought in a moment of passion is blinded by emotion. I cannot slay her without a reason," she said. "If I were to slay her before you face your challenges, then the Elders will believe that I am going out of my way to protect you."

"So?"

"So there has been talk."

"Of what?" I asked.

Her look sank into my bones. "My death, Epiphany."

"That is what you would not tell me?"

She gave the slightest of nods.

My heart gave a fierce thump against my ribcage. I would not stand idle if they tried to hurt her. Despite being cast out and despite whatever reasons she had, I could not find it in my heart to sit back and watch her be assassinated.

"Oh, Epiphany," she murmured, shaking her head. "You cannot protect me."

"No," I said determinedly, "but I would die trying."

She touched my cheek again.

"Now it is I that does not understand you. Earlier, you seethed with hatred of me. Now, you are willing to lay down your life to protect mine? Is it that you accept my reasoning at long last, or that you have forgiven me so soon?"

When she said it like that...I didn't understand it myself.

"I do not know," I said. "I only know what I feel."

"Emotions are misleading," she said. "They are not a thing to die for."

"Love," Vasco said, "love is a noble thing to die for."

"The days of poets and knights are long gone, my Silver Prince," she said matter-of-factly.

"Look at the woman before you and tell me you believe that."

She did and what she thought in that moment, I could not say.

CHAPTER FIVE

I was sitting on the edge of Renata's great bed pulling my leggings back on. I didn't know exactly how I felt about Vasco implying that I was anything like a poet or a knight. Renata had left us with instructions. She'd given Vasco permission to tell me about the challenges.

"The challenges will take place over the course of seven nights," he said leaning against the bedpost. He watched me slip my naked foot into the first boot.

Thanks to Renata, I didn't have any stockings. It unnerved me that I couldn't remember hearing the thin material rip. I didn't have time to go back to my room to find another pair.

"What's tonight?" I asked.

"Physical," he said. "You won't face the more metaphysical challenges until the end of your trials. It will be the metaphysical trials you need to prove yourself impressive in."

"What about Lucrezia?" I tied the boot with a sharp jerk.

He rested his head against the bedpost. "That is something I have been giving some thought to. She is powerful." He paused and stood straight. "Did you taste her power when she…" He motioned at my back.

I shook my head. "No. She used brute force."

"She is a creature of fear," he said cryptically. "I presume she will be one of the metaphysical trials."

"Do you think she will try to find a way to kill me and make it look like an accident?"

"What do you want?" he asked.

I gave him a perplexed look.

"Truth, or would you like me to, as the Americans say, sugar coat it?"

"Truth," I said. "I need truth. I'm sick of cowering like some wounded puppy dog."

I tied the other boot off and stood, smoothing my skirts over the leggings.

"I agree with our Queen. I would not put it past her to try."

"And what happens if she tries to kill me and I kill her instead?"

To that, all he had to offer was a shrug.

I walked past him to the door that led back out into the hallway. He barred the way with his arm. "Colombina, you need to remember everything, absolutely everything I have taught you in the past. Tonight, you will have to duel with Gaspare. He is quick and light on his feet. Do not underestimate him or overestimate yourself. Be aware. The Elders are a tricky lot. If we can tiptoe around something, we'll do it."

"It is strange to hear you count yourself as one of them," I said.

"I am an Elder, Epiphany. You need to remember that now more than ever."

I touched the silver tinsel in his long black hair. "You are one worthy of the title," I said. "I always remember it."

"Good." He grabbed the back of my head and pulled me to him. I had a moment of panic before I felt his lips press against my forehead. "Show them what you're made of," he whispered, "show them the thorns hidden amongst your beautiful petals, bellezza."

We stood there for several moments. I was about to pull away when he held my face in his feminine hands.

I stared into those eyes and it was like gazing out over an azure ocean. Vasco bent his head, but not like he was trying to steal a kiss. He opened his mouth and breathed his power on me like some great dragon. I felt his power curling around my face like invisible smoke. I inhaled that power, drew it into my lungs, pulling its metaphysical essence up into my mind until it felt as if I would burst with it.

I saw sunlight glinting on metal. The sounds of steel against steel rang like some heavenly song in my head. I was light on my feet, quick and agile. I was fast. Gods, so quick! My father was a great warrior and king, and few in his realm could catch me. I knew when to push forward, when to fall back. I knew how to twist my blade and how to spot the weaknesses in my opponent's defense. It was why they called me the Silver Prince, the Sword King's son.

When I opened my eyes, Vasco's grin loomed in my vision.

I licked my lips, as if I could taste the knowledge and power lingering there.

"What did you do?" I asked, but this time I was quite aware of myself.

"A gift," he said. "Tell Gaspare I send my regards."

He turned and offered me his arm. I slipped my hand in the crook of his elbow. "I get this feeling he's not going to be happy."

He patted my hand. "He won't be. Gaspare never could best me in a fight," he said.

I laughed. "I could get used to this empathy thing."

"Sì," he said, "it beats the hell out of spending years trying to train you."

I nodded and hoped. No, I prayed. I prayed that the power Vasco had given me was enough. That I would not falter.

I had to beat Gaspare. I had to beat the others.

How was I supposed to defeat the others when they were all so much more powerful than me? I couldn't absorb everyone's power.

I had to stand on my own two feet.

I forced myself to focus on beating Gaspare one step at a time. If I worried about the others, especially Lucrezia and whatever mind tricks she'd pull out of her hat, I would only discourage myself.

Thorns.

It felt pretty much like a handful of petals to me.

"The Silver Prince?" I broke the long silence, cocking a brow in his direction as we walked arm in arm.

"Ah," he said, grinning. "That was a long time ago."

"Promise me something, Vasco. One day, if I survive these challenges, you will tell me your story and how you came to the Rosso. In all the time that I have known you, you've yet to share such things with me."

"You will live through this, colombina, and one day, if you wish, I will tell you a very boring story."

I laughed. "With a title such as the Silver Prince, I highly doubt it's boring, Vasco. It sounds a little peculiar, but somewhat adventurous."

"Then you've something to look forward to."

I smiled despite myself. "So it seems."

CHAPTER SIX

I dug my nails lightly into the bend of Vasco's elbow. Two guards standing like massive statues opened the mahogany double doors as we made our approach. The torchlight flickered in the spacious room beyond. There was enough light to completely illuminate the room, but even so, the shadows danced in corners like eerie specters.

At the northern wall was a row of small thrones reserved for the twelve elders. The eleventh and twelfth chairs were empty. One, I knew was Vasco's place. The other must've belonged to Gaspare.

Renata sat in a throne made out of some type of ebony wood. It was placed higher than the others, the back was high, and the arms were intricately carved and curling. Behind the fall of her skirts she was long enough of leg that her heeled feet touched the floor.

Vasco led me dumbly before her. He went to his knees and I followed.

"Padrona," he said in his court voice, a voice that was at once charming and untouchably cold. "I bring forth your scion, Epiphany."

"Vasco, rise and take your place," Renata said smoothly.

Vasco rose and only then did I take my hand from his arm. I forced myself to stare at the stone floor. If I looked at him I knew my expression would betray how I felt. I was afraid. I was nervous. I hated court politics, but if there was one thing I knew to be true, it was that you did not show weakness to those that would delight in exploiting it.

I sensed Vasco take his seat. It left me feeling suddenly and undeniably very alone. I raised my head enough to look at Renata.

A woman laughed and every hair on my arms stood on end. I didn't want to look at her, didn't want to see the face that went with that unmistakable laugh.

I turned and met Lucrezia's wild eyes, eyes that were the color of fresh spring grass. The bodice that cinched at her waist was a few shades darker. She smiled with lips that were as red as her flaming locks. "Greetings, Epiphany."

I forced myself to go completely still. I would not give her the benefit of a reaction.

"No hello?" Her red brows arched high. The look she gave me was predatory and amused.

I opened my mouth to follow the protocol of court etiquette when Renata's voice flowed like something lethal into the silence. "Lucrezia."

Lucrezia mouthed something. I think it was, "Good luck."

"Epiphany." I must've been staring at her because Renata's voice called me out of my thoughts.

I bowed my head. "Yes, my lady?"

"Do you wish to face the challenges?"

"Yes."

"Do you accept the challenge of a duel from the Elder Gaspare?"

"I do."

"Rise and choose your sword."

Dominique was suddenly by my side. He offered his hand to me, to help me stand, but I did not take it. Again, it would be another sign of weakness for the others to exploit. He went to the far wall opposite the thrones, flicking back a tapestry that bore a crest of a griffin on it. There were swords, so many of them. Broadsword, short swords, and twin daggers all gleamed in the torchlight like a deadly bounty. I didn't own a sword, and thus, I was forced to pick one.

I didn't want to.

I didn't want to handle a sword that had been handled before. I went to the wall, trailing the tips of my fingers over the blade of one of the longer swords. The swords had been taken care of, oiled and cleaned. I could smell the faint scent of the oil that had been used on them and knew that they had been cleansed very recently, probably in preparation for the challenge, but one thing they retained were memories.

My fingers faltered as a brief image of masculine hands gripped the pommel. The pommel sported the design of an eagle. I drew the breath in through my nose and moved to the next sword.

Cleansed or no, my powers of empathy were picking up on psychic impressions, memories that had been left behind that no cloth could wipe away. The swords seemed to whisper their histories to me. I knew Lucrezia's blade before my fingers even brushed the polished steel. It was a modest blade, medium length, with thin crescent guards. It reeked of blood and violence, of death and decay. I shuddered, drawing my hand away. I didn't want those memories.

It was a shorter blade that caught my attention. Despite its small size, it was the most uniquely crafted blade of the lot. Etched into the shining steel were patterns of spiraling vines, and curled around the pommel was a metallic fox, sleek and sly. I closed my eyes, touching the fox with tentative fingers, feeling its metallic body.

Empty. It was the first sword that was empty of memories. It would do.

Somewhere in the back of my mind were Vasco's memories, but I kept them pushed back, allowing what knowledge I needed to handle a sword to come through naturally. I took the sword down from the prongs that held it, wrapping my hand around the pommel.

"Is it done?" Renata asked.

Dominique nodded beside me. "It is."

"Vasco," she said.

I turned to watch as Vasco crossed the open area. He smiled faintly, but instead of coming to me, he turned and drew his sword. He lowered his blade, tracing an invisible circle in the middle of the room. The double doors clanged opened as a tall figure entered. His black hair was pulled back tight at the nape of his neck. I met his light brown gaze.

He strode into the room like it was his party, full of an arrogance that was not unknown to our kind. It had to be Gaspare. I'd seen him before, but never spoken with him. He wore a dark purple jacket with black lace at the throat. His hand lifted, fingers stroking the little black beard hanging from his chin. "A slip of a girl," he said, talking to himself. I ignored the comment.

"Inside the circle," Vasco said, "both of you."

"Gladly," Gaspare said striding into the midst of the circle Vasco was creating. I wondered how Gaspare managed to walk in boots that were heeled and went up to his thighs. The fashion seemed a little silly for a duel.

He bowed to me as I cautiously made my way. "Poor child," he said in heavily accented English. "Poor little rabbit in the wolf's den."

"We'll see," I said.

"Indeed!" His eyes lit with an inner flame. "We shall," he said and I heard the sound of steel sliding from its sheath a second before he rushed me.

CHAPTER SEVEN

G aspare was quick. He was almost as quick as Vasco, but I had Vasco's memories. I whirled backward, keeping my body out of reach as I dodged the tip of Gaspare's blade like it was second nature to me. I held the fox sword in both hands, driving it upward at an odd angle for defense. Gaspare's blade met mine in a loud clash of steel. The impact shook my arms. He inclined from the waist up, forcing me to widen my stance as I tried to hold him at bay.

"Hmm," he mused, "I wasn't expecting that."

In truth, neither was I.

Gaspare withdrew his sword in a move almost too quick to see. He tried to bring it down over my head. This time, I didn't bother trying to block his blade. I dropped into a low crouch, placed my left hand flat on the stone floor, and tucked my head down. The blade cut the air where my head had been only moments before.

I reared up and kicked my right leg out in a sweeping motion.

My foot connected with the back of Gaspare's left knee. He lost his balance and stumbled, but recovered quickly, springing from foot to foot like a jack-in-the box ready to pop.

He smiled beatifically. "Little one, little one, where do I go?"

I made no reply, instead, I watched him, trying to anticipate his next move.

"Remember," he said as I dodged the thrust of his blade as it brushed past my cheek, "you can't stay on the defensive forever. We are fighting 'til third blood." He flashed fangs. "I get to bleed you twice before defeating you."

I tried to anticipate his next move, ignoring the baiting remarks he cooed at me. Even with Vasco's memories like a past life of experience in my skull, Gaspare was better than I was. How could it not be so when they were Vasco's memories? Vasco was taller, longer of leg and of arm, and the memories I was using were of arms that had more reach.

I clutched the pommel tightly. The memories helped some, when Gaspare pressed me I knew instinctively where my sword needed to be, but I wasn't confident going on the offensive. Gaspare showed me why when I tried to take advantage of his opening. His sword parried mine smoothly. I had to get past his guard, but couldn't see how when he kept making me back-step into defense.

A spurt of warmth flickered between my palms.

The sword that had been empty of any memories or any remembrance of what it had been seemed to awaken in my hands. In the back of my mind I saw the image of a very large fox opening its maw in a yawn.

The fox's brown eyes widened. It yelped, *UP!*

My arms went up. The vibration of my blade meeting Gaspare's sang through my body.

It was hard to focus. I tried to see Gaspare, but for a moment, all I could see was the sleek orange fox in my vision.

The fox gave me a considering look and if a fox could smile, that's what it did, showing its sharpened little canines.

Epiphany. It whispered through my mind in a gentle androgynous voice.

"How do you know my name?"

"What?" Gaspare asked, hesitating as we circled one another like caged tigers.

I shook my head. "Nothing."

Ye have but to think. The fox eyed me curiously. *I know everyone that touches me.*

Chills shot up and down my spine.

Whoops! The fox gave a little yip of pain as I hissed through my teeth.

I touched the cut Gaspare had dealt me on my upper arm, fingers coming away with blood.

Gaspare grinned widely.

Bugger that! the fox murmured, licking its injured shoulder. *Let go, will ye?* He eyed me. *Ye seem to have a problem.*

What do you mean?

Give me control, my lady.

Why?

The fox sat up, and even sitting he was much taller than any fox I'd seen. His elongated ears swiveled forward. *Because, my lady. As ye can see I am a—*

His ears flattened in concentration and the sword was suddenly pulling me with it. I followed the blade, trying to match its movement with some measure of grace. *As ye can see,* the fox growled as Gaspare charged me. The sword pulled me left, right, around, and down as the blade bit into Gaspare's thigh. He screamed, but I ignored it, using my own strength to pull the blade out while I concentrated on the fox.

Well, bugger, the fox said again. *We'll talk later. All right?*

Fine.

Good girl. Now! The fox beamed. *Let's play a little game of cat and mouse!*

Before I could ask which role we were playing, the blade thrummed in my hands as we deflected yet another attempt on Gaspare's behalf. I saw the fox in my *vision* as if he were curling over my body and taking control of my very being through the sword. No, not control…

Collaboration! The fox yipped in happy delight. I lifted the blade parrying Gaspare's much longer sword.

The fox smiled a wicked smile that I felt spread across my own lips.

Gaspare's eyes showed a little too much white around the edges.

And then we went on the offensive. The fox was clever. So clever! He moved through my body like liquid honey, slow and steady, and then like water, quick and nimble. Gaspare sought my neck with the blade and I bowed my entire body back, springing up and driving the tip of the fox blade into his stomach.

Second blood! The fox's words echoed my thoughts, but he added, hastily, *One more drop to go!*

It didn't take long. We played cat and mouse, falling back, then suddenly going on the offensive when Gaspare least expected it. We allowed him to wear himself out, and I found myself so in tune with the fox that I completely forgot about Vasco's memories.

Gaspare gave an inhuman growl of frustration and tried to drive the point of his blade into my face. With the fox's aid, I saw the opening. We skipped to the side on the tips of our toes. I stopped the flat part of the blade with an open palm, the fox blade steadily balanced in my right hand, my hand went back, and the sword sang forward and into Gaspare's stomach.

I rode the sword through his body, until I felt the tip of the blade hit the stone floor.

An echo of power dripped into my words as the fox and I hissed, *"Third blood!"*

I jerked the blade free and Gaspare fell over, clutching the wound. Already, his body struggled to heal it.

Renata's voice carried throughout the room. "Epiphany has drawn third blood. Are all in agreement that she is the winner of this duel?" She glanced down the row of Elders and the look on her face challenged them to defy her.

They didn't.

Slowly, fists went out and thumbs went up.

Lucrezia eyed me across the distance. She held her thumb up, in agreement with the entire party.

The wound on my shoulder had already healed. Unfortunately, the sleeve of my dress hadn't and blood was still trickling down my arm. Vasco smiled brightly and then sent a questioning look at Renata. She inclined her head. He rose and as he had earlier, traced his sword around the circle Gaspare and I had fought in, this time, counter-clockwise.

Gaspare was getting to his feet, but the sour expression on his face was all for me. "I do not know how you did it," he whispered, "but the next battle we fight, I assure you, little rabbit, you will not be so lucky."

"I'll keep that in mind," I said softly, holding the sword against my skirts with the blade pointing down. A droplet of blood fell and hit the stone floor.

Gaspare stood with an effort, wiping his blade on the trim of his jacket.

As if there's much blood to wipe off, the fox crooned in victory.

Hush, you.

'T is all right to gloat a little.

I've got bigger things to worry about.

Ahh, yes, he mused, *like that one there and the look she is giving ye...*

Renata's beautiful eyes met mine. Her voice whispered through the confines of my skull. *We need to talk.*

Oh, yes, the fox said, *we most definitely should!*

Renata's eyelids flickered in surprise

Fox, I thought.

I closed my eyes, blocking out the sight of Renata.

The fox lowered his head. *My lady, I am Cuinn,* he said with a lilting tongue. *Ye do not have to keep calling me "fox."*

Cuinn, then, I said. *Please, stop doing that right now.*

Stop what?

Jabbering.

He inclined his head again. *As ye wish, but I am going nowhere.*

What do you mean?

Ye woke me, Cuinn said yawning. *It was your power that woke me, and now I and the sword are in your keep.*

I watched him give a lazy smile as he curled up, nuzzling his nose into his fluffy tail.

Wonderful.

It is, he said. *I like ye.*

I shook my head and jumped when a hand touched my shoulder.

"Colombina, are you well?" Vasco asked.

"I'm fine," I said and realized that we were the only two vampires left in the room. "Where did everyone go?"

"They left."

"When?"

"A few minutes ago," he said. "Are you sure you're fine?"

I nodded.

He gave me a look that told me he didn't believe me and then held out his hand.

I arched a brow.

"The sword," he said.

At that, Cuinn leapt to his feet and screamed, *NO!*

I shook my head. "It's mine. I can't."

"It's not yours, Epiphany. The sword doesn't belong to anyone." His voice was tender, as if I'd lost my marbles somewhere during the fight.

"It does now!" The fox made my words a whispered growl.

Vasco actually took a step back. He held up his hands. "I'm sorry."

Good, Cuinn seemed to settle down.

"Renata wishes to speak with you. She bid me to escort you to your room," he said, gazing intensely at me. "If you hadn't been wherever you were in your mind, you would have heard her inform me that she would meet you there."

I nodded. "Sorry, Vasco. I'm not feeling quite like myself right now." I touched his shoulder with my free hand, trying to be reassuring. "I'll be fine."

I couldn't find it in me to let go of the sword, so as we walked to my room I kept it close to my skirts, hidden against my leg, disguised by the folds of material.

"You fought well," Vasco said.

"Did I?"

"You had a bit of an unstable beginning." He stroked his chin with his thumb and index finger idly in thought.

It reminded me of what Gaspare had done earlier, so I said, "Don't do that."

He stopped, either because he got it or because he still thought I was off my rocker and was merely appeasing me.

"If I had thought you knew how to fight I wouldn't have given you my memories."

I didn't know what to say as I approached the door to my room.

"I need to be alone for a while, Vasco. I'm sorry. I'm having trouble focusing right now."

He drew in a deep breath, not because he needed it, but to steady himself. "If you need me…"

"I know." I opened the door. "I'll call upon you if I need you."

He bowed and was gone. I shut the door behind me.

Ah, alone. Cuinn stretched and yawned. *Might I rest now?*

Can I put you down?

Yes, he said, *just don't leave me.*

I won't, I said. *I'm in the same room. Are you ever going to explain?*

I shook my head. Cuinn seemed to be fast asleep.

Lazy fox.

Lucky fox.

CHAPTER EIGHT

Vampire or no, my feet were sore from all the fancy footwork. The fox blade, Cuinn, was sitting on my dresser. I had changed into a pair of black silken pants with a matching blouse.

I sat on the edge of the bed, lost in thought, staring at the fox blade. How had my power woken him?

Someone slipped a key in the lock in the door and I was suddenly on my feet. I saw Cuinn alert and on all fours and the blade was suddenly in my hand. I didn't know how it had gotten there.

Renata entered the room and it seemed as if Cuinn and I let out a collective breath.

I couldn't imagine what I looked like, eyes wild and startled with a sword in my hand.

The corner of her mouth twitched.

I laid the sword gently back on the dresser. Cuinn didn't argue, content to curl up and pretend to be more concerned with sleeping. He was curious enough to keep one ear cocked.

It was unnerving. At once seeing him and not seeing him.

Renata came to me and took one of my hands in hers. "Epiphany," she said. "You are trembling."

"I know."

"Why?"

I didn't know what to tell her so I shrugged.

I should've known that she was smarter than that. She had years of reading others. Her beautiful gaze flicked to the sword and she went to it, picking it up in a one handed grip. As soon as her skin touched the metal the sword burst into bright light. A plume of smoke rose and the smell of burnt flesh hit my nostrils. Startled, she dropped the sword on the dresser. It hit the wood with a loud thud.

Cuinn narrowed his eyes. *Not yours, Queen.*

Renata gazed down at her hand. The startled expression was already gone, replaced by something quick and calculating.

"The sword," she said. "Is that it?"

"If I were to tell you it is?"

She sat on the edge of my bed, watching me intently. "Then you need to understand what it is."

"I know what it is."

"Do you?" She arched her brow inquisitively at me.

I nodded. "Cuinn," I said. "He's a fox."

"Mmm." She leaned back on her elbows, showing off the length of her torso in a distracting manner. "Not entirely."

Cuinn chose that moment to interrupt.

Me thinks your Queen has taken a liking to ye.

"Be quiet, Cuinn."

Renata's head tilted to the side. "He is speaking to you?"

"Yes," I said. "He's eavesdropping."

Eavesdropping? he asked, appalled. *I do not eavesdrop!*

I rolled my eyes in disbelief.

His next words made my heart fall to the floor.

Kiss her.

WHAT?

He smirked. *Ye heard me. Kiss her.*

Why on the God's green earth would I do that?

Well, Cuinn began, talking quickly, *so that I may speak with her and that she may speak with me, but most importantly*—he gave me one of those sly smiles—*'cause ye want to.*

I almost tried denying it, but Cuinn shook his head and said, *I know ye,* and I knew without a doubt that he spoke truth. It wouldn't get me anywhere arguing with him.

Instead, I questioned further. *Why do you wish to speak with her?*

Ah, it'll be easier and she won't think you've completely lost your wits.

"Epiphany," Renata was still on my bed searching my face. "What is it?"

I opened my mouth to explain, when Cuinn got impatient with me. *Ye don't have to explain everything ye do!*

I moved toward her, spreading my legs and straddling her body between my thighs. I had a moment to see the startled look in her glorious gaze before I pressed my lips to hers.

Renata put a palm against the back of my head and the kiss turned into something deeper, more unbidden. Her hands cradled my hips and as her tongue expertly explored my mouth. I wrapped my legs around her body, my arms lacing about her neck.

Someone cleared their throat.

Renata pulled away from the kiss, whispering my name.

What I saw was not my bedroom.

We sat in a clearing. I, in Renata's lap, her arms wrapped loosely about my waist. Moonlight cast an enchanting glow on the wooded area that surrounded us. The trunks of the trees were dressed in skirts of rich green moss. Beneath the fallen trunk of a tree, the ground sank into a den, and from that den came Cuinn. Moonlight hit his orange coat, catching the fiery highlights. There were streaks of coal-like shadows at the corners of his snout. His ash tipped ears swiveled as he dipped his head, kneeling in a fox's version of a bow.

I had never seen anything so magical.

His eyes like sunlit molasses met mine and a crooked smirk curved oddly over his animal face.

Greetings, Epiphany. He sank lower. *Greetings, Queen of the Rosso Lussuria.*

Renata gave Cuinn a very long look. "So this is the spirito animale that lies hidden in the sword?"

The words were simple enough to comprehend, but it was strange to hear her speak her native tongue.

Aye, he said. *Do ye see now that she is not mad?*

He stepped forward and his ears flattened against his skull. He was treading cautiously.

"I did not fear she was touched by madness." Renata's fingers traced circles against my lower back and I shuddered.

Ah well, Cuinn said, *now ye know for certain she is not.*

Renata dipped her head in acknowledgement.

Cuinn asked, *What do ye know about my kind?*

I didn't know who he was talking to, but Renata answered.

"Very little," she said. "I know that there were once swords of great power, and within them, within every fiber of their making, they were infused with a spirit." She tilted her head. "Celts, was it not?"

Aye, he said, *It was, druids namely.* He set back on his haunches. *I must admit I am curious to know how I fell into the hands of a vampire.*

"I've no aid to give there, volpe. I only know that it has been with the Rosso Lussuria since before I was Queen."

"Why wouldn't you know how you got here?" I asked him.

I have been sleeping for a very long time.

"Well, why didn't you wake up?"

He shook his head. *That is not the nature of a spirit sword,* he said. *We awaken when one worthy wields our blades.*

"You're starting to make all of this sound so very sword-in-the-stone-esque," I said.

The comment made his face burst into a delightful little fox grin. *Aye, with every myth there's a grain of truth.*

"You're not going to start spouting some, 'you are the chosen one,' lines, are you?"

Renata laughed. "You have been spending too much time in the library."

Cuinn shook his head. *Nay, but you were in the right place at the right time.*

"Or you were," I said.

Aye.

"I had wondered," Renata mused, "how Epiphany had beaten Gaspare."

Cuinn's eyes narrowed. It wasn't a human gesture, but it was a gesture of defense nonetheless. *Are ye accusing her of cheating?*

"I could," Renata said blankly.

The fox slowly began to smile, and then he let out a bark of laughter. My ears seemed to hear the barking, but my mind heard a boy's laughter, not quite a man's, but it was the closest thing my mind could make sense of. I realized, though I had been thinking of Cuinn as male, he had an amazingly androgynous voice.

"Why do you laugh, volpe? It could very well happen if any of the Elders figure this out. Epiphany could be accused of cheating."

Cuinn clicked his jaw shut, but he was still smiling. *Nay,* he said and stood on all fours again, coming closer. I felt the line of his furred body sliding against my back, over Renata's hand. *'T was not cheating if it was her power that called me. If I remember your laws correctly.*

"How would you know our laws unless you once belonged to a vampire?" Renata asked. I too, wondered.

Nay. I did not.

"How do you know then?"

'Cause I know you are not believing what you're saying.

"Clever and intuitive," she said dryly.

Aye, not so easily fooled, am I.

"Epiphany," she said and I looked at her. "A word of advice. He may have saved your life, but he is a fox."

"What is that supposed to mean?"

We're notorious tricksters. That's what she's trying to tell you. I am bound to you and through that binding I cannot, unfortunately, lie. If ye knew anything about spirit swords ye'd know that.

Renata appeared thoughtful enough that I asked, "Is this true?"

She shrugged.

Cuinn began walking back toward his den.

"Where are you going?" I asked.

Now that I've helped to clear everything up with your Queen. He yawned. *I'm going back to sleep.*

I opened my eyes to find we were still in my room. I was still straddling Renata, but she had fallen back in the bed. My stomach sank. She looked up at me from where she laid, hair spilling out like dark waters. She touched my cheek.

Somewhere in the back of my mind, I heard Cuinn give a little yip of laughter.

CHAPTER NINE

I couldn't tell whether Cuinn was sleeping or whether he was merely giving us the illusion of privacy. I got to my knees and Renata's fingers laced around my wrist, stopping me.

"Epifania," she said it softly, almost tenderly.

I struggled, caught between uncertainty and desire.

"It has been years since you've said my name that way."

She propped herself up on elbows, bringing our bodies dangerously close.

"What way?" she breathed the words.

"Like it's something sweet on your tongue." I turned away, willing myself not to look at her.

She touched my cheek much as she had earlier.

"It was always more than your name that was sweet upon my tongue."

An unseen vice gripped my chest. I tried to pull my hand away, and Renata's grip tightened at my wrist. As if we were doing a graceful dance, she followed me as I sat up, trying to get out of the bed. I moved back once, twice. My right knee caught the edge and I lost my balance. Renata caught me before I toppled over the edge. She pulled me in against her body, close enough I could feel the swell of her breasts against mine.

The smile I had seen in so many memories curved in soft amusement. Her eyes danced with unexpected passion and curiosity. I remembered that look. How could I forget? It was a blessing that I did not dream. I feared that if I had dreamt in the past two hundred years, they would've been filled with that knowing smile, that spark of unrestrained passion and amusement.

"Renata, not again, not this game."

She held my face in her hands gently, touching my cheeks with tentative fingers, as if I would break, as if she could feel some fragility etched in my bones.

"Yes," she said, trailing her nails lightly down my skin, using the opening of my blouse to mark a path on it. Her hands traveled lower, until I felt her fingers working deftly at the buttons.

I swallowed past the burning stitch in my throat.

"Epiphany," she said, her fingers stilled on the last button. "Look at me."

I did, feeling her free the last button. Her hands moved to my shoulders as she brushed the silk aside. So light, so gentle, so very careful. I'd tried to force myself to forget Renata was capable of such tenderness.

The silk fell in a caress of fabric halfway down my arms. The air was warm on my skin. She trailed the tips of her fingers over my collarbones and her nails dug in lightly, carving an invisible path over the tops of my breasts. I shut my eyes.

"Do you want me to stop?" It was the last thing I expected to hear from her. But lightly, hesitantly, I shook my head.

Had I been stronger of will, I might've said yes. But somewhere inside of me was a moth that craved the burn of her flame, that didn't want her to stop.

I moved toward her, letting the silken shirt fall to the bed.

"No." It was the barest of whispers.

"Lay back."

I did, waiting.

Renata slipped her fingers beneath the waistband of my pants. She drew the material down my legs, watching, as if some part of her savored the sight of the dark fabric sliding away to reveal my pale skin underneath.

Once, she had told me she took pleasure in such a thing. Whether the look in her eyes now was a truth or lie, I did not care.

I simply wanted that look.

Her fingers hesitated at my ankles. "You will not accuse me of rape?" Amusement lilted her tone.

My words came out strangled. "You broke my heart once. How much worse can it hurt than the first time?"

Renata laughed, but it wasn't a happy one. It was a laugh filled with sorrow, of things that had been lost.

"Oh, Epiphany." The look she gave me was the closest to sympathy I'd ever seen from her. "I never meant to break your heart."

Tears burned at the corners of my eyes. "But you did." I almost choked on the words. "I craved death's sweet kiss when you cast me out."

The look she gave me was compassionate and sad. "You are already dead, my sweet."

I shook my head as a tear broke free. The cool dampness of it tickled down my cheek. "You know what I mean. I wanted to die for good, Renata. I lay in bed for hours. I thought of you and wished you had never spared me my fate." I gave a bitter laugh, choking on it. "You broke me in a way, even to this day, I do not understand."

Renata placed a finger over my lips. "I did what I did out of care for you. Do you not see that?"

"I remember too much," I spoke around her finger. "I feel too much, too much of the emptiness you left behind."

"Then feel me," she said climbing my body and sliding her thigh between my legs. "Feel this."

She pushed the hair out of my face, fingers shadowing the path my tears had taken. Her palm cupped my cheek and I turned my face, brushing my lips across her skin.

With trembling fingers I drew her head down to me, whispering her name.

"What do you want?" she said.

"Make love to me," I said, my words trembling only slightly less than my hands. "Fix what you broke inside of me."

Her long lashes fluttered like raven wings. "I will try."

I sank my hands into her hair, twining the darkened tresses around my arms like silken shackles. She kissed me, a gentle brush of her lips. I used the grip I had in her hair to raise off the bed. I kissed her, opening my mouth and exploring the hot cavern of her with my tongue. Renata kissed me back, using her body to pin mine to the mattress below us.

She broke the kiss, catching my wrists in her hands. Her fingers cinched tightly and I unclenched my fists. Slowly, she drew my hands out of her hair.

"I thought this was supposed to be healing?" She guided my arms behind my back and jerked me against her. Her lips slid over my brow.

I shuddered. "Is it not?"

She drew away with a devious glint in her eyes. "It will not be if you taunt me into losing control."

I wiggled and her grip on my wrists tightened, encouraging my blood to pump faster.

"Please," I said.

"Please what?"

"Please," I pleaded.

She laughed, slipping her hand between my legs. Her fingers splayed and parted me.

"Please?" Her voice dripped with honey as she touched me. "Please this?"

"Yes." I moaned as she slid her fingers inside me.

I had forced myself to forget how good it felt, forced myself to forget how her fingers worked me, how my body reacted to her touch, how she read it, how expertly she played me. She began drawing her fingers out, pleasantly coaxing a whimper of protest from my mouth. She withdrew, and at the absence of her touch, I nearly wept. The fear that she was going to pull away made my throat tight.

Instead, she touched my thigh.

"Spread your legs."

The look in her eyes was enough.

I opened to her as she moved down my body. Her mouth sought me and she kissed me lightly, brushing her lips across the flesh between my legs. A shiver of pleasure curled my toes. Her lips parted, catching on my skin as she raised her eyes to gaze up the line of my body. I clutched the sheets.

"Harder."

She obliged, sucking me into her mouth until I could feel the dents of her fangs digging into my skin. Her fingers found me, and I moaned, hips rising and falling against her mouth and hand. The pleasure tightened my body, and at its resistance, her pace quickened. The thrust of her fingers became something hard and fierce, a sharp blow dealt to the core of my being. Her tongue circled my clit and she sucked harder, faster, until she brought me to climax writhing and crying her name.

I fell back against the pillows. Renata moved, bringing my attention to her. A look of sorrow and regret etched her features. Somewhere in the beautiful contours of her face was passion and lust, but there too was love.

Renata loved me. No matter what she said, in that moment, I knew it. That knowledge crept over my skin and burrowed into my heart.

❖

I woke gasping the first ragged breath of life. As always, it took a few moments to gain my bearings. I didn't move until the pain subsided, and then slowly, ever so slowly began to sit up in the bed.

An arm flung out across my chest.

"Not yet," she said in a purring voice that held the edge of amusement and command.

I sensed Cuinn's ears perk, but did not sense him stir further.

"He's awake," I whispered.

Her lips spread in a lazy smile, as if she had just woken from a very pleasant dream. "I care, because?"

"I haven't fed."

She grinned, nestling her leg between mine underneath the silken sheet. "I have."

I blinked. "How?"

She traced my brow with a lazy finger. "I have always risen earlier than you. Do you not remember?"

Once I thought about it, I did. "Yes." I lowered my gaze to the pulse beating against the side of her neck.

She laughed, her hand moving to the back of my head. "Come here."

I thought she was pulling me toward her for a kiss, but she didn't. She offered her neck to me, drawing me close enough that I was able to bury my face in the bend of it. The smell of her skin was sweetly alluring, but the smell of warm blood pumping beneath it was far more intriguing in that moment.

I kissed the skin over that tiny drum and felt a shudder go through her.

"You're offering blood?" I said.

"Suffice it to say, you did very well last night."

I licked my lips as a fierce pang of hunger hit, writhing in my gut.

"No catch?" I panted, uncertain if I was going to be able to pull myself away even if there was one.

"None," she said, playing with the hair at the nape of my neck.

I caught her skin between my teeth and bit down, feeling my fangs pierce her skin. She cried out, but not in pain. The borrowed blood in her body hit my tongue like fire and ice, at once hot and cold, burning and melting in my mouth like molten chocolate. I locked my mouth around her skin, swallowing quick enough that none of the blood went to waste. Her heart beat, pushing the blood into my mouth. My body grew languid with life and warmth. She whispered my name and I knew what she wanted. Her arms encircled my body, lifting me while I fed at her neck. I wrapped my legs around her waist, feeling her breasts brush mine. Her nipples hardened against my skin, causing an echo reaction within my own body. I moaned over her pulse.

It was one thing Renata and I had always had in common. We liked blood. We liked blood a lot, especially in the bedroom. Sex and blood mingled well for us. Then again, being what we were, how not?

I snaked my arm between our bodies, found the little tuft of hair between her thighs, and touched her with the tips of my fingers.

"Piph," she murmured, grabbing a fistful of my hair and holding me prisoner against her body.

I parted her lips and found her clit, slick and swollen with desire.

She jerked my head back and I had to open my mouth wide so I wouldn't tear her skin. I swallowed quickly, trying not to lose the mouthful of blood, and only managing to swallow half of it. Blood spilled down my bottom lip.

Renata caught my face in her hands, holding me still, licking the blood from my chin like a cat. She licked my bottom lip, sucking, grazing me with her teeth and then kissed me, this time deeper, taking in the taste of blood and desire. I kissed her back, tongue matching the rhythm my fingers had taken between her legs.

I broke the kiss, climbing down her body. I kissed her shoulder, her collarbone. I caught her nipple between my teeth lightly, drawing her breast into my mouth and sucking. She moaned, her grip tightening in my hair, pulling hard enough I winced in pleasure and pain.

Renata's hand twined in my hair to the point where it bordered on nothing but pain. She fell back on the bed, pulling me down with her before her body went rigid and she cried out.

"Are you satiated?" she asked.

"Yes, are you?"

She smiled like a contented cat. "What do you think?"

I rested my head on her breast, kissing the soft and delicate skin there. "I think you are."

She laughed and kissed me. "Then you would be correct," she said. "Though I shall never in a million years think that I could ever get enough of you."

My heart gave an expectant leap. I touched her face. "It's hard to believe this is how it once was. Hard to believe we ever lost this."

"I know," she said and I felt the pang of sorrow and regret inside her. The look she gave me was somber. "Yet, it feels as if nothing has changed at all, except for you."

"And you," I said.

"I have changed?"

"A little."

"How?"

I tried to pinpoint what exactly was different but couldn't. "I don't know," I said at some length. "It just feels...different. It's a better different, but it feels different."

"Perhaps it is only different because of your growing powers and not some change in me. My feelings for you never wavered."

I remembered her mouth between my legs. I had felt her love then, felt her love and lust that was so much like my own, but at the same time so very different. It hadn't been my body or the sex she wanted to possess.

It was me, and in her own way, that was love.

I knew without doubt.

Everyone loves differently, Cuinn mused. *Methinks your Queen is right. Ye did not see her love because ye did not know that in her own way she loved ye.*

Cuinn...

Aye?

I don't need relationship advice from a fox.

He seemed to think that was amusing, because he gave a startling bark of laughter that rang in my skull, making me flinch.

"What is it?" Renata asked.

"Cuinn," I said.

Her eyes narrowed suspiciously. "What did the little volpe say?"

I shook my head. "Nothing," I murmured, "he's agreeing with you, is all. Volpe?"

The corner of her mouth twitched. "Fox in Italian. And I may very well like him after all."

"I would like him much better if he weren't in my head."

"Well"—Renata nestled back against the pillows—"you are the one that picked the sword."

She's r—

Cuinn, I warned.

I don't need to say it.

No, I thought, *you don't.*

CHAPTER TEN

A s strange as it may sound, I was loathe to wash the scent of our lovemaking from my skin. The idea of walking before the entire court and smelling of her claim upon me sent a little thrill through me. In the end, I was reluctant to be so brash and baiting. I wore a wine-colored dress that cinched at the waist. The sleeves were long and wide, but not so much that they would get in the way. It was something comfortable that I could move freely in.

There was a knock on the door and I stood from my perch in front of the vanity table.

Epiphany.

I sighed and took the fox blade from the dresser, since Cuinn made it clear I had to.

It's only Vasco.

I was close enough to the door that I could smell the crisp scent of his cologne.

Caution before folly.

I rolled my eyes, opening the door.

Vasco strode into the room and I closed the door behind him, laying the fox blade back on the dresser.

When I turned around, I got an eyeful of his attire. He looked like a white and silver wrapped present.

"Damn." I stared at him for several moments. "Is it Christmas already?"

The pants he wore were very tight. The only darkness was his hair and the black leather boots that hit just below his knees. There was a slight heel to the boots, making his legs look longer. The silver thread was still twined in his hair, but the braids had been pulled back, held captive in a low clasp.

Vasco grinned at me.

"Don't even start," I said and motioned with a hand at his outfit. "That was worth a stare or two."

He laughed one of his low, rumbling laughs. "Even from a woman that loves women?"

"If those pants were any tighter, Vasco, you'd be a woman."

He gave me a serious look. "Sì." He wiggled his hips. "They are a little tight."

I crossed my arms over my chest and caught my bottom lip between my teeth. I shook my head at him.

He gave a quick grin and returned to seriousness. "We do not have very long to talk. I am to escort you before the Elders."

I nodded, already guessing as much. "Are you going to tell me about the upcoming challenge?"

He spread his arms out. "That is why I am here."

I went back to the vanity table, watching his reflection in the mirror. He sat on my bed.

His nostrils flared and he turned toward the pillows like a hound on a scent trail.

"Vasco," I said before he could pick the sheet up and hold it to his face.

His hand hovered. "Who did you sleep with last night, colombina?"

"That's none of your concern."

He started grinning again.

I pointed the brush at him like a weapon. "Stop it, Vasco."

He was still grinning when he picked the sheet up and inhaled loud enough that I could've heard him without the supernatural hearing.

As quickly as the grin had appeared, it vanished. He dropped the sheet to the bed with a look of shock and horror.

I folded my hands in my lap with a sigh as Vasco leapt to his feet and started cursing in a slew of Italian. Although I couldn't understand what he was saying, I understood what he was feeling. He was afraid, not just for me, but for Renata too.

I managed to catch the word, "Foolish," and then that too was sucked in and drowned out by another long line of fast and indecipherable Italian.

"Great," I said. "That's nice, Vasco. Can you repeat that? In English, please?"

He froze. Apparently, he hadn't realized he'd been speaking Italian.

After a moment, he blinked. "What have you done? What have you both done? You heard what she said last night!"

Impatiently, I started pulling the curls of my hair back, tying it off with a long black ribbon.

"I heard a lot more than you did, Vasco."

He sat back on the bed heavily. "What is done is done."

"It is," I said. "Now tell me about the next challenge."

"Signore dei Sogni. Lord of Dreams."

"Sognare?" I asked, remembering the Elder's name. Sognare had never been, in my opinion, one of the crueler Elders. In fact, in the past two hundred years I couldn't remember him bothering me at all.

"Sì," he said.

"Lord of Dreams?"

Vasco nodded. "His power has to do with dreams, inspiring them, controlling them."

I tilted my head. "But that's impossible. We don't dream."

"If Sognare wants you to dream, you will."

That was interesting. I'd never heard much about Sognare. Actually, come to think of it, I hadn't heard much about the Elders and their specific powers. I'd seen Sognare several times. And if you ask me, he reminded me an awful lot of the way humans portrayed their fictional wizards. However, that was probably because he was the oldest vampire that I'd ever seen. His gray beard was long enough to sweep the floor.

"That doesn't sound very physical," I said.

"Mental." He shrugged. "Physical. It is both."

I picked the fox blade up. Call it a hunch, but I had a feeling Cuinn wasn't going to let me leave him behind.

Vasco eyed the sword. "It is true?"

"This?" I lifted the blade.

"The volpe spirito," he said.

"Renata told you?"

"Sì," he said. "She explained some. I have been assured that you have not gone deliriously mad and that your wits are still about you."

"Well, not yet," I said.

He offered his hand. "May I carry it? I know they are peculiar about such things, but you cannot walk into this challenge armed, as it is not a challenge of weapons."

Not visible ones.

I waited for Cuinn to add more, but he didn't.

Cuinn?

Aye?

Will you let Vasco carry you?

He seemed to consider it.

Then he surprised me by saying, *Aye, I suppose.*

I handed the sword to Vasco, hilt first.

Vasco took it. I turned toward the door when a heavy thump made me turn on my heel. The fox blade was planted firmly in the floor. I watched as Vasco struggled to retrieve it.

I heard Cuinn give a little snicker of laughter.

"Cuinn," I said, this time aloud.

Vasco gave me a look and tugged on the sword again, bracing his booted feet several inches apart. The sword wasn't budging. I had a feeling it wasn't going to, either, supernatural strength or no. Vasco swore and this time I heard him say, "Volpe!"

All he needs to do is ask nicely.

"Vasco, ask nicely."

"What?" He looked startled.

"You're going to give yourself an aneurism; just ask him nicely!"

He blinked. "Why?"

I moved toward him and the sword and Vasco moved out of the way. I pulled the sword out of the stone in one fluid motion. "I'm not handing the sword to you until you ask nicely."

Vasco blinked again. "Per favore?"

That'll do.

I handed the sword to him. Vasco removed his own sword from his back sheath and laid it on the bed. He slipped the fox blade into his sheath, checking it with his hands. He seemed satisfied that it fit.

I let the surprise show. "It fits?"

"The sword and sheath were blessed by one of the Stregheria."

"The what?"

"Stregheria," Vasco repeated. "An Italian Witch. The sheath will fit any sword."

"And the sword?" I asked.

"The sword will kill a vampire."

"That's a nice thing to be carrying on your back."

"Right now I am carrying your volpe spirito trapped in steel, and this too is a nice thing to carry on one's back."

I didn't know if he was teasing or not. "You're saying my sword can bring true death to one of our kind?"

"Sì, or anything that you wish it to kill, for that matter."

Cuinn, I mentally purred at him.

Aye? he said again, but this time he sounded irritated.

Is this true?

His ears swiveled back as he rested his maw on his forelegs.

It is.

You didn't think to tell me, why?

'Cause ye'd find out eventually.

I shook my head. "Let's go."

Vasco bowed. The pommel of the fox blade was hidden behind the long braided tresses of his hair. I opened the door and stepped out in the hall, too busy giving in to my irritation to be particularly afraid.

CHAPTER ELEVEN

R enata turned toward the doors as I made my way before her. I caught a flash of her dress, blue velvet so dark it was almost black, before I sank gracefully to my knees and fixed my gaze on the stone below me.

"Vasco," she said and he rose from his kneeling position, knowing her will and taking his seat among the other Elders.

To me, she asked, "Is it your will to proceed?"

I dipped my head lower. "It is, my lady."

"Lucrezia," she said, "summon Sognare."

I sensed more than saw Lucrezia get to her feet. She moved past me, and as she passed, the bulk of her heavy skirts brushed the side of my body.

A spark of anger flared through me and I fought to conceal it. The double doors clanged closed and the room was suddenly filled with eerie silence. It was a silence that belonged to an empty room, but it was not. It was only a room full of vampires that had no real reason to make any noise. Or so I thought.

A rustle of material sounded. Someone whispered, "Little rabbit."

I looked up then, turning my face toward the sound of Gaspare's sour voice. He sat beside Baldavino, who reclined at ease, rolling his eyes at Gaspare's comment. The hair brushing his shoulders was as gold as a lion's mane. Both of the Elders wore deerskin breeches, but where Gaspare's velvet jacket was black, Baldavino's was the solid color of pine needles.

I met Gaspare's eyes and the look of taunting malice in them.

Cuinn's androgynous voice crooned through my head, *Your mother was an ogre and your father the dribble from a goblin's arse.*

I gave a short and unexpected laugh.

On the dais, Gaspare's hands clenched into fists. "You dare to laugh at me?"

Aye! Cuinn's voice was a deadly hiss in the confines of my skull.

"Perhaps," I said, "or perhaps it occurs to me that you would dare loathe the rabbit when you yourself are a terrible huntsman, Gaspare."

I heard the sound of his chair clatter to the floor a moment before his fist balled in my hair. He jerked my head back and drew his other hand back as if to strike me.

Renata's voice cracked like a whip, full of heat and command. "Gaspare!"

I narrowed my eyes in defiance.

He used the grip he had to pull me up high on my knees. "Wretched little bitch!"

I heard the hiss of steel sliding from a sheath.

"Let her go." Vasco's voice dripped with cold fire as he pointed the fox blade at Gaspare.

Gaspare snarled and spat, "You would protect her?"

Vasco's eyes brightened with power, rocking waves of an azure ocean. His voice dripped with unrelenting challenge. "Sì."

I took the opportunity the distraction presented, catching Gaspare's hand between my fingers. I am a vampire and we are all supernaturally strong. Though I have been an Underling for two-hundred years, I used my strength against him, digging my fingers into his skin between his thumb and index finger like a vice. Gaspare reacted by loosening his hold. I caught his hand, pushing it back toward his wrist until I felt the bones grinding. Something in his wrist popped and he screamed.

Such a small noise for such a loud scream.

I moved as I had seen Vasco move, too quick for the eyes to follow. A strike of lightning that never strikes twice. The throne room was a blur around me. I was motion. I was liquid. I caught

Gaspare's shoulders and he tried to move, tried to see it coming, but he was too slow. I threw my body into it, ramming my knee high up between his legs as hard as I could. I used the grip on his shoulders to pull his body into the collision, and then I turned, as if dancing the steps of a dance that my body knew and had performed a thousand times before. I used his weight against him, used the momentum of the impact to push him facedown on the stone floor.

I shoved my knee hard into the back of his spine. He tried to reach for me, and I caught his wrists, jerking his arm up high behind his back until I heard the ball and socket joints of his shoulders dislocate in a sickeningly thick sound.

Gaspare screamed for me again. On the edges of his scream I heard Baldavino's laughter, heard him say, "Looks like someone's been teaching the little Underling how to wrestle."

Baldavino didn't speak often. On the rare occasion that he opened his mouth, I could not remember a time when anything good came of it. He was a prick, in much the same way that Gaspare had always been, and yet not. I had always been fairly certain that Baldavino simply hated everyone with an equal passion. Gaspare, on the other hand, relished belittling and demeaning those he deemed beneath him. It was two different types of arrogance, but still, it was arrogance nonetheless.

Gaspare tried to get up and Vasco was there, placing a booted foot hard against the back of his head.

"Signore, I would not advise struggling any further," he said.

Gaspare went incredibly still beneath me.

"Epiphany?" Vasco made my name a question.

"Yes, Vasco?" I asked sounding polite and calm and not like I was holding a man captive.

"Are you well?"

I looked up at him and felt a dark smile tug at my lips. "Yes."

The corner of Vasco's mouth rose in a half-smile.

An eruption of noise battered my ears as someone clapped, hard and rapid.

Lucrezia's voice slithered like a whispering snake throughout the throne room. "Brava, Epiphany," she said. "Molto bene."

I didn't turn to look at her. The space between my shoulder blades tensed as I heard the sounds of her skirt slithering across the stones. She knelt beside me, leaving only a few feet between us. Her eyes sparkled with delight and she tilted her head to the side to look down at Gaspare.

"That was nicely done, wouldn't you say?"

Since it seemed she was speaking to Gaspare, I didn't say anything.

Gaspare didn't either.

Lucrezia reached out, as if to touch me. I moved from the waist up, keeping my face out of her reach. Her eyes closed, and as if slipping on a mask, when she opened them again she smiled oh-so-sweetly at me.

I forced myself not to recoil.

"Do you still fear me?" she whispered in a small voice, like a monster pretending to be cute and cuddly, when you know full well it will slit your throat the minute you turn your back.

I met her gaze and said, "I do not like you."

"Buono," she said in a darkly pleased voice, "molto buono."

I felt a touch at the back of my neck that nearly made me jump out of my flesh. "Lucrezia." Renata's voice dripped behind me like something even more deadly than Vasco's and Lucrezia's combined. The tips of her fingers rested at the base of my neck like an anchor.

Lucrezia looked up at Renata's face.

I felt the movement travel through Renata's body and knew when Lucrezia flicked her eyes to her empty seat on the dais that Renata was pointing at it.

Lucrezia stood and gave an elegant curtsey. "Sì, mia padrona." The serious tone to her voice didn't match the sparkling amusement in her expression.

Renata knelt much as Lucrezia had.

"Dante," she said. "Dominique." She called their names like a cool command.

Gaspare spoke then, his voice thin and frantic. "Mia padrona! No! Per favore!" he pleaded.

I tried to follow and only managed to catch, *my mistress, no, please.* You'd think that after two hundred years I'd have learned more Italian. Well, guess again. Considering the only time Vasco spoke it was when he was cursing at something, and the only time the others spoke it was when they were trying to be sneaky, my knowledge only went so far. Very quickly spoken Italian was too far. I'd never been adept at translating that.

Dante and Dominique came to us. Dante was naked from the waist up, wearing only a pair of red leather pants and dark boots. Dominique wore black leather, with a plain white T-shirt stretched over the bulk of his chest. For the sake of my own survival and health, I wouldn't in a million years have started a fight with either one of them. Supernatural strength or no, they were both built like their bodies were made for throwing people around. As guards, that was pretty much what they did. They protected the Queen. If that meant throwing people around, I'd no doubt that either of them would not hesitate to do it.

Dante reached out to touch my shoulder and Dominique stopped him, shaking his head and sending his dark braid swaying down his back.

Gaspare pleaded relentlessly. Renata ignored him. Vasco still had his foot on the back of his head. I wondered if he was getting a leg cramp, but highly doubted it.

Gaspare tried to wriggle out from under me and I pulled his arms up even higher, slamming my knees down into his back. Vasco shifted his foot to the back of Gaspare's neck, leaning his weight into it.

I dropped my gaze to the black velvet of Gaspare's back and said through gritted teeth, "He's going to fight you."

Dominique responded loud enough that I could hear him over Gaspare's slew of frantic Italian. "Let us worry about that, piccolo."

I ignored the fact that he'd called me a nickname that meant "little." Dominique had never been rude to me or treated me badly.

I slowly started to get up and then realized slow wasn't going to work with the way Gaspare was struggling.

I got up in one fluid stretch and moved out of the way.

Dominique and Dante moved in unison, as if they instinctively knew what Gaspare would try to do and they'd rehearsed beforehand just how they would react. Dante grabbed Gaspare's kicking feet while Dominique caught him by the arms.

They carried Gaspare out of the room like that, with Gaspare stretched out like a wiggling eel between them.

Only then did Vasco sheath the fox blade.

Relief and tiredness left my body in the form of a sigh. It occurred to me why I had never stood up and defended myself against the Elders. I looked out over their faces and saw that half of them held contempt while the other half held either disinterest or curiosity. Sognare's wizened eyes met mine and I guessed that he had taken his seat for lack of anything better to do, for I had not heard Renata order him to do so. There was a certain amount of curiosity in his gaze that I did not understand.

I never stood up and defended myself against them, because some of them I would always have to defend myself against. I had thought it better to be as quiet as a mouse hiding in the long grass and hoping the predator would pass me by than a tiger whose very bold colors and stripes invoked challenge.

I turned to Vasco, who gave a slow nod, as if to let me know that he understood my thoughts and had seen the looks too.

I had just declared my very bold colors by standing up to Gaspare.

Aye, Cuinn said softly, *but this is the way things are meant to be.*

I hope you're right.

I am right in that I know ye are more than ye seem, Epiphany, and these vampires have not reckoned the half of it.

CHAPTER TWELVE

Renata waited until Dominique and Dante had returned to proceed. Vasco was sent to admit two lesser attendant vampires into the room. The girl was only a few inches taller than the boy and they both appeared to be about some twenty years of age, though I knew they were much older, not yet two hundred, but older still.

They kept their heads at an angle so that their long hair hid their youthful features. The girl's hair was a blond so light that it was almost white. The boy's hair was a honey blond so dark it bordered on brown. They set about preparing the dream trial area. I watched, curious, as they arranged large fur rugs on the floor.

I turned in time to catch Sognare hobbling over on his cane. His silver beard trailed the floor as he made his way to me. Thick brown robes covered him from neck to foot. Sognare's eyes were almost as gray as the hair on his head, but not quite, for there was a dusting of blue in them.

"Come," he said, "sit."

I sat crossed-legged on a thick gray rug. What animal the rugs had once been, I did not know, nor did I particularly care to find out.

"You have fed, yes?"

I could still taste Renata's blood in my mouth, something faint, but sweet and metallic. I closed my eyes trying to hide the remembrance. I inclined my head and said, "I have."

"Good," he said, using his crooked wooden stave of a cane to help lower his elderly body to the ground.

It took long enough that I couldn't help but smile and say softly, "That body of yours doesn't seem very convenient."

Behind his long beard, I thought I saw the flash of a smile. "Ahh, the folly of the old," he said, "I feared death, and now I find myself stuck in a perpetual state of it, bag of brittle bones." He chuckled, crossing his legs to mirror mine.

I seriously doubted the old wizard of a vampire was that brittle of bone. One of the benefits of being a vampire, the body heals at a supernatural pace. It'd taken a great deal of strength for me to break Gaspare's wrist, and had I been human, I probably wouldn't have been able to do it. It'd probably take as much strength to break Sognare's wrist, despite appearances to the contrary.

Vasco began walking a circle around us; only this time he did not use his sword.

"We shall begin while Signore Vasco sees to the anello di protezione," he said. "Close your eyes, Epiphany."

I did as told, hoping that the area of protection would protect me as well.

Sognare, the Lord of Dreams, began humming a solemn tune that was at once haunting and melancholic. I let go of my thoughts and listened to him.

When all was quiet, I waited, flinching when I felt his gnarled fingers brush across my eyelids.

"Exoculo," he murmured.

"Consopio." His fingers touched my brow.

"Alucinor." His touch stopped at my temples.

Sognare's power reached out toward the center of my being like some great clawed hand. I found myself dizzy and sick.

There was nothing, nothing but complete and utter darkness. As soon as I thought it, there was cold, a cold that cut to the very bones of my body, fierce and sharp like needles. I reached out with my hands and felt nothing, nothing but air and darkness, nothing but that stabbing cold. I shivered with it, my teeth chattering and rattling my skull.

That was wrong.

As a vampire, I should not have felt the cold like a killing thing. I forced myself to focus and reached down, feeling the ground beneath me. Frozen blades of grass cut my hands and I raised them, feeling the blood trickling, but unable to see into such impenetrable darkness. I should have been able to see, at least enough to make out certain shapes.

I held my hands to my chest and got my feet under me. The darkness in my head spun like an invisible vortex. A light kissed the edge of that darkness, a light that spread its pink and orange fingers across the sky.

I saw the green field frozen, frozen beneath layers of crystalline ice.

I looked for the source of that pink-orange hand, and fear lodged in my chest.

Sunlight, coming to burn me alive. It was rising and when it rose…I ran, blades of iced grass cutting my feet. I slipped and fell, scrambled back up again, running with sheer terror, encouraged by centuries of instinct.

You cannot run!

I looked back to see Cuinn's sleek form running toward me. His long body seemed to cut through the air, his paws never making a sound.

Cuinn was suddenly next to me. I buried my hands in his fiery fur, shielding my face in his scruff.

Cuinn, I thought, terrified, *Cuinn, what do I do if I cannot run?*

Ye break the Dream Master's hold.

Cuinn faced the sun and his muscles rippled in anticipation beneath my hand. He gave a fierce warning yip that seemed to echo out over the land. The light seemed to hesitate, rays wavering. He took a step forward and a growl unlike any I'd ever heard from a fox slipped past his blackened lips. Again, the sun's power hesitated, as if unsure whether or not it wanted to face the fox spirit's power.

I opened myself and felt Cuinn's courage. I filled myself with the fox's courage until it felt I would burst with it. I turned to face the light. Cuinn's tall head bumped my hand, and when I took a step forward, he followed.

With each step the sun began to sink back. I focused on the cold, on drawing it inside myself. The crescent of something darker and larger than the sun began to rise.

"Now!" Cuinn yipped with happy delight and we were running, running full out toward the sun and the moon our power had conjured.

❖

I came to myself and found my attire soaked. The throne room spun wildly in my vision, and I had to close my eyes to keep from wavering on my knees.

Sognare's voice came. "She has broken my hold," he said and his voice was empty, but his eyes held something I couldn't read and wasn't sure I trusted. "She has passed my test."

I wondered if he knew that I had passed his test with Cuinn's aid.

Cuinn's voice filled my mind. *I remain unseen when I wish.*

When I stood, a chorus of small glass shattered to the ground at my feet.

There was blood on my hands. I realized the tiny shards on the floor were not glass, but icicles. "You could have killed me."

Sognare, leaning heavily on his cane, inclined his head. I saw Vasco retrace his steps, taking the circle of protection down.

A rock of fear dropped to the pit of my stomach. I had not known that his visions were powerful enough that he could inflict harm with them.

Yet again, it seemed Cuinn had saved my life.

Nay, he whispered, *I merely give ye the tools.*

Vasco touched my shoulder and I flinched, coming back to myself with a flurry of thoughts.

"The Queen is addressing you, Epiphany."

I turned to Renata. "Yes, my lady?"

There was a look on her face that I couldn't quite fathom. Her eyes searched my gaze, but what she said was, "You are excused, Epiphany."

I bowed my head. "Thank you, my lady."

Vasco gave me his arm and I took it.

We were almost to the doors when Renata's voice stopped us in our tracks.

"I did not give you permission to leave, Vasco."

Vasco sank gracefully to his knees, bowing his entire body forward. "Forgive me, Padrona. I sought only to escort the lady to her chamber."

The fact that he hadn't called me by name meant that he was as worried about being stopped as I was. Why had she stopped us? Was she reasserting her control, reinforcing her position as Queen in front of the Elders?

"Then ask if you may leave, Vasco. Do not assume when I have not granted you permission."

He sank a little lower into his bow. "Sì, my lady. I apologize. Might I escort the Lady Epiphany to her room?"

"No."

Vasco looked up then. I tried not to let the surprise show on my face. Would she seriously forbid Vasco to see me to my room? It was a gesture he had done for so many years.

Vasco didn't bother with trying to keep the question from his face. He gave Renata that wide-eyed stare and told her with his eyes that he could not believe she would be so petty. Before he could open his mouth to argue, Renata's lips parted.

"No," she said. "Escort the lady to my private chambers."

Vasco bowed again. I think, this time trying to hide his expression. Though he hid his expression from the Rosso Lussuria clan, I felt the emotions unfurl inside him—astonishment, shock, and then a deep-seated worry. His emotional reaction overshadowed my own until I wasn't quite sure what I felt.

Lucrezia made a displeased noise low in her throat. "So she is indeed your little pet bitch again."

Renata turned on her like the raging sea. "Many of you seem to have forgotten that I am your Queen."

"I have not forgotten, my lady," Lucrezia said in a voice gone flat.

Renata's voice held power like a crashing wave. "Hold your tongue, Lucrezia," she said, splendid and frightening. "I did not ask you to speak. Be careful that the madness you do so enjoy inspiring in others is not a madness which spills from your lips and to my ears again, for the next time you speak out of turn, I will cut your tongue out myself."

If I had thought Vasco the fastest of us, I had sorely underestimated Renata.

Lucrezia's mouth opened and Renata never gave her the chance to speak. She sent her flying down the steps as if she weighed nothing, and I might've believed Lucrezia weighed nothing, if she did not fall with such a messy and heavy thud.

Renata stepped down, meeting Lucrezia's wild-eyed look. Lucrezia didn't move. She remained on her side, propping herself up on her hands and looking up at Renata.

The look in her eyes was venomous.

"Dominique, Dante," Renata said and her voice still contained power like the sharp edge of a blade.

Lucrezia's eyes were slits of challenge.

Dominique and Dante moved quietly toward Lucrezia.

"No," she commanded coolly. Her red lips curved into a cruel smile that was directed at Lucrezia. "Fetch Gaspare. It is time to remind the Rosso Lussuria of what their Queen is capable of. Vasco," she said, eyes never flicking from Lucrezia's, "escort your lady."

Vasco gave a quick bow of his head. "My Queen, if it is no trouble, I would very much like to remain at your side this night."

"Escort Epiphany," she said. "Then, if it is your will, return to my side."

"It is, my lady."

"Go."

Vasco caught my arm. He tried to turn me toward the double doors that Dominique and Dante held open, but I dug in my heels. Renata noticed my reluctance.

Go. What I will do here tonight is not something I wish you to play witness to, her voice whispered through my mind like a breeze tickling dry leaves.

I turned with Vasco and did as I was told.

CHAPTER THIRTEEN

I paced the length of Renata's chamber. Vasco reclined on the bed with his legs crossed at the ankles. His longs arms were tucked back behind his head. I was aware that he was watching me, aware of the flickering sense of curiosity that emitted from him. It seemed that my powers were growing, for me to be able to sense such a small thing as curiosity. As he said he would, Vasco had escorted me to Renata's bedroom and then had left to stand at her side. An hour and half later, he returned with a smile tugging at the edges of his mouth. I hadn't understood his look of pride and satisfaction.

"Colombina," he said.

I paused. "Hmm?"

"You are pacing like an impatient cat," he said. "Why?"

"What is she doing, Vasco? Why order me to her chambers in front of the Elders? Why is she placing both of us, all of us, at risk? I felt your fear. I sensed your dread, your worry."

"Did you sense anything from the others?" he asked and the tone of his voice was almost casual.

I shook my head. "No, but I wasn't trying to sense anything from them either."

"What about Lucrezia? You heard her words. What did you sense behind them, colombina?"

I gave a bitter laugh. "Lucrezia is filled with anger, hatred, and envy. She always has been. It's hard to sense anything beyond that."

"Why?" he asked.

"Why?" I blinked, giving him an uncomprehending look.

"Sì," he said. "What motivates those feelings?"

I pursed my lips in thought. "I don't know. Where are you going with this, Vasco?"

He smiled wide enough to flash the length of his canines. "Know thy enemy."

I started pacing again. "Power and envy," I said. "She craves power. I've watched her try to take it from others for years. She's envious of Renata's power, of anyone that has more power than she does."

"Sì," he said. "It is hard for you to have the perspective the rest of us have, as we have been together far longer."

His words made me stop in my tracks. "By human definitions, I am not so young, Vasco, not as young as some of you treat me."

"I know," he said giving me a look of silent understanding. "But you were not there when Lucrezia came to the Rosso Lussuria, seeking sanctuary from her maestà. Her mind was a fragile thing. We did not think she would survive, and if it had not been for her own blossoming power she would not have."

"What do you mean?" I sat on the edge of the bed.

"Lucrezia and her master shared a similar gift," he said, "both carry the Kiss of Madness."

"The Kiss of Madness?"

"She can break a person's mind with a single kiss, mortal or immortal. Her king tried to use the kiss against her, to punish her when she sexually abused one of his lovers."

I had known that Lucrezia liked her sex spiced with pain. For decades with Renata, our lovemaking was often the intermingling of pleasure and pain, her dominant will eliciting my total surrender. Yet, I hesitated to compare Renata's desires with Lucrezia's. In a sense, Lucrezia's idea of sex wasn't sex at all. Torture and rape seem more appropriate terms in regard to Lucrezia's style.

I fought the shudder that started at the base of my spine. The memory of Lucrezia's hands was one I longed to forget.

"Renata refused to allow Lucrezia to take a lover among the Rosso Lussuria, didn't she?"

Vasco's brows went up a fraction. "Sì," he said and I realized he was impressed that I'd come to the conclusion all on my own. In a way, so was I. "Renata banned Lucrezia from ever taking a lover as a result of her…bedroom manners."

"Or lack thereof," I added dryly. "Why did Renata agree to allow Lucrezia to join the clan in the first place?" It was incredibly rare for a clan to accept a vampire that had been sired by another, most especially one that had never originally belonged or been sired among the clan. "Why was Lucrezia not declared Il Deboli?"

"I would say that our Queen took pity on her but fear that would be a lie," he said. "It was not pity that motivated the Queen."

"It was a political move," I said, "another vampire to add to her ranks?"

"Sì, Lucrezia was another powerful vampire to bind to the clan."

"I would've sent her back the way she came," I said. "I would have declared her Il Deboli."

"Truly?" he asked, searching my face. Declaring Lucrezia Il Deboli was a death sentence. Contrary to popular belief, vampires did not thrive well in cities. We preferred to keep to ourselves and lived our lives separate from that of the humans. The only time vampires ventured out into the city was when they were hunting prey or when they were the prey.

"Yes, truly. Lucrezia's as mad as a hatter. I would not invite that into my clan unless I was absolutely confident I could control it."

Vasco's face erupted in a grin. "Your mind is getting better at court politics, bellezza. You just answered your own question. Once Lucrezia began to surface out of her madness, she agreed to swear blood oath to Renata. We agreed to spare her life thinking that her power would discourage any that threatened the security of our clan. We thought we could control her."

"I would have had her executed. That's what happens when you live so long, Vasco. A few centuries of immortality and the arrogance starts going to your head."

"I never thought I would see the night when you would be both ruthless and practical. I think it is more than just our Queen who has underestimated you."

"I don't think it is ruthless, Vasco. I think it's practical, yes. If a thing proves to be dangerous one night I will not wake the next expecting that its nature has completely changed." I fixed him with a hard stare. "If Lucrezia was mad when she showed up on the Queen's doorstep, why risk it?"

"Because power is an important thing to our kind. Surely you know that by now. Lucrezia narrowly averted slipping into the madness inspired by her master's kiss. When she showed up, she should have been completely taken by it. As it was, she only had bouts of it, and until her mind was healed, Renata kept her under lock and key."

I shook my head again. "I find it hard to believe Lucrezia's mind ever fully healed, Vasco."

The look in his eyes was sad, so terribly sad. "So do I."

I changed the subject. "What did Renata do to Gaspare tonight, Vasco? What did she do that put that prideful step in your walk and satisfied smile upon your lips?"

"The Queen dismissed you for a reason. I am your friend, Epiphany, but I am no fool to go against my Queen's orders. If she wishes you to know, then she will tell you."

"No," I said, unable to keep the anger out of my words, "you are no fool to go against your Queen's orders." I looked at him and knew the vacancy in my eyes did not match the heat of my tone. "If the Queen had not appointed you as my protector, would you have befriended me, Vasco?"

"I, like you, keep to myself. I will not lie to you, Epiphany, because you are my friend, and I value our friendship more than you know. If our Queen had not bid me to watch you, to protect you, then I would have continued to keep to myself."

And there was the truth. If Renata had not told Vasco to protect me, he would never have befriended me. I stood abruptly, giving him my back. I was afraid that I couldn't hide the hurt and resentment I felt.

The weight of his hand fell on my shoulder, and though I stiffened, I made no move to shake him off.

"It would have been my loss, colombina. You are a wonderful friend," he said. "You are la sorella del mia spirito."

"If you don't want me to think that what you just said could potentially be some Italian insult," I gave him a very displeased look, "then you should repeat yourself in a language I understand."

"You are the sister of my spirit," he said. "You are the sister of my mind and heart, and I would have regretted never knowing you."

"Well," I said, sparing him a sidelong glance, "that's good to know."

He took a step that brought us facing each other and sank to the carpeted floor on his knees. "I ask your forgiveness, Epiphany, my sister."

I touched his serpentine braids with their thread of silver, like stars and blackness intertwined. I exhaled deeply, not finding it in my heart to be angry at the one person, the one vampire, who had ever truly been my friend.

"I forgive you, my brother."

"It seems I am interrupting." It wasn't the words that made my blood run cold. It was the veil of threat the words held that made me drop my hand from Vasco's braids.

The smell of sweet metallic blood flooded my senses before I saw her. Renata's body was covered in blood like she'd just about bathed in it. The blue velvet of her gown was black with it. The long waves of her hair were matted and clumped.

The fact that most of the blood was on her body, rather than in it, meant that her purpose had been to cause someone a great deal of pain.

She had tortured Gaspare in front of the Elders. She had used him as an example, as a well sent message. A reclamation of her power, as it was.

It is time to remind the Rosso Lussuria of what their Queen is capable of.

Staring into her eyes framed by the mask of drying blood, I had no doubts that she had indeed reminded the Elders of what she was capable of.

Even so, even knowing what she was capable of, I found myself wanting to cross the room, wanting to go to her, yearning to drop to my knees and lick the crimson patches from her moonlit skin.

"Did you execute him?" I asked and my voice was calm, giving away no hint of my desire or thoughts.

"No." She stepped into the room and her gaze flicked to where Vasco knelt. She gave him a dangerous look that made me tense and uneasy.

"Renata." I moved to bring her attention back to me. "There is no reason to be angry with Vasco. He has done nothing wrong."

She gave me a look as cold as winter's silent fury. "I told you to stay out of my head."

I took another step forward and sank to my knees. "Please," I whispered.

"Please what, Epiphany?"

"Please do not turn your power and anger on Vasco."

I looked up at her then.

Renata gave a slow blink, her expression sliding into something calmer and more calculating.

"Vasco," she said.

"Yes, my lady?"

"You are dismissed."

Vasco stood without question and went. The doors shut with a quiet click behind him.

She said my name and I rose to take the hand she held out. She turned me, pulling me in against her.

Too close, too close to the smell of the blood. Too close to the intoxicating smell of her skin.

My vision blurred as my eyelashes fluttered.

"Epiphany." Her lips brushed my ear and I fought the anticipation that ran through my body. Her hand trailed a path down my stomach, summoning a tremble of remembrance and longing from deep within me.

I went to my knees, catching her hand and feeling the drying blood on her skin. I raised it to my mouth and pressed a feather soft kiss against the tips of her fingers.

She caressed my lower lip and I opened to her, taking the taste of blood and flesh into my mouth.

I rose up high on my knees as another of her bloodstained fingers slipped past my lips. I sucked, locking my mouth at the base and licking it clean.

Her calm expression never wavered. Her hand twisted in my hair, twining the tresses until her grip was tight. A moan escaped me, but I did not stop. I had endured far rougher play than this. I set my tongue against her skin, licking up her hand, across her knuckles.

She pulled me back, holding me at bay while her eyes held me captive.

"Is this what you want?" she asked, using her other hand to unlace the stays of her dress. She began peeling it down her body.

The blood had soaked through the velvet and to her white skin below.

I made a strangled sound. "Yes."

I had spent enough years as her pet to know what she expected of me.

With her fist balled in my hair at the back of my scalp, I drew the dress down her body. She used the grip she had to guide my mouth across her skin and I let her. Where my lips brushed, my tongue flicked out, until the red was white once more, until the rich coppery taste of blood and sweet-salt taste of her skin coated my mouth like some delectable wine. She led me off my knees, guiding my mouth to her breast. I sucked, drawing her nipple lightly between my teeth and setting the tips of my fangs to glide dangerously close to piercing her tender flesh.

Her grip tightened and I whimpered in submission.

Renata pushed me down on the bed until I was sitting. She propped one long leg on the edge of it. Obediently, I tucked my legs under me, rising enough to kiss the mound of flesh between her thighs.

I parted her with my tongue. Her wet skin was like some silken fruit against my lips. The tip of my tongue found her opening and I pushed against her, hands anchored at her hips, and slipping as much of myself as I could inside her.

My name was a strangled cry as she gave a fierce jerk that sent my scalp to tingling. "Stop teasing."

Wordlessly, I gave a nod of compliance. She allowed me to seal my lips over her again and I licked and sucked until her body went rigid and a cry of pleasure announced my victory and her defeat.

"Epiphany," she said in a voice that smoldered with pleasure and amusement at the same time. She steered me to face the bed.

I knew what she wanted. I leaned over and placed my palms on the gray blanket. The movement brought my buttocks up against her. She raised my dress up over my hips. Her hands lingered before slipping past the line of satin to caress my bare skin. I quivered as she parted me.

"You're wet," she said, tracing the swollen flesh between my legs.

"Yes," I gasped as she circled my clit with an expert touch.

She released my curls, trailing her nails down the back of my neck. Her fingers dipped lower and she pierced me, rough and sudden. I cried out, clawing the coverlet.

"Mmm, yes," she said, flicking her wrist until I made a sound that was half-moan, half-whimper. "Very wet. Wet enough."

"For?"

I heard her steps leading across the room before the sounds of the heavy armoire doors were flung open. I didn't turn to look to see what she was retrieving. If I turned to look while we played such a game, she would use it as a reason to punish me. I remembered them well, the games we once played.

She returned with a strand of black silken rope and used it to bind my wrists.

While she was tying the knots she glanced at me. "I would do a karada"—she squeezed my bound hands—"but that would take more rope and more time than I've the patience for."

I trembled with remembrance. A karada is a diamond shaped body weave, a rope harness that travels from the neck, between the buttocks and legs, and up the length of one's back and torso. It's a type of Kinbaku, Japanese erotic bondage. It sounds simple until one sees the many different types of weaves and patterns. It is one of the great erotic arts.

A karada does not restrain the submissive. It fits snugly to the body and gives one the feeling of being trapped without the actuality of it. There are ways to tie knots in places that would make a less conventional woman than I blush. Amongst other things, Renata had always been very proficient when it came to ropes. I had not forgotten that and found myself a little disappointed that so little a length of rope would be involved. It had been a long time since she had truly bound me.

"You look a bit crestfallen, cara mia." Her eyes glistened deviously in the candlelight. She traced the line of my brow. "There will be other nights."

"What are you going to do with me?" I asked.

The smile she gave was full of pleasant confidence. She moved, trailing her hand up my arm and across my shoulder. She stopped behind me and I felt her nails tickle over the fabric of the dress. She bowed her body over mine, pressing the stiff length of an ivory olisbos against my buttocks.

"Epiphany," she said in a voice that was light and playful.

A muscle in my jaw twitched. I clenched my teeth together while she rubbed her toy against me.

"I kept this," she whispered, hands slipping over my hips and to my stomach, "just for you, cara mia."

Her hands swept across my breasts and I balled my hands, clutching the coverlet in my fists. She caught the neckline of the gown and pulled, tearing the front so that my breasts spilled free.

"Much better," she said, pinching my erect nipples hard enough that I gasped.

She gave a low and throaty laugh.

"Up," she said and I obeyed, crawling onto the bed.

When I didn't put my cheek against the mattress and rise like I knew she wanted me to, she grabbed a handful of my hair and pressed me down herself.

Once, for the simple adoration of her reaction, I used to feign defiance. True defiance she would not tolerate, and it was not in my nature to be defiant where she was concerned, but feigned defiance fanned a fire in her that left me breathless and panting. It was a way of challenging her to push my mind further, to ride my body harder. I did it then, forcing her hand, giving her no other option but to pin me to the bed.

In all of her dominance, Renata was positively magnificent.

Her hand that was capable of such tenderness was also a promise of cold strength.

"You do remember how I like you to do this, don't you?" she asked, both of us knowing I knew what she expected.

A vibration of anticipation whipped down my spine.

"Yes."

"Then do it," she said, and my body jerked with the force of her hands tearing the back of the dress open.

The cool air kissed my skin. Her long nails moved down my back, over the thick line of fabric bunched at my waist.

This time, I expected the movement and held myself against the force of my lesser garments being wrenched off.

Renata took me by the hips, pressing the end of the olisbos against me. She played the tip over me until she parted me and was able to slip past my opening and to my clit. I cried out then, surprise and pleasure sprinkled with just the right amount of humiliation I at once hated and had longed to endure at her hands again.

Her hips rocked slightly, causing just enough friction between my legs that my breath grew eager and shallow.

She shifted and pressed against my opening, working slowly inside me. Her body bowed over mine and I felt her breath at the back of my neck. Her lips trailed a path down my spine, hands resting at my hips. She made no move to penetrate me further, only sheathed inside me and sheltered my body with the weight of hers. A second later, I felt her cool fingers tracing the scars engraved between my shoulder blades.

When I felt her rise, I remained passive, waiting. Her breath eased out in a sigh. "Oh, Piph," she said. I writhed as she pulled out. Something heavy hit the floor and I knew it was the olisbos. Her arms circled my waist.

"Come here," she said, and I followed her hands as she pulled me to sit with her on the bed. Her eyes glistened with unshed tears. "Come here." Her long arms enfolded me. "I'm sorry," she whispered against my hair.

I froze, uncertain how to react. "What are you apologizing for?"

"For making you feel like you meant less to me than you ever really did." She touched the scars at my back with the tips of her fingers. I moved and she let me go. The dress was still bunched at my waist and I stood, tugging it down past my knees and kicking it carelessly to the floor. I crawled back onto the bed.

"I know," I said, sensing the truth behind her words. "But why did you stop? Just to apologize?"

Her bowed mouth curled slightly. "Because," she said, hands steadying me as I climbed onto her lap, "I desired a better view."

I looked at her and searched for the meaning beyond her words. I touched her cheek. "That's not all," I said. "You stopped because some part of you cannot bear to look at it."

Her smile wilted. She buried a hand in my hair and brought our faces close enough that her breath caressed my lips. She placed the flat of her palm over the scarred flesh and her skin was warm.

"No," she said, "it is not all. I do not enjoy gazing upon Lucrezia's handiwork, especially not on your body." She was silent for several moments. "I can heal you."

"How?" I asked.

"I made you. Two hundred years ago, when you died you woke to the call of my power. My power is the life in your veins. You doubt me, why?"

"I do not doubt your power, Renata. I have never doubted your power."

"But still, you do not trust me?" she asked. "A hundred and fifty years ago you would not have questioned me."

"Trust once broken is not so easily mended."

She nodded, loosening her grip. Her fingers played over the skin of my back. "Fair enough. Then what would you have of me? What will help you to trust me again?"

The question caught me off guard. Time was the obvious answer, but what I said aloud was, "You can tell me how you would heal me."

The look she gave me was almost sad enough to be worthy of Vasco. "In a way in which you will not enjoy."

"And what way is that?"

Cuinn chose that moment to startle me so thoroughly that I actually jumped where I sat in her lap.

Renata gave me a strange look.

What your Queen is not telling ye is that she needs your blood to heal it.

But it can be done? I asked him.

Aye, if you're willing to pay for it in blood.

"And what does the little fox say?" She didn't sound exactly happy that Cuinn was eavesdropping again. I couldn't really blame her. He'd been so quiet for so long that I'd thought he'd well and truly gone to sleep, or at the least, out of my head.

"You need my blood to heal it."

"That is only partial truth," she said. "What is true is that I will have to remake the wound in the same way it was created."

I surprised us both by saying, "So be it."

Chapter Fourteen

R enata cut the binds at my wrists first, and while she did, her thoughts seemed far away. I realized that as much as I didn't want the wounds reopened, Renata didn't particularly care to be the one re-inflicting them. The knowledge surprised me a little.

When my wrists were free of the silken cord I spoke. "You do not seem very eager to do what you are about to do."

"I am not."

I touched her cheek, caught her attention enough that she stopped to look at me. "Then why did you offer?"

"It is what needs to be done," she said and her tone was so very matter-of-fact that it made me try to sense the emotions behind her words.

She caught my wrist in her hand. "Epiphany," she said, "stop trying to read me."

"If you would but tell me then I would not have to try and read you."

Her chest fell in a quick sigh. "You were more right than you know when you said I could not bear to look at it," she said. "I cannot, not only because it is a mark on your shining body, but because it is a mark that is not mine. Do you understand, Epiphany? Do you see how selfish your Queen truly is?" she asked, unflinching.

"I do not think that you are as selfish as you wish others to believe, my Queen."

"I thought you naive once, Epiphany, but you were never naive, not really. You were different, yes. Beneath the surface, your desires ran darker than others, is all. Do you think you were naive when first you came to me?"

"No."

She clasped my smaller hands in hers. Her long, tapered fingers twined with mine. For a moment, she stared at our entwined hands. "Do you want me to hurt you?"

"The way Lucrezia did?" I kept my voice as even and mild as I could make it.

She inclined her head.

"No," I said. "What Lucrezia did to me is not a pain I wish to remember. Though suffering at your hands is a great deal better than having to endure her attention ever again."

"But you like pain," Renata said. The corner of her mouth rose on one side. "Considerably more than either of us reckoned, I think. Don't you agree?"

"Yes, but you were right when you said I would not enjoy this."

She raised our entwined fingers, brushing her lips across the side of my hand. "I will try to make it as pleasurable and as painless as I possibly can."

"I know."

"Lie down on your stomach, Epiphany."

I moved to lay with my cheek resting against the mound of pillows. Renata climbed on top of me, using her knees to hold her body off mine. She swept my tangled hair to the side and I closed my eyes, focusing on finding some still and quiet place within. Instead, I found myself listening to Cuinn.

Ye might as well just accept that it's gonna hurt.

Words of comfort I'll accept, but reminding me of what I already know is only irritating, Cuinn.

Cuinn gave a little snort and grumbled, *Someone woke up on the wrong side of the coffin.*

Renata's warm hands moved down the sides of my torso. "You're tensing. It will hurt far worse if you do not relax."

I let out a long, unnecessary breath and tried to relax, one muscle at a time. The back of her fingers swept across the base of my spine. I knew that the knife she'd used to cut the bindings was somewhere in the bed, hidden within the folds of the coverlet. In essence, it wasn't so different from the things we'd done before.

Then again, it was.

Renata had cut me up a little in the bedroom, but never had she cut me simply for the sake of causing pain. It had never been the raping of flesh that it had been with Lucrezia. Renata never forced me to surrender. I surrendered to her ways of my own free will.

It made all the difference, or should have, but the memories of Lucrezia's voice at my ear, the feel of her silver blade sinking into my skin as she carved her art into my back pushed against the surface of my mind.

So many years ago and still it haunted me. It was not Renata that bothered me, nor was it necessarily the fact that she was going to reopen the wounds in order to heal the scar, but the memories of Lucrezia's hands made me feel nauseous and unsettled.

I looked forward to the reminder of such abuse being erased.

What I did not enjoy was dealing with the memories that were resurfacing, tightening my body in fear and making my limbs stiff.

"What is wrong, Epiphany?"

"I don't think I'm going to relax."

"It is not so different than the things we once did together." I turned my face enough to look at her. It was a little too close to what I had just been thinking.

"Now who is in whose head?" I asked.

Her hands swept distractingly over the back of my left hip. "I am not Lucrezia, Epiphany. You know that. I do not gain pleasure from pain alone."

"I know," I said. It was true. Oh, she enjoyed my pain, but only because I enjoyed it.

She bent, pressing her lips against my shoulder. "Then why are you unable to rest?"

I closed my eyes, blocking out the darkened curve of her splendidly arched brows and the twin blue jewel-like fragments that glistened beneath them. "I cannot help but remember, Renata."

"Yes, you can," she said. "You have but to let go and make a new memory with me, Epiphany."

"I have many memories of you. None of them have tainted my soul in such a way as Lucrezia's hands."

"Shh," she said, "Think of me."

I tried. Her mouth worked at my shoulder, lips parting as her breath eased out, cool and warm against my skin. The soft fullness of her lips marked a path like falling rose petals down my body. Her hands cupped my buttocks. Only then did I turn as much as the position would allow to look at her. Her mouth sealed around my flesh, her fangs threatening to pierce me.

I ground my hips into the mattress and she bit down until my skin broke beneath the pressure. I gave a strangled sound as I felt her mouth sucking at the wound.

Her fingers traced my thighs and I opened to her. She stroked my clit, back and forth, allowing it to catch on her skin before dipping into my wetness and spreading it like salve. I groaned as she traced me. Her jaw cinched tighter, until I rose up off the bed, groaning.

Satisfied, she withdrew, catching the languorous flow of my blood with a sweep of her tongue.

Her hands slipped under my hips as she raised me. I rose to my knees, using my elbows to support the weight of my upper body. She inclined her head, settling her mouth between my legs. She pulled me against her lips like my body was a chalice she would drink from.

I sank into the feel of her mouth. The tip of her tongue circled me, curling like a wave dancing over me. I moaned, spine lengthening in pleasure. Renata sucked harder, hard enough that her teeth dug into me. Her tongue flicked and the muscles in my abdomen went firm as her tongue sent shockwaves of ecstasy through me.

She was quick…so terribly quick. I didn't even feel her move. The tip of the blade pricked the scarred tissue, parting my skin. With my mind still fogged by the aftermath of pleasure, it took a moment for my body to register the pain. When it did, I automatically hissed and tried to crawl out from under her. Renata drove her knee into my back, using her strength to pin me to the mattress. I expected the second cut and the expectation made it all the worse. My body tensed, and with the pain stinging like a thousand bees against my skin, I cried out.

Renata pressed her hands against the X-shaped cut and my entire body grew rigid. The pain was so intense that it stole the scream that built in my lungs and held it trapped in my throat. Her hands burned like sunlight.

Somewhere, distantly, as if the pain had detached me from my body I heard my own strained voice pleading with her to stop.

It was worse than what Lucrezia had done to me. Even while she'd drawn her dagger as achingly slowly as she possibly could across my skin, this was by far worse.

The pain spread like a phoenix bursting against my back, traveling up my spine, down my spine, through my limbs like a fire that threatened to eat me alive.

Then, it was no longer flame, no longer heat, but a cold more terrible than Sognare's vision. Then, I did scream.

Gradually, the cold began to ease from something fierce and biting to something soothing and cool. I was left gasping.

Her fingers swept the damp curls from my face. "Epiphany?"

I turned my head, realizing I'd been smothering my face with the black velvet pillow. If I had been human, would I have passed out? Would I have unintentionally suffocated myself?

I didn't make a move to roll onto my back, which ached more with the memory of pain than the actual pain itself. My entire body was dewed with sweat, as if I had broken a fever.

I found my voice and it was raw and hoarse. I wondered how much screaming I'd actually done.

"That hurt like bloody hell," I said, realizing the words didn't quite convey the agony of the experience.

"I know," she said, laying down beside me. "I told you the healing would come at a price."

Aye, that she did, Cuinn said, sounding somewhat disturbed.

I ignored him, touching a strand of Renata's still matted waves.

"You kept your word," I said, almost idly while I tried to push the memory of the pain aside. "You tried to distract me."

"As much as I could." She played with my hair, coiling it around her fingers. "The endorphins, even for a vampire, make the pain a great deal less than what it would have been."

"Did it work?" I asked.

"Yes," she said, cupping the back of my neck in her hand. She drew my mouth to hers. "Yes, it worked."

"Good," I said. "That is good." In the back of my mind I sensed the rising sun, like the promise of a dreaded heat against my skin. "The sun is about to rise."

Renata wrapped her arms around me and I settled in against the gentle curves of her body, a welcomed respite. "I know."

While she held me, I awaited death. Dying at dawn was not like waking when the moon rises. It was at once more intense and less intense. What I could only describe as an invisible force began to seep into every corner of the room, building and waiting like a serpent for the right moment to strike. It was nothing to see with the eyes, but with the soul. That unseen force stretched and grew like a great dragon unfurling from its sleep. The energy rose and I had a moment to brace myself, a moment to will my body to submission, before that invisible dragon slammed into me. It hit, and like falling from a great height, knocked the life from my lungs, my body. In such a moment, one does not think that the world is going black. One does not have time to think.

Chapter Fifteen

A dancing light sprang to life in what seemed like an infinite darkness. The darkness did not scare me. An orange and white glow flickered, casting a halo of light that aroused my curiosity. The light wavered and spoke my name. Intrigued, I moved toward the light. The edges of the flame burned black. The flame stretched and reshaped itself until the outline of a glowing orange fox took form.

Cuinn? I wondered.

Aye, it is I.

Cuinn moved and it was as if he had swallowed a bright orange sunset, but this sunset was dim enough that it did not hurt my eyes. The orange glow surrounding his aura illuminated the endless dark.

Ye must rise, Epiphany.

Rise? I asked.

Aye, he said, *there isn't much time. Ye need to wake!*

Wake? I asked, wondering again what the little fox was up to.

Cuinn lowered his furred body to the ground and leapt at me. His paws hit my chest and I was falling, falling in that vast darkness, falling so fast that my stomach lurched.

I woke, bolting upright, clutching my stomach against the pain and dizziness.

I felt the soft sheets against my nude body. Renata's chamber. The thought made me turn and look for her. She laid beside me, beautiful in her death.

"Cuinn," I whispered his name aloud as the panic squeezed my chest like a vice. "Cuinn, what have you done?"

I felt the threat of sunlight hanging unseen over my head.

We need to wake your Queen.

Why, Cuinn? The sun is still up! Why did you wake me? Stop!

I froze, clutching the sheet to my body in a trembling grip.

I will explain, but there is not time. Ye need to wake your Queen and ye can only do that with me in your hands. Get up; get the sword.

The thread of urgency in his voice made me scramble from the bed, but it was dark and though I could see shapes, I could not make out where Vasco had last left the sword.

A flash of silver and amber light burned and then dimmed. I went to the armoire and found that the soft glow was that of the sword. The sword was glowing.

Why is it glowing? I hesitated in picking it up.

'Cause ye summoned it with your thoughts. Take it, Epiphany. We haven't much time. Again, his soft voice was filled with urgency and something close to panic. Somehow, Cuinn panicking didn't seem to bode well. I let go of my questions and grasped the sword.

How do I wake her, and promise me, Cuinn, give me your oath that you have a very good reason for this.

Ye have my most solemn oath that I've a very good reason. You've only to prick yourself with the sword and offer your blood to your Queen.

I pressed the tip of my index finger against the sharpened point and hissed as it broke the skin more quickly and easily than I had expected. A tiny drop of blood welled and I squeezed, forcing more of the red richness from the nick.

Offer how? I asked.

Put it against her lips.

I touched the silken flesh of her bottom lip, tentatively smearing the blood across the bowed crevice of her mouth. Nothing happened.

She has to taste it!

I put the sword down long enough to clutch the soft angled line of her jaw in one hand. I used my fingers to part her lips, squeezing the blood out. A drop spattered across her perfectly white teeth, and still nothing happened.

"Shite." I grabbed the sword, raising its tip to my face. I didn't think about the fact that there would be pain involved. I merely acted, bringing the blade to my mouth. I tucked the tip of my tongue against the back of my bottom teeth and drew the metal tip across the flat part of my tongue. It stung, immediate and fierce. I covered my mouth with a hand and fought against every instinct in me not to swallow the blood.

I pried Renata's lower jaw open and kissed her. I forced my injured tongue between her teeth, sliding it over the cool velvet of her. I pushed my blood inside her.

A slight intake of air sounded and I made to draw away. Renata made a sound low in her throat, catching the back of my head with her hand. She held me against her, feeding at my mouth. There was no skill to it, no contained passion. The kiss was wild and reckless, driven only by the taste of my blood and her desire for more of it.

I tensed and Renata felt my resistance, pressing her lips against mine as if she would weld our mouths together by the sheer force of her kiss. I opened wider to avoid being injured further.

She shoved her tongue toward the back of my mouth and I pushed at her shoulders, trying to get her to ease up a little. She didn't and so I pushed into the kiss, using my own strength to drive her back against the pillows.

Under other circumstances, a kiss like that probably would've driven me mad with desire. Having just risen to the call of my blood, she was not yet herself. Though I too am vampire and it is unlikely that she could wound me so severely with her own body that I could not heal it, I felt her desire and shuddered against the shadows there.

In her bloodlust, she wanted to consume me in ways that had nothing to do with conscious thought and everything to do with animalistic force.

A lash of power hit my body like a fiery whip. I broke the kiss, hissing against the pain.

We do not have time for this! Cuinn's words rang inside my head like some great bell.

I watched Renata battle her own bloodlust.

"Epiphany," she said. It was the first time I had ever heard her voice wrought with uncertainty. "What happened?"

I sat back on my heels as she sat up. She glanced around the room and I realized that she wasn't just looking around the room. She was scanning it, searching for a potential threat. If I could feel that the sun hung heavy in the sky, then so could Renata. She was my creator, my Queen and Siren, and far more powerful and sensitive to such things.

"Why am I awake, Epiphany?" There was something suspicious in the look she gave me. The flicker of a thought crossed my mind that I could try to read her, but I didn't. Cuinn had said we didn't have time. Whatever he had woken us for, it was not to sit and chat.

I stood from the bed, thinking to find clothes. I went to Renata's closet, opening the wide doors.

"Cuinn woke me. I do not know why, exactly, as he has not yet explained himself. Whatever it is, he felt it was pertinent that I use the fox blade to wake you."

"You used the sword?"

"Yes," I said stepping into the closet that was the size of a small bedroom. I heard the rustle of the sheets a second before Renata appeared in the doorway.

"Some of your clothes are in that chest." She dipped her head in the direction of a chest that was tucked neatly into a corner. It did not surprise me that she still had some of my clothes. When she had disowned me as her pet I had only received the dresses and clothes that she had decided to return. Why she'd kept some of them, I could not say. I raised the latch and opened the lid to find a crimson dress neatly folded on top of the pile. I picked up the heavy material, running a fold through my hands.

We do not have time, Cuinn said again, but this time, as if he shared my memory and moment of melancholy, his voice held sympathy.

I felt Renata watching me from the doorway.

Cuinn, I thought, setting the dress aside and finding a knee-length black tunic to slip into, *if I have time to dress then you've got time to explain.* I found a pair of gray trousers that were a few shades lighter than the tunic and pulled them on, lacing the ties over my hips. I made to move past Renata, when she caught my elbow and started to speak, but what she said clashed with Cuinn's voice in my mind. I had a moment to hear her say "Why" before Cuinn chimed in with, *There are ancient magics at work.*

I raised my hands. "Wait," I said to Renata, "one at a time. Cuinn is explaining." I said aloud, "Finish, Cuinn. I heard ancient magics. What about them?"

Someone in your clan has summoned something, Epiphany.

Are you sure?

Aye.

How are you sure?

I sensed magic...dark and ancient.

Do you know what it is?

Behind my eyelids, I saw Cuinn give a shake of his head.

Nay, I cannot tell from so far away.

I looked up at Renata and said, "You should dress. I'll explain then, but whatever it is that Cuinn is sensing scares him."

Renata went very still. "I may not trust the spirit, but I will trust your judgment, Epiphany."

"Why else would Cuinn wake us?" I asked. "He is bound to protect me, is he not?"

She gave me an incredulous look. "One does not know how deep the binding goes with fox spirits."

"I remember, but I sense his fear, Renata, and it's genuine."

She went to dress. I laced my boots and retrieved the fox blade.

I heard something then. The sound was faint, as if it had come from somewhere deeper down the labyrinth of halls. It came again, an inaudible whisper like a breeze in the night.

Renata emerged from the closet, her dark brows drawn together and head tilted.

"Did you hear that?"

"Yes," I said.

"There is no wind here. There should be no sound whatsoever in the Sotto other than that of the Donatore and their Watchers."

She was right. Nothing in the Sotto should've been alive during the day to make a noise as strange as that.

If what Cuinn had said was true, and it seemed it was, something or someone was out there. Did that mean that he was also telling the truth about something dark and ancient summoned? I closed my eyes.

If ye combine your energy with mine, we can see what it is.

I was about to think my answer when Cuinn showed me that he was not going to give me the time to frame a mental reply.

The force of his energy hit me and I staggered, feeling the vague sense of falling. I felt Renata catch me at the elbow before the room fell away. The gray stone of the hallway came into view. We were running, running the hall on four paws, feeling the invisible wind raise and carry our tail high behind us. We rounded a corner, following the breeze of power and a cold, cold energy.

At first, I couldn't make sense of the shape at the end of the hallway. It appeared to be an incredibly tall human. From Cuinn's height it was hard to guess exactly, but the cloaked figure must've been around seven feet tall. The figure moved, stepping into a spill of torchlight. The torchlight caught the glossy surface of its cloak, making it appear like black leather. A spur graced each slim shoulder. The figure turned and I realized it was no incredibly tall human. The cloak was actually thick wings that the creature had enfolded around its body. Two elongated black ears swiveled, and a mouth that was more feline than anything else I could compare it to, opened. The creature hissed, flicking a red ribbon of a tongue out from between very sharp upper and lower canines.

That much, I saw before I came back to myself on Renata's floor. My head was resting in her lap and she touched my forehead with gentle fingers. I moved, getting to my feet.

"Epiphany, what is it?"

The fox blade was still in my hand. "I don't know. Someone summoned a…" I hesitated to call it a demon. But if it wasn't a demon, what was it? "A demon…"

"That is not possible."

"Apparently, it is," I said, "because I just saw it."

She grabbed a handful of my hair and jerked me down to my knees. Her eyes were wide with fear. "Do you understand what you are telling me, Epiphany? Do you comprehend what you are saying? If someone in the Sotto has summoned anything, they have to be awake to summon it."

I spoke through gritted teeth. "Yes, I understand that. Renata, let me go."

She didn't. "Why? What are you going to do?"

I licked my lips. What was I going to do? I hadn't thought about that. What would Vasco have done? The thought made me think of him.

"Renata," I said, swallowing, suddenly horrified. "Vasco. I have to check on him."

"If he were truly dead I would sense it, Epiphany."

"The sun is up. You cannot sense the death if one is already dead."

Her grip tightened harshly, making my scalp ache. "I would sense it."

She has not sensed the other.

You know for a fact it has killed?

I see more than ye, Cuinn said. *It has devoured the life energy of its prey.*

I met Renata's gaze and held it. "You can't sense them die if they're already dead during the day. Whoever conjured the beast did so for a reason. More than likely, just to kill us, but they are being clever. Think about it."

She let me go, her rich lashes fluttering. "If what you say is true then they summoned it during the day for that reason alone, that I would not sense their deaths."

"Yes. Renata, we don't have time and you don't have guards." I left the room before she could stop me, heading toward the hall at a full out run. As I left the shelter of her bedroom, I felt her dread and worry like a dart in my side. Cuinn, understanding me, was silent.

Would she follow? Undoubtedly, but I didn't wait to see and she didn't stop me.

❖

I reached the hall where Cuinn and I had last seen the creature. I rounded the corner and held the sword aloft in a two-handed grip.

"Stop."

The creature's clawed hand paused in mid-motion where it reached for the door handle. The wide curve of its ears swiveled in what I sensed was irritation. A spaded tail swept the floor as it turned to face me.

Its eyes were angular and seemed large set in a feline-like face. I saw myself reflected in black mirrors. The creature had no irises to speak of.

The creature, caught somewhere between human, feline, and bat, spoke in a voice that was atrociously slow and lingering.

"You ssshould be sssleeping, vampire."

Epiphany, Cuinn said, *back up slowly.*

I took a very slow step back, but thought to ask, *Why?*

Ye do not want to know. Trust me on that.

Cuinn...

The creature tilted its massive head.

It took a step forward on its bowed leg. I brought the sword up between us, pointing it at the demon. "Stop," I said again.

Onyx eyes blinked and lowered to the sword's point. A ripple of anger rolled through the demon's cold energy, making it seem warm for an instant.

"You dare to challenge me, dessscendant?"

"No." It was Renata's voice that made me turn my head. She strode toward us in a dress of black velvet, her hair still matted with blood.

She sank to her knees in the stone hallway.

I had never, in my entire existence seen the Queen kneel, to anyone or anything. She took in the creature's face for the briefest moment, before she lowered her gaze in a gesture of respect. A gesture most reserved for her.

In that one move, Renata acknowledged the creature as someone of higher status than herself. I did not understand it.

"The lassst thing I expected to sssee from you half-breedsss isss ressspect."

"I know what you are," she said, "Epiphany does not."

The demon-creature turned the full weight of its dense stare back to me.

"Eeepiphanyyy," it said, carefully enunciating each syllable, "that isss what you are called?"

I sank to my knees. If showing respect would keep the creature from killing any of us, then I would do it for survival's sake. I averted my eyes, not because I was acknowledging its status above Renata, but because the endless black pools were utterly unnerving.

"Yes."

"You do not know what I am?"

I opened my mouth to say, "demon," and Cuinn's voice blared through my mind, *Do not call it that!*

I closed my mouth and tried truth instead. "No, I do not know what you are."

I sensed more than saw the creature's attention return to Renata.

"You do not teach them their hissstory?"

"Only the Eldest of us know. It has been long since your kind walked among us."

"Thisss isss true," the creature said in a voice that was almost thoughtful. "Tell your daughter what I am. Name me, vampire."

The fact that it had called me daughter meant that it knew Renata was my Siren. I wondered if the demon was capable of telling such a thing just by looking at us.

"You are one of the Great Sires."

"That isss not my name," the creature's voice hissed like nails on glass. "I sssaid name me, vampire."

"It is not wise to speak your name."

The creature's long obsidian tail swept the floor in agitation. The spaded tip hit the wall with a heavy thump.

"Fairy talesss," it said, hissing. "Name me!"

I turned just in time to see Renata's head jerk upright. Her eyes blazed with power, like the deepest ocean and clearest summer sky meeting and melding.

"You are Dracule."

A spurt of satisfaction emitted from the dark being.

"Wasss that ssso hard?"

"Who summoned you, Great Sire?"

The creature was silent. I used the silence to my advantage.

Cuinn, do you know what the Dracule are?

Aye.

Tell me.

"Firssst, tell your daughter what I am."

A distant relative. Your Queen will explain.

Renata sat back on her heels, looking for all the world like she was relaxed, but I sensed the tension coming off her.

"The Dracule are our Sires, Epiphany. They are the oldest of our kind."

"It's a vampire?" I asked.

"It'sss?" the creature hissed, taking a threatening step toward me. "You call me an it'sss?"

I realized that, for the first time in two centuries, I'd made one of the biggest political blunders I could've ever made at what was more than likely the most inopportune of moments.

My pulse leapt fiercely. I bowed my head.

"I meant no offense, Great Dracule."

I heard its tongue flick out, tasting the air. "You ssspeak truth, but there isss more."

"I did not mean to insult you." I sank a little lower into the bow, curving my body toward the floor. "Simply, instead of saying he or she, as I am not certain of your gender, I defaulted to it's. I give you my sincerest apologies and beg your forgiveness."

The creature made a sound somewhere between a hiss and grunt. It took a moment for me to realize that it was laughing.

"Would you like to sssee, vampire?"

I bolted upright. "What?"

The creature was walking toward me on its gracefully arched legs. The claws of its talon-like feet appeared very sharp indeed. I forced myself not to fidget or move away.

The Dracule stopped in front of me, leaving an arm's length of a space between us. I did not like that it had moved so close.

"Would you like to sssee?"

If ye want to win its favor, say aye.

I wasn't entirely sure what I was saying yes to and prayed Cuinn had not led me astray.

"Yes."

One furred black shoulder raised. The leathery wing drew aside like a curtain. The creature turned its face to Renata and hissed.

"I did not sssay you could sssee."

I watched as Renata casually averted her gaze.

The Dracule spoke my name, calling my attention back to it. I sat on my heels, refusing to look away, refusing to allow myself to give in to the fear that sent my heart drumming against my ribcage. The other leathery wing rose and was drawn aside to reveal a surprisingly sleek and elegant body.

In truth, the Dracule were not such hideous things. They were a wild beauty, yes, and perhaps some would think them the things of nightmares, but as I looked at the Dracule, I did not see something that was monstrous.

The Dracule's body was covered in shiny black fur. The fur glistened like silk and looked soft to the touch in the flickering torchlight. My eyes dropped from a slim neck to the two mounds at its chest. It was hard to tell through the fur, but I was fairly certain the mounds were breasts. I looked lower, past the flat plains of a stomach, over the arched curve of its hips, and to the slope below.

There, at the Dracule's groin, was a small furry node of flesh. It did not look male, though it did not look entirely female, either.

The Dracule ran an almost human hand down its stomach, lightly touching the top of the fur between its thighs. As it had five fingers and opposable thumbs, it was almost human. The sharp silver claws that unsheathed from the tips of those fingers were terribly contrary to human.

"You wonder what thisss isss?" the Dracule asked.

"Yes," I said, hastily adding, "Forgive my ignorance."

The Dracule sheathed its claws in a soundless move. It parted its legs slightly and pressed two fingers to the base of the little mound.

"It isss like yoursss, only more."

Does that mean it's female?

Aye, Cuinn said, sounding amused. *'T is a girl.*

I held the Dracule's bottomless gaze and tried not to show the awkwardness I felt in regard to the situation. Beneath the awkwardness, I admit, was a fine thread of curiosity that I also tried not to reveal, having no idea what effect it would have on her.

"Thank you, Dracule," I murmured, inclining my head respectfully. "I do appreciate your forthrightness."

It was hard to tell by looking at her, but I sensed distantly that she was amused with me.

Renata broke the silence that followed my words by asking, "Who summoned you?"

The Dracule kept looking at me. The corners of her furred mouth raised in what I thought was a smile, albeit, a disconcerting one.

"Sssomeone classse and not ssso classse."

"You speak in riddle."

The Dracule looked at her then. "And you have not given me reassson to ssspeak otherwissse, vampire."

"What would make you speak otherwise, Dracule?"

Its ears swiveled and I realized it was thinking. The leathery wings snapped like a clap of thunder and I jumped. It settled those wings like a cloak around its body.

"Her."

CHAPTER SIXTEEN

For the first time in my undead life, I was sincerely too frightened to speak. I heard Renata's voice, as if coming from the other end of the hall.

"You are implying that the joy of Epiphany's body would be worth the name of the one who summoned you?"

"No," the Dracule said. "The joy of your vampire'sss body will be worth the protection of three I wasss sssummoned to take."

"You have already taken the soul of one of my vampires," she said and made it clear that she was not happy about that transgression. "Will you trick her and only spare her two?"

"I will ssspare her three."

The dimly lit hallway went unbelievably silent. I realized they were both staring at me. I met Renata's inquiring look.

"I do not know what to say."

"Yesss or no," the Dracule said.

Renata spoke to the tall creature. "On one condition, Dracule, as I know your kind are a bargaining lot. If Epiphany agrees to bed you, as her Queen, I am to be present."

"Fair enough." The Dracule raised her shoulders in an awkward version of a shrug. "It isss not like I could not have already taken her sssoul if that isss what I wanted."

"Why haven't you?" I asked.

The Dracule did not answer.

Renata's voice flowed through my mind, like something liquid and touchable.

Curiosity, she said, *it has and will always be the Dracule's greatest virtue and greatest vice.*

Still, the Dracule did not answer.

You speak like one who has had experience, I thought.

Epiphany, if you agree, I do not advise letting it touch you between the legs with its hands.

I remembered the tiny silver claws that the Dracule had unsheathed and shuddered to think of the possibilities.

Guide me, I told her. *What do you want me to do?*

Her voice seemed to sigh in my mind. *As much as I despise sharing, this seems the lesser of two evils. The Dracule are honorable, in a way, and they do love to barter. Once summoned, only a bargain of more worth will lead them astray of their original intent.*

Can we trust her?

We do not have much of a choice. I would advise you to decline if I thought your little fox spirito was a match for one of the Greater Dracule.

Cuinn?

I didn't have to ask the question as he understood my thoughts.

Your Queen is correct. Ye can kill the Dracule with the blade, but ye'd have to catch her first.

I turned to Renata.

Are you afraid of her?

If she turns against us, oh yes.

Renata could have forced me to do it. She could have ordered me to accept, but she didn't. She left me room to decide what was right and wrong on my own. I turned my face up to the Dracule. "Is it true that you enjoy a good barter?"

"Yesss."

"Then"—I got to my feet—"barter we shall."

"Lead." She made a sort of sweeping gesture with her body, as someone would when inviting a guest into her home. The gesture was more like a half-bow with her arms tucked behind the shield of her wings.

❖

We had spent a good half hour bartering with the Dracule. I admit, Renata was a great deal better at it than I was. I did not know how the Dracule killed their victims, nor did I particularly care to find out. The Dracule was not allowed to scar my body, maim my body, or remove any of the flesh from my body. While Renata bartered and discussed the terms with the Dracule, I wondered just how intimately she knew their kind.

"Do I have your word that when I am mounting your vampire you will not ssstab me in the back?"

I heard the Dracule's words and began paying close attention to the conversation again.

A dark smile curved over Renata's lips from where she sat in a chair next to the armoire. The Dracule stood at the foot of Renata's great bed. I sat on the edge of it, watching them both.

"If you hurt her in a way she does not enjoy," she said darkly, "then yes, oh yes, I will cut out your heart myself, Dracule."

"If you can," the Dracule said, empty black eyes slipping from Renata's dark smile and to my still form on the bed.

The Dracule started moving toward me and my heart leapt into my throat.

"You both need to feed," the Dracule said, continuing in a dry tone, "I am willing to feed you both, at a price."

"The blood of a Dracule," Renata said arching her dark brows, "that is no small offer. What say you the price?"

Not only were we bargaining my body, but we were suddenly also striking a bargain about the Dracule's blood.

Well, I thought to myself, *at least the Dracule is willing to open a vein.*

Aye, Cuinn said, reminding me of his presence, *your Queen is right again. 'T is no small offer.*

Why did it seem like Cuinn was starting to agree with Renata more and more?

I can't do this if you're going to be playing around in my head, Cuinn.

He fell silent. I sensed that he was curling up for a little nap, but knew he would not truly sleep. He would, as usual, eavesdrop. Is it really eavesdropping when the spirit communicating with you mind-to-mind is magically bound to protect you? In truth, I didn't think he could help it. He could no more block me out than I could him.

"Did you hear her, Epiphany?" Renata touched my shoulder and I startled back to myself.

"Hear what, my Queen?"

"The Dracule has offered her blood on the condition that I make you ready."

"Ready?" I asked, unable to keep the suspicion out of my voice.

"She has offered to feed us so long as I use my hands and my mouth to prepare you for her."

I licked my lips, considering. Renata had never shared me with anyone before. It was never something we'd had cause to discuss, as we'd never put on a show for another woman, let alone one of the Dracule.

I couldn't decide. Would it excite me or make me uncomfortable? Would being touched by Renata in front of the Dracule make me feel a little safer? I honestly had no idea.

"That is up to you, my Queen."

Renata was silent a moment. I think she was allowing me more time to give it some thought.

When she realized that I was leaving the decision up to her, she made it.

"Agreed," she said, "it has been long since I have tasted the blood of the Dracule. It is very heady stuff."

"It isss."

I didn't disagree with her decision, mainly because the pangs of hunger were beginning to tighten my stomach. I was beginning to feel hollow and empty, easily distracted. I felt tired, and that alone was warning I needed to feed. We did not feel tired, not truly, but we did begin to feel a kind of physical and mental lethargy that had to do with having gone too long without feeding.

Renata went to the wall, pulling aside a plum colored curtain that hid two double doors. The two doors opened into a decent-sized sitting room that connected to one of the back halls. When she emerged, she was carrying two crystal wine glasses. She held the glasses out to the Dracule. The Dracule's black eyelids blinked.

"You will not take my blood with your mouth?"

"The Dracule have two shapes," she said, offering a cutting smile. "If you are unwilling to change your form then I think this way best."

The Dracule took the glasses and flexed her hand. Those tiny claws shot out and she drove them into the artery at her wrist, holding it steadily above the wine glass. The smell of blood made my nostrils flare. It smelled more strongly metallic, higher and richer in iron than mortal blood.

"Two forms?" I asked, resisting the urge to rise and jerk the Dracule's wrist to my mouth.

"Yes," Renata said. "What she did not tell you is that she has a form that is…less intimidating."

The Dracule handed Renata the first glass. Renata's long, tapered fingers wrapped daintily around the stem.

"And isss your vampire sssome human I have to pretend to be lesss frightening for?"

Renata took a sip of the blood, her eyes closing. When they opened, her pupils had constricted to tiny specks.

"My Epiphany does not scare easily, Dracule."

The Dracule offered the second glass to me and I stood in order to retrieve it. Her clawed fingers brushed my hand and I gave pause, but not out of fear. No, I was strangely calm. If the Dracule had meant me harm, wouldn't a being such as she have already caused it? Her fingers touched mine, light and gentle. Her black eyes held a thread of uncertainty.

She withdrew her hand, claws tickling along my skin.

"Ssso I sssee."

Her fur had been as soft as it seemed. I couldn't help but wonder, no matter how much I tried not to, what that furred body would feel like sliding against mine. I attempted to ignore the shiver that shimmied down my spine and distracted myself by pressing my lips against the rounded edge of the glass, draining the blood.

The Dracule reached out, brushing a curl out of my face with the back of her fingers. I felt Renata move up behind me. Caught between the two of them, I shut my eyes, as if that would stop desire's heat from building between my legs.

"Isss it your Queen or isss it me that you crave?"

"Both."

The emotions that flowed through the Dracule's being were like tiny streams, veins of emotion. There was eagerness and anticipation, but also sorrow and a cavernous well of longing. I was about to raise my hand to touch the Dracule's cheek when I felt Renata's fingers at my neck. She guided my hair to spill down my back.

"The Dracule must wait her turn," she whispered, her breath warm at my ear. Her tongue traced the curve of my earlobe, making my skin prickle.

"Disrobe, Epiphany."

I did, taking the hand she offered and allowing her to guide me to the bed. She used her body to encourage me to crawl toward the head of it, raising the black velvet of her skirts and straddling me.

She kissed me and I swayed back against the pillows, offering my mouth and forgetting all about the presence of the Dracule. Renata's lips burned against mine, her tongue filled me. Her hands swept across my waist and spilled over my breasts.

She drove her fangs into the sensitive skin of my breast until I made a sound for her.

Renata used her hands and mouth to tease me. The tresses of her waist-length hair slid across my body and I writhed at the sensation of it. She kissed my hips, licked my navel, nipped at the skin in the bend of my elbow. Her fingers stroked the dampened lips between my legs enticingly.

She rose, moving to lay beside me, touching a lock of my hair with a libidinous smile.

The Dracule came to us then, crawling across the bed. She crouched above me and I saw myself reflected in the strange pools of her eyes.

Her wings unfolded and she lowered, pressing her sleek furred body against mine.

"Silk," I breathed the word, rubbing the side of my face against her chest. "You are like drowning in silk."

The Dracule said nothing while she used her knee to part my legs. I yielded, opening to her. Her satiny hands moved at my waist. She looked at me with an expression of tender surprise and yearning. She raised that inhuman face, revealing the rawness of her want.

She put her hand between my legs and it was like being caressed by a woman wearing silk gloves. The creature that had been so frightening was amazingly gentle as she moved her hips and angled the flesh of her groin against mine.

That mound of silken flesh brushed my clit and I gasped, raising my hands unthinkingly. I touched the furred softness of her shoulders, the only thing I could reach, and buried my fingers in her fur. That mound of flesh moved again, summoning a wave of pleasure from within me. I lowered my gaze to find that her hips moved ever so slightly, but not enough to cause such a sensation.

"How?"

"I told you, it isss like yoursss, only more."

She pressed her lower body against mine, raising enough that with her height, I could no longer hold her shoulders. Her genitalia pressed more solidly against me and I wrapped my legs around her hips. A moment later, she drew back, and as she drew away, that soft flesh clung to me, clung like it had suctioned to my skin. Her hips moved again, enough to tug lightly, but that light tug was an immensely pleasurable gesture that bowed my spine.

I cried out as her body clung to mine like a mouth, the pleasure almost unbearable. Almost.

She bent, her red tongue flicking out against my breast in a way that caused my hips to buck unwittingly. I turned my head and met Renata's amused expression.

"Mmm," she said silkily, "who'd have thought you'd have a penchant for the Dracule's particular brand of pleasure." She reached out, idly touching my brow.

The Dracule chose that moment to nip my breast, hard enough to bring my attention back to her.

I stroked the tip of her elongated ear. Her pace quickened and the pressure between my legs ignited, sending my head back against the pillows. The heat built, making my thighs clench tight.

The Dracule spoke with an effort. "Sssoon."

The muscles in my stomach went rigid. "Very soon."

Before the orgasm took me body and mind, the Dracule's body arched like a bow. She threw her head back, exposing the line of her silky throat. Her wings stretched out behind her, casting a terribly beautiful shadow in the dancing candlelight. A cry like nothing I had ever heard before spilled from her mouth, a woman's cry of ecstasy mingled with a screech that was too low and raspy to be that of a bird. I saw as much, before I too became the victim of pleasure and echoed her.

The Dracule collapsed on top of me, wings spread out across the bed. Her spaded tail rose, swaying from side to side. The movement shifted her hips, making me very aware that her groin was still connected to mine. I rubbed against her and she groaned, grabbing a handful of my hair. Her sharp claws threatened to pierce my scalp. For fear of injuring myself, I stilled.

"Ssstop." The Dracule used her grip to raise me up on my knees. She moved to lay on a bed of those leathery wings. "Ssstraddle me."

I climbed her legs and reached down. I couldn't help it. I wanted to touch it. I wanted to feel her sex in my hands. I wanted to investigate it, to know what it was, what it felt like…to see how it reacted to my touch.

I cupped her in my hand, feeling her slick skin stiffening against my palm.

"This," I asked, massaging her, "what do you call it?"

I squeezed, watching her eyes shudder closed.

"Nod Dragoste."

I let her roll out of my hand, dipping my fingers lower in exploration.

I found her opening, easing my fingers inside.

There we were very much alike.

"What does that mean?" I said, fingers curling.

"In Englisssh?" she asked, her body tight around me. "It would transsslate to sssomething like, ah—" She shuddered again, spasming as I pushed deeper. "Love knot."

She caught my wrist and pulled my hand away from her groin.

"Ssstraddle. Put your sssex againssst mine. I want to feel you sssliding over me. I want to watch you dancing above me."

I held myself above her on hands and knees, rubbing the side of my face against her stomach. I wanted to bite her. I wanted to lick her. But though the fur was as soft as silk, there was no flesh to lick and bite. If the Dracule shed as much as any cat I'd ever known, I was not going to make the mistake of biting her.

"Show me your other shape," I said, brushing my cheek across the curve of her hip. "Show me your other form, Dracule, and I'll grant your request."

I would have never said such a thing to Renata. I would have never spoken such bold words laced with demand to her, my lover and my Queen. But the Dracule was not my Queen, and though we made love, she was neither friend nor lover.

Though Renata had broken my heart, something in me wanted to trust her again. Yes, even at the risk of being broken again. In love, there were always risks. I was not blind. I had no doubts of the risk I took. But if I were honest with myself, I found my longing far outweighed those doubts. Whether that was the deep soul binding of Siren and vampire at play, or the years of engrained servitude, I did not know. Then again, perhaps it was simply my nature.

Love had a strange way of discombobulating the self and breaking any preconceived notions. The Dracule was not my Siren. She had not earned my complete and utter surrender, let alone the submission of my body and heart. I was not bound to her through magic, passion, and politics in the way that I was with Renata.

The Dracule sat up and moved toward me. I realized she was about to kiss me and had a moment to fear, to think that the mouth in which she was about to kiss me with was not a mouth made for kissing, when the silk of her fur brushed my lips. Her maw opened and the ribbon of her tongue tickled my bottom lip.

"Kisss me, vampire." Her voice was a whisper of a hiss that sent her breath tickling against my mouth almost as much as her tongue had. "Kisss me and I will change for you."

Her tongue danced against my mouth and this time, I opened to her. Her tongue slipped past my lips like some long and thin piece of candy. It flattened alongside my tongue, dancing a wet ballet in my mouth. I pressed my lips to her furred mouth and found it was too large for me to do what I wanted to do. I was not capable of returning her kiss. So instead, when she withdrew, I traced the black line of her lips with the tip of my tongue.

The Dracule growled, deep and rumbling. It was a sound far more animal than the serpentine hiss of her voice.

She pressed her mouth roughly against mine. I did not feel her change. One moment, a mouth too large to kiss was pushing against me and the next I felt the soft fullness of human lips. Her tongue spilled into me, velvety and warm. I opened to her, kissing her back.

The Dracule spoke with a woman's sensuous mouth. "Is that better, vampire?" The blackness of her eyes receded to reveal gold irises slashed with branches of onyx lightning. Although her face was that of a beautiful woman, the long spaded tail that swayed behind her and the leathery wings stretching from her back were not. I leaned back to fully see the pale body against mine. A dusting of obsidian fur covered the mound at her groin.

We knelt on the bed in front of each other. She looked down at me, craning her neck slightly. I pressed my stomach against the slight bulge between her legs, rubbing against her. "Yes."

The Dracule turned away and I touched her cheek.

"Show me your fangs."

Slowly, she opened her mouth. Her fangs were not so very different from a vampire's. The only difference was that she had elongated canines on both her upper and lower jaw.

She closed her mouth with an unhappy snap.

"Satisfied?" Without the long, thin tongue, it seemed easier for her to speak.

I gave her shoulder a light push and said, "I will be."

She sank back on a bed of her incredibly long black hair and wings. I straddled her, brushing my groin over hers. That node of furred flesh hardened slightly. I spread my legs wider, sinking lower on my knees until her sex was nestled against mine.

The Dracule watched me with unnerving intensity.

I skimmed her sex with mine, shuddering as her flesh swelled between my legs, gliding through my wetness. I felt her against me and wondered if the flesh was large enough, sturdy enough.

A shudder rippled through the Dracule's alabaster form.

"Will you fit?" I asked, circling my hips, dancing my flesh over hers.

The Dracule gave a breathy reply, "A little."

"Do you want me to take you inside me?"

Her eyes fell from my face to our touching groins.

Her hands found my hips, nails digging lightly into my skin. That one touch was sufficient. I shuddered, sheathing her engorged clitoral knot inside me, taking in as much of her as I could. I sat back on my heels and used the muscles between my legs to cinch like a snare around her. It would not work for long, for she was female and not a thing meant to be sheathed and cinched. But for foreplay, it worked considerably well.

The Dracule's nails dug in more roughly. I cried out, grinding myself into the pain. The move made her slip out of me and I gave my own version of a frustrated sound.

"Rub against me," she said, removing her nails from my flesh. She left little tiny crescent imprints on my skin, but had not drawn blood.

Those magnificent eyes flicked over my shoulder and I turned to see what she was looking at.

Renata crawled in all of her pale, nude glory toward us.

"The Dracule makes a wondrous distraction," she said. "Would you cast me from your bed?" she asked the Dracule.

"I did not bargain for you," the Dracule said in a voice that was warm with agitation.

Renata's hand swept across my ass and I shivered.

"I am not for you, Dracule," she said, turning an icy stare on the Dracule beneath me. "Do you not want Epiphany to writhe betwixt us? To watch her, trapped, a prisoner between our bodies?"

The Dracule licked her lips.

"When you put it that way, half-breed, it does not sound so bad."

I felt Renata move up behind me, felt the olisbos we had abandoned the night before pressing against my lower back. She buried her hand in my hair and jerked my head back, forcing an encouraging whimper from me.

Her breath at my ear made of my name a command, "Epiphany."

I lowered myself, trying to hold the Dracule's gold and black eyes while Renata sheathed herself inside me. Renata guided me upright, tickling her nails down my back. Her hands anchored at my hips and I lowered myself, guiding my sex over the Dracule's mound. Renata followed, burying the olisbos inside me. The Dracule pressed against me, catching me by the shoulders and pulling me down on top of her. I caught myself and was about to suggest a better position when Renata took me by surprise. Withdrawing the olisbos, she thrust her hips, impaling me with it. I gave a startled cry, body arching.

The Dracule seemed to pick up on some unspoken command, for her flesh rubbed my clit and the pleasure was so intense that I squirmed.

Renata held me by the hips, held me still by turning her supernatural strength against mine.

Trapped between the two of them, one like a wave of the sea and the other like the wild night breeze, it was no gentle lovemaking. I am vampire. I do not see shame in the acts of love between women and what they desired, I gave eagerly. When they pushed, I yielded. What they demanded, I surrendered. With their bodies connected to mine, I gave every inch of myself in passionate abandon.

Renata found a rhythm, pounding between my legs as if she would leave her mark etched deep within the flesh of me. I tightened around her, full, so full. The orgasm felt as if it would burst, tearing me apart in a finale of bravura rapture.

The Dracule found her own rhythm, something slower and more sinuous than Renata's exquisite force, but no less dominant, no less as claiming. Caught between their shining bodies, between the forces of them, I came screaming, body tightening like an arrow ready to fly free of its bow.

When the orgasm passed, I felt the Dracule writhing against me, beneath me, her pale and slender body stretching under my face and torso. I swept my hands across her ribs and cupped her breasts, driving my nails into her skin.

Her body went rigid as she cried out.

On the edges of her cries, Renata's laughter followed, thrumming through me.

CHAPTER SEVENTEEN

Afterward, we lay across the bed. Renata discarded the olisbos and climbed in to rest her body against the line of my back. The Dracule stretched out in front of me. She started to rise and I caught her wrist, pulling her back down. Her tail brushed my leg, curling around it. In human form, her tail was as white as her skin. Renata reached out, idly stroking that alabaster tail with her fingers.

"Whose deaths would you have me spare? We bargained the rules of the bedroom, but you've yet to give me the names of those lives you seek to protect," the Dracule said at length.

"Did I please you so little as to only warrant the protection of three of our people?"

I raised my eyes and found the Dracule staring at me. Her expression was not a light one. I scooted forward, moving closer to her. I nestled my knee between her thighs, brushing the love knot between her legs.

Of course, she could've gotten angry with me for invading her personal space, especially after the bargain had been fulfilled. However, I did not think she would. There was more to the Dracule than anger and killing. So much more.

"If I ask the gender of the vampire who summoned you," I said, "will you tell me?"

Asking the gender would narrow down the possibilities. I wondered, in the back of my mind, if Lucrezia had done it. She was power-hungry and mentally unstable enough to pull such a stunt. The Donatore, though stronger than normal humans and somewhat immortal, did not have any magic by which to summon the Dracule. If it were not so, I would not suspect a vampire had done the summoning.

The Dracule seemed to consider it. Slowly, she dipped her head forward and said, "I will grant you that."

I traced the line of her jaw with the tip of my index finger. "And will you still grant the protection to three of those I care about?"

She blinked. "Yes."

I felt Renata's body tense next to mine. Her fingers stopped idly petting the Dracule's tail.

"Will you extend that protection to the clan?" I asked. "What do you gain by killing our people?"

The Dracule's eyes flickered nervously, as if she wasn't sure how to answer the question.

"I will spare all of your people…at a price."

Renata gave an abrupt laugh. "At a price," she said, "that comes as no surprise, Dracule."

The Dracule shot her a displeased look.

I traced the slight swell of the Dracule's shoulder, trying to distract her from her anger.

"What be the price?"

Ignoring the fact that Renata's arm was draped across my waist, the Dracule snaked an arm around the base of my back, lower than Renata's. She pulled me closer to her and whispered, "I will spare your people if you agree to bear my sigil."

"Sigil?" I asked. I knew a sigil had somewhat to do with magic, but I did not know what it meant for the Dracule. "What does bearing your sigil entail?"

Renata's cheek brushed my shoulder, her lips pleasantly and distractingly grazing the slope of my neck. "She is offering to bind herself to you. If you bear her sigil you will be able to call upon her whenever the whim strikes your fancy." She was silent for several seconds. "The only reason a Dracule would offer to bind themselves to a vampire is out of love. Truly, you have not fallen in love with my Epiphany so soon?" The words themselves were serious, but her tone held a thread of light amusement.

The Dracule narrowed her eyes. The look on her face made me shiver to the core. "I am not blinded by love of your Epiphany," she said in a voice gone low and rough. "I offer because she pleases me."

Renata sat up, nude and glorious and boldly facing the Dracule's look of challenge. "You think to take Epiphany away from me?"

"Your claim runs deep in this one, half-bred Queen or no."

"If you think to win Epiphany's favor by referring to either of us as half-breeds, you are mistaken."

"I can speak for myself, Renata," I said, albeit softly.

The Dracule offered a triumphant look.

"Don't look so pleased with yourself," I said to the Dracule, "as I haven't agreed to anything yet, and my Queen speaks the truth. You will not gain my favor or my compliance by calling one I care for a derogatory name such as half-breed. I'll not be wooed by petty insults."

The Dracule didn't look happy. I ignored it. "Why do you keep calling us half-breeds? She said that your kind were the beginning?"

"Would you like me to tell you a charming little tale?" the Dracule asked.

"If you wish."

"Once, long ago, the leader of the Dracule fell in love with a mortal woman."

"And?" I prompted.

"And the Dracule cannot love mortals," she said. "We crave their blood, and to love them eventually leads to their death. Such is what happened with our King. He seduced his mortal lover and took her to his bed."

"And killed her?" I asked.

"While they were making love the thirst for blood came over him. He bled her to death. When he realized what he had done, he wept. He tried to return the blood he had taken by slitting his wrist and holding it to his lover's mouth."

When Renata had taken my life and had given it back to me, she had offered her wrist. It was one of the major acts in the rite of death and rebirth, in the siring of a vampire.

The Dracule continued. "He tried to sacrifice his own life for hers, and when he did not die he screamed his fury and cursed God himself. Azrael, the Angel of Death, heard the King's cries."

"What happened?"

"Azrael took pity on him. He asked the King if he would give his immortal life for the mortal woman to rise again. The King agreed and Azrael took the King's immortality and placed it inside the woman he so revered. Her name was Lilith. She was the mother of your kind."

"The King of the Dracule gave his immortality to us?"

"Yes."

It made me think better of the Dracule that once they had a king that had sacrificed his immortal life for a mortal woman he had loved and not meant to harm.

"That is why you call us half-breeds," I said. "It upsets you that the youngest of us do not know our history and the eldest seem to forget. Your king sacrificed himself for our rebirth and none of us honor or acknowledge that, do we?"

Her eyes closed.

"Very few make the acknowledgement these days."

"We did not withhold our history to shame your kind, Dracule. There are still those of your kind that regret your King's sacrifice," Renata said from behind me.

"But," the Dracule said, "the vampires should know of their origins. Despite those of us who hold you in contempt, we are the beginning and deserve to be acknowledged as such. Your pretty little vampires would rather pretend they were not born of the King's sacrifice than show lineage to us." She gave a bitter laugh. "Monsters and demons, they call us. Did you know?"

Renata gracefully bowed her head. "I am not one of the vampires that agree with that, Dracule."

"Neither am I," I said. I placed my hand on the Dracule's hip.

"Then will you bear my sigil?" she asked. "Will you honor my mark?"

I sat up, resting my back against the pillows. I started reaching for the gray coverlet and stopped myself, realizing why I was doing it. Surely it was not for modesty's sake, for once you sleep with someone you lose some sense of that modesty. I had slept with both women, reaching for the coverlet was merely a thing to do to distract my mind and hide myself. I didn't need to distract my mind or hide. I needed to consider my options and to comprehend what the Dracule was offering and what would happen if I declined that offer. It was obvious, looking back on their meeting in the hallway, the way that the Dracule had initially acted toward Renata and me, that there was bad blood between our kinds. I had not known then that the history of vampires was so tightly wedded with that of the Dracule. It was no small disrespect for the vampires to turn their backs on their true Sires.

"If what you say is true," I said, "then should not the Dracule honor and respect the angel Azrael?"

Her expression told me plainly that she did not grasp why I would say such a thing.

"Azrael did not strip you of your immortality, no?"

She looked at me then, as if I were a spider weaving a cunning little web and she was wary of setting foot in it. "No, he did not strip us of our immortality, only the King."

"Then should you not, as you expect our kind to honor and respect yours, honor and respect the angel Azrael?"

"What are you saying, Epiphany?" Renata asked.

"I am saying only that the Dracule should pay their respects to Azrael, for he is the one who gave them, as well as our kind, the ability to bring mortal lovers over."

"There is wisdom in your words," the Dracule said. "You are saying that the vampires are not the only ones who have acted in slight and disrespect?"

"Yes," I said, "that is what I am saying."

I forced myself to hold her incisive gaze.

"You are avoiding answering my question."

"You haven't answered mine," I said, "not fully."

"And what question is that?"

"What does bearing your sigil entail?" I tilted my head to the side. "If you expect me to bear it, to allow you to mark me, then I need the details. I will be able to summon you, to contact you?"

"Yes."

"Will it make me your slave?" I asked. "Will it take away my free will? Will you be able to hear my thoughts? Will you be able to communicate with me telepathically?"

Renata touched my thigh then, but not to distract me sexually, to warn me to tread cautiously.

The Dracule apparently caught the meaning of the gesture, for she said, "I know you have the death blade and I know that you are able to communicate telepathically with your Queen. I will not invade your thoughts unless you so wish me to. I will not take away your free will. I will not make you my slave." Her dark brows furrowed thoughtfully. "Think of it as an alliance, if you will. If you bear my sigil and wear it with pride"—she placed her hand flat on my stomach—"and do not hide it from others of your kind, then I will not lay a hand on any of those you care for. I will spare them, Epiphany."

"Is that all?" I asked.

"You will have my protection," she said, the pupils of her eyes expanding and shrinking as a wave of frustration emitted off her.

"And what will you have?" I asked. It was imperative to state specifics when discussing such a matter.

"You," she said.

"But you said you would not make me your slave. Am I to be at your beck and call, then?"

"No," she said, lightly shaking her head, sending the dark tresses slithering about her waist. "We will merely have an agreement. I would prefer that you come to my bed and body willingly." She cast that gold and black stare at Renata. "There has not been an alliance between our kinds in many years. Would you prefer that your pet reject my offer?"

Renata's eyes were full of intellectual calculation. "I would advise her to at least consider it," she said very carefully.

"You think I should take it?"

Her shoulders rose in a shrug. "As she says, there has not been an alliance between our kinds in a very long time, and to have such an alliance on our side is not necessarily a bad thing. When considered, the price does not seem so very high."

"And if the price was losing me to the Dracule?" I asked. "You have never been willing to share me, Renata. I remember that very clearly."

Renata cupped my cheek in her hand. Her fingers stroked the hair at my temple.

"Would I lose you to her, Epiphany? Have the past two centuries meant so little to you that you would turn from me and give your heart wholly to the Dracule?"

It was almost the same exact thing I'd pulled on the Dracule. Had I spent too many years as Renata's pet that I'd accidentally picked up some of her political maneuverings, her subtle manipulations? If so, had she noticed? I looked at the Dracule. She was beautiful in a heartbreaking sort of way. Then again, so was Renata. They were both dominant and powerful, both brunette beauties with porcelain skin and unrealistically magnificent eyes. I looked at them, really looked at them, and realized that out of the two, the Dracule was surprisingly the softer beauty. She was taller than Renata, which certainly said something of her height. Yet, in her human form, she seemed closer to six feet than seven. It was not the Dracule's body that made her the softer one, for the spaded tail and leathery wings made her appear more like some dark fallen angel, but the bones of her face. Renata was feminine in every sense of the word, but her features were positively striking. Her beauty was sharper, more immediate. The Dracule's was more subtle, slowly creeping over one.

Would my harsh and beautiful Queen lose me to the touch of the Dracule?

"You know me. Do you think you will lose me to her?"

Renata smiled gently. "No. You are attracted to her, intrigued by her. I would expect nothing less." The gentle smile stretched into something more wry. "As I do know your type, Epiphany."

"And what is your type?" the Dracule asked. "Do I not fit it?"

Renata laughed and leaned over, tracing the Dracule's obsidian brow.

"If you did not, she would not have bedded you."

"Is that true?"

I licked my lips, because she was staring at me, which made me feel strangely uncomfortable. "Yes. It is true."

"Not many vampires would admit to such a thing," she said, gold and onyx eyes so intense that I wanted to fidget.

"I am not one of them."

"Prove it," she said at length. "Accept my mark."

"You will spare all our people?"

"Yes."

"You will tell me the gender of the one who summoned you?"

"Yes."

"Tell me the gender first. Was it a woman?"

The Dracule began moving closer. "No." She shook her head.

"A man?" I asked, as if there were any other options. If it was a man then obviously it was not Lucrezia. If it was not Lucrezia, who then?

"Yes."

I bowed my head. "Then give me your mark, Dracule."

I had no idea what to expect when the Dracule took my wrist. She raised my wrist to her mouth and before her lips touched my skin I knew she was going to bite me. I forced my body to relax. Fangs like oversized thorns sank into my skin. I gasped, eyes fluttering as the blood pumped out of my wrist. With her fangs sheathed inside of me, she locked her mouth around the wound and sucked at it, encouraging the flow of my blood.

It was, and wasn't, similar to what Renata had done to my back. What was similar was that the wound began to burn. It burned with a power that was as hot and piercing as the fangs that had been driven into my flesh. The Dracule unhinged her fangs like a snake and I balled my fist in the blankets, fighting not to cry out in pain. She locked her mouth around the wound again, only this time the tip of her tongue darted out, dancing through the red blood on my white skin. I felt the wounds closing, felt the blood no longer flowing out of each hole every time my heart beat. It seemed as if time had slowed. I watched the Dracule back away from my wrist. Her eyes opened and her lips parted. She let out a breath that was as warm as a summer breeze.

The blood burned and pain returned like fiery needles. I drove my teeth into my bottom lip, sealing my mouth on a sound of pain. My blood bubbled at my wrist as if it were boiling. It burned like a brand before it sank into my skin, like water poured over earth.

The Dracule's eyes met mine and the gold in them seemed like liquid flowing around black marble strokes. The look she gave me was darkly ardent. Her eyes flicked to my wrist and I looked. The blood darkened until it was as black as ink. It began to move as if it were crawling beneath my skin. Her sigil shaped itself like black vines flowing and curving on my skin.

What the sigil was of, I could not comprehend. I thought it was letters, but no letters I knew were quite so strange. The last black shape arched like a scythe spreading out toward the base of my wrist. When the lines stopped moving it looked like nothing more than an elegant tattoo.

"What is it?" I asked, admiring the dark ink against my white skin.

"It is the mark of my name."

One long line curved symbol like the delicate arch of a flower's stem.

"What is your name?"

"Iliaria."

"It does not look like your name to me," I said in a puzzled whisper.

"It is in no alphabet you would understand."

"So it is an alphabet?"

Gracefully, she dipped her head.

"Why does it tingle?"

It tingled and itched very unpleasantly. It wasn't painful, but it was uncomfortable enough that I wanted to scratch at my wrist.

"To let you know I am near. You will feel the mark whenever I am near. You may use that mark to call upon me." She ran the tip of her finger over the graceful flowing letters.

"How do I do that?"

"You have but to think of me and I will know it."

"You said that you would not invade my thoughts."

"I said I would not invade your thoughts unless you wanted me to do so. By thinking of me, you invoke me."

CHAPTER EIGHTEEN

I liaria left. Fretting for Vasco, I had asked questions about the vampire she had taken. Based on the description she revealed to Renata, it was blessedly not Vasco and had been some Underling I did not know. Mayhap, I should have cared more, but the truth was I didn't, not as much as I would have had it been Vasco. It was regretful, yes, but I was relieved that it was not my only friend.

Renata and I were alone in her room. Renata stood. She paused by the two solid black doors that led to the bathroom.

"I need to bathe, Epiphany."

I cocked my head to the side. "Is that an invitation?"

The corner of her appealing mouth rose. "Once, you would not have had to ask such a question. You would have simply followed." She held her hand out to me. "Yes, Epiphany, it is an invitation."

I took the hand she offered and allowed her to lead me through the doors. The Sotto did not have electricity. However, there were those of our kind some years ago that saw fit to invent some kind of crude plumbing. There were toilets, for us as well as the Donatore. Though we vampires did not excrete solid waste, there was water in blood that was released in a rather humanly fashion. When the Sottos had first been built, away from the rural places and hidden in nature, the earliest of our kind had seen the necessity of having water and grounds to hunt. It was not for us, but the Donatore, for they were human and needed to eat and drink.

Following the advancement of the modern world, we learned to dig and bury pipes, connecting them to rivers that were in constant rich supply. It was for that reason Sottos were almost always found near a natural water supply, no matter where they were in the world.

I had never seen the pipes myself, nor did I know how they had obtained the materials, though I imagine that had somewhat to do with the Cacciatori.

The water was cool or warm, never hot. When one took into consideration that we did not feel the cold as mortals do, it was not such a great downside. Of course, I'd never asked the Donatore if it bothered them overmuch. They did have more rustic means to heat whatever water they needed, if they so desired.

Renata set the stopper in the tub before turning the chrome handle. The water spilled in a rapid flow from the carving set into the wall. The carving was of a lion's head and the water spilled from its gaping maw.

She stepped over the high edge of the bath and beckoned me with a glance. Renata swept her hair aside, guiding the cloak of silk over one slim white shoulder.

The sight of her nude body had always pleasantly distracted my mind and scrambled my wits, but seeing her curvaceous form reclining in the bath, even after having sex with the Dracule, still called to my body.

"Epiphany," she said, half-laughing, with a smile that made her eyes sparkle with mirth, "come here."

I went, obediently sinking into the wide bath. She swept the curls from my back and placed a kiss against the sensitive skin at the back of my neck. I shivered. Her arms wrapped around my waist, pulling me against the front of her.

"Do you remember when I turned you?"

"Yes," I said.

"Do you remember what I said before I gave you the kiss of death?"

I nodded.

"What did I say to you?"

I remembered the words as if she'd only just spoken them yesterday. "You said that you would always take care of me."

Her hands guided me and I turned, sinking to my knees in front of her. My hair spilled across my shoulders, spilling over my breasts and into the water.

She touched my face and gave me a look of tender affection.

"I meant what I said."

"I know," I said, for I felt in my heart that she spoke truth. In spite of the many misconceptions I may have had, I felt her sincerity in those few words.

Renata took my hand, touching the sigil at my wrist.

"I do not want to lose you to her," she said and there was vulnerability in her eyes that I never expected to see. In some distant part of her being, she felt threatened by the Dracule. I touched her neck, tracing her skin.

"You won't."

"Do you give me your oath?" she asked with a thread of amusement in her voice.

"You have my oath. You always did."

"Epiphany."

I lowered my face, brushing my lips across the arch of her brow.

"Renata," I said.

She held me until I moved to turn off the faucet. Afterward, we bathed in silence. Renata ran her fingers through the heavy mass of my hair, rubbing soap into the strands. I relaxed under her hands, feeling strangely at peace in spite of the knowledge that someone in the Sotto had summoned a Dracule to kill us. If it had not been for the Dracule's single-minded curiosity, we both might've been dead. When offered moments of peace, one should be worthy and aware.

I took a normal pace down the stone hallway, carrying the fox blade in my right hand. When I mentioned that I wanted to leave to check on Vasco, it was not only Cuinn who had protested, but Renata had also insisted that I kept the blade at my side.

Cuinn was silent, allowing me to walk the long hall in relative quiet, with the exception of my thoughts. I wanted to run to check on Vasco, even though I believed the Dracule. I would go to Vasco's room and wait for him to rise. I had to see him to be sure. I was unaccustomed to being awake before him. The older and most powerful vampires always woke first.

I tried to distract my mind by the feeling of that power as I navigated the deserted hallways before the sun had set. When would I have another chance to be awake before the others? I frowned as the stick of optimism was washed away. If it hadn't been for Cuinn alerting me to danger, I wouldn't have been walking the halls. Still, the danger was out there. The Dracule may no longer be a threat, but someone had summoned her. Someone had asked her to kill the vampires of the Rosso Lussuria.

I made it to the end of the hall and turned right down a smaller adjoining hallway. I walked past the wide-open sitting room and continued until the hallway spilled open into the Elders' Quarters. The walls of the Elders' Quarters had been placed in such a way that each of the black wooden doors seemed welcoming and inviting. The stone walls formed an octagon connecting to the narrow hall. I headed for the door on the far right, but a voice brought me to a halt.

"Isn't it a little early for you to be awake?"

I turned on my heel. The last time Lucrezia and I had met without the company of another's presence, I'd ended up with scars and painful memories. A sense of dread unfurled like a serpent in the pit of my stomach. I willed myself to stillness.

I had not known she was powerful enough to wake so early.

She leaned against the doorway clothed in nothing but a white sheet. She smiled as if she were pleased with herself, as if she'd gotten the exact reaction she was hoping to get out of me. She took a step forward and my fist tightened around the fox blade, forcefully enough that her eyes flicked from my face to the blade.

"Are you going to kill me, Epiphany?"

"Are you going to try to hurt me, Lucrezia?"

Her voice fell into a breathy whisper. "Do you want me to hurt you, Epiphany?"

I struggled not to shudder against the memory of that voice in my ear. "If you try to hurt me, Lucrezia, I will try to kill you."

"Truly?" she asked, taking another step forward. She looked me up and down. "I heard you liked pain, Epiphany. A great deal, if I'm not mistaken."

"I have never liked your kind of pain."

She smiled genuinely enough. "Oh, I remember, my dear. I remember very, very well." She kept moving toward me and I fought every instinct in my body that screamed to take a step away. I kept my grip tight on the sword, ready to raise it if provoked. I would not let her hurt me again.

"What's the matter?" She stopped leaving a few feet of space between us. "You seem a little edgy. Do I make you uncomfortable?"

"Yes."

I didn't see her move. She disarmed me in a matter of moments. My back hit the wall as the blade fell to the stone floor with a clatter. She caught my wrists and used her strength to raise my arms above my head. She ground my wrists into the rough stone.

"Mmm, you smell of fear." Her lips brushed my neck and I flinched. She kissed my neck, softly, so softly, betraying the harsh reality of her own sadistic desire. Her lips trailed a path over my exposed throat, threatening to travel lower. I twisted my body away from her, away from the wall. I managed to break away, but Lucrezia was too fast.

She caught my wrist and tried to use it to jerk me back to her. In order to avoid being brought up against her body, I sank to my knees in defense. She turned my wrist in her hand, clinging with fingers like hard shackles. She looked down at the Dracule's mark embedded in my flesh and her eyes widened.

Lucrezia was afraid of the Dracule. I saw it, and saw my way clear of her.

She regained her composure, her expression closing down to show nothing but bitter malice.

"What is this, Epiphany?"

"What does it look like?"

Her fingers cinched tighter and I fought the urge to make a sound of pain. It felt like she was trying to pulverize the bones of my wrist.

"It looks like the mark of one of the Great Sires," she said almost casually, "but what would one of the Great Sires want with an Underling like you?"

To that, I didn't have an answer. Lucrezia's hold loosened. She let me go. I got to my feet in a painfully slow move and forced myself not to go for the discarded fox blade. It would amuse Lucrezia if I showed fear by lunging for a discarded sword.

I did not understand her expression. The white sheet stayed wrapped around her, and I realized that before she opened the door she had known I was out in the hallway. If she had not known, she would not have bothered tucking the sheet into place. I looked at her and knew she would not attack me for fear of the Dracule's wrath.

The Dracule had been right to some extent, bearing her mark alone already proved to be some sort of protection.

Nonetheless, it did not erase Lucrezia's desire to inflict pain. She would only have to come up with better ways, more clever ways, of hurting Renata and me than outright challenge. It took me a moment to realize that I was sensing what Lucrezia felt. My thoughts were only the translation of those feelings. We stood there, wrapped in silence.

"Why do you want to hurt the Queen?"

She scoffed at me, but she wouldn't meet my eyes. "Who spews such blasphemy that I would intend harm to the Queen?"

"Others do not have to do the telling," I said, "Your emotions do an adequate amount of telling for them."

"Are you accusing me of betrayal against the Queen?" she asked, adding harshly. "Against your precious mistress?"

I went to retrieve the fox blade then, remaining carefully alert while sure in the knowledge that she would not try a direct attack when I bore the mark of the Great Sire.

"You crave power, Lucrezia, everyone knows," I said blandly. "I am simply saying one should be wary of which powers they chase, for some powers have a way of chasing back."

"Are you threatening me?"

I gave her as blank a look as I could muster, because being this close to her was still terrifying.

"You little cunt." She took a step forward, hands clenching into fists at her sides. "You *are* threatening me."

I turned the fox blade in my hand without raising it. It caught the flickering torchlight. The movement also caught her attention, giving her pause.

"It is you who should be wary, Epiphany. You and your precious mistress." She practically spat the words before turning to return to her room.

I stared at her door long after it had closed, thinking furiously. Were her words merely a spiteful threat or did they hold some weight? I strongly sensed that her dislike of Renata and me was genuine, though I did not understand it.

I approached Vasco's door and stepped into the safety of his room. My head was full of thoughts. Unfortunately, none that made me feel any wiser.

CHAPTER NINETEEN

Vasco's room was without light. I tried to move gracefully, tried to remember my way around furniture, but despite my best efforts, ended up banging my left hip roughly into the corner of his cherry oak dresser. I hissed through my teeth, cursing myself for not waiting until my vision adjusted to the dark. I felt along the wood's smooth polished surface for a box of matches. The fox blade began to glow, casting sufficient light by which to see. I wasn't worried about the noise. Vasco was still dead to the world. I was a little surprised he had not woken yet. If Lucrezia had already risen for the night, surely he would have as well? I gave up searching for a box of matches and sat on the edge of Vasco's bed. I placed the fox blade in my lap.

His hair was still in its multitude of little intricate braids, his features serene and peaceful in his daylit death. He was naked from the waist up, with the blankets shielding his lower body. Two small silvery hoops glinted at both of his nipples.

I pulled my legs up to sit cross-legged, waiting.

I didn't have to wait long. Vasco's body bolted upright as he gasped, taking the breath of life into his lungs.

By the sword light I saw his pupils were constricted.

Little by little, his pupils expanded.

"Colombina?" He frowned. "What are you doing?"

I leaned back against the wooden footboard. "Waiting for you to rise, il mio fratello."

Vasco's face erupted in a ferocious grin. "You do not have to say *il*, mia sorella."

I couldn't help but smile. "Duly noted," I said. "I only know what I've picked up here and there."

"Sì."

"Obviously, there is room for improvement."

"Your Italian is a great deal better than what it was."

"Thanks to you."

"I get all the credit?" he asked, blinking at me. "Does our Queen get none?"

"You know she rarely speaks Italian. Every now and then, she'll throw in a few choice words if the English equivalent escapes her."

He kept grinning. "That is a rare occurrence."

"Yes," I said, "it is."

He glanced at the sword glowing in my lap. "You need light?"

"No, but it would be appreciated."

Vasco leaned over and opened the top drawer of his nightstand. He lit the lantern on top of it with a match. If there was one thing the Sotto was well stocked with aside from human blood, it was matches. The sword's glow began to gradually dim, until it stopped glowing altogether and we sat in the warm glow of firelight.

"You are up early," he said.

"Yes. I rose much earlier than usual. Do you wish to hear why, my brother?"

"Sì."

I touched the sword's blade with the tips of my fingers. "Cuinn called me to rise and I woke."

"The spirito would not do such a thing unless you were in danger."

"That is true," I said. "Cuinn sensed something lurking in the hallways."

"And our Queen?" he asked.

"He bid me wake her," I said. At the look of perplexity on his face, I continued, "I used sword and blood to wake her."

"I had forgotten the spirito blades were capable of such a thing."

"It would have been nice if someone had told me they were."

"What was in the Sotto?"

I raised my right hand. The sleeve of the tunic fell back to reveal the dark sigil embedded in my flesh. At first, it didn't register. He stared at the mark for a long moment and when he realized what it was, his eyes widened.

"Is that…?"

"The mark of one of the Great Sires?" I asked.

"Sì, is it?" He leaned forward, tilting his head like a crow that was inspecting something shiny.

"It is," I said. "Someone summoned one of the Dracule to kill us, Vasco."

"That is treachery," he said, clearly appalled. "Who would do such a thing? How could they do such a thing?" he asked, though it sounded more as if he was thinking out loud. "How could anyone be awake to summon one of the Great Sires?"

Cuinn whispered through my mind.

The Stone of Shadows.

Since he didn't explain or add anything more, I asked Vasco. "What do you know about the Stone of Shadows?"

"La pietra di ombre?" He sat back with a thoughtful expression, his lips pursed. "It is a magical relic forged with the blood of the Great Sires. The legend is that the Great Sire who created the first placed his blood in the stone so that his immortal lover would not die when the sun rose."

"It was created with the sole intent of keeping a vampire alive during the daylit hours?"

"Alive and protected from the sunlight itself, sì."

Why hadn't the Dracule bothered to tell me as much?

"Do the Dracule die at dawn like we do?"

"No."

"So whoever summoned the Dracule must have the Stone," I said.

"Which complicates things."

"How does it complicate things?"

"Because the *stones* do not belong to our kind, colombina. The only way a stone could have fallen into the hands of one of our kind is if one of the Great Sires gave it to them."

"That doesn't make sense," I said. It was obvious there was an old underlying feud between our two kinds, but I had not grasped how deeply embedded that feud was. "Some of the Dracule resent us greatly," I said, "I know this, but why would—"

Vasco answered my question before I'd finished asking it. "Think about it, colombina. If the Dracule has bound his or herself to one of the Rosso Lussuria, their agendas must coincide."

"Their agenda being the destruction of our kind."

"Sì."

"Could it be the same Dracule that bound herself to me?" I didn't want to ask it. I didn't want to know, but I had to ask. I had to know.

"A Dracule can only be bound to one lover at a time." A look of melancholy crossed his face and I sensed the thread of heartache in his voice.

"You had a Draculian lover?" I asked, managing to sound only a little surprised.

The corner of his mouth raised in a half smile that didn't reach or match the well of sorrow in his eyes. "Sì, his name was Pantaleone. He was my lover many years before you were even born."

"What happened to him?" I asked.

"He was murdered," Vasco said. It hurt to hear the pain in his voice.

"Did Renata have a Draculian lover, Vasco?"

"Our Queen had her alliances with some of the Dracule. To my knowledge, she never took one to her bed. That would be a question better directed at our Queen, Epiphany. Why do you ask it of me?"

"She's a little hush-hush on the subject."

"In other words, she is being vague with you?"

"Yes."

"She will give you an answer when and if she's ready to give it to you."

"I know that. I was her pet for fifty years, remember?"

"Are you saying that you are no longer her pet?"

"You know what I mean. Tell me about Pantaleone. Were you bound to him?"

"Sì," he said, and again his expression took on a sad look. "I felt his death when he was murdered."

"Did you ever find the murderer?"

He turned away from me then. "No, and it is a bitter torment that still gnaws at my heart."

"I'm sorry, Vasco."

"Do not be sorry, bellezza. I have had a fair amount of time to grieve." The smile he conjured was etched with bitterness and sorrow.

"I never saw a sigil on your skin."

"The sigil faded when Pantaleone died."

I nodded. I wanted the answers that Vasco seemed to have, but it was a sore subject, and I didn't want to rub verbal salt in his wounds. How do you find the answers you're looking for when the only questions you have are painful ones? Vasco chose that moment to question me.

"How did you come to bear the mark, Epiphany?"

"Renata and I bargained with the Dracule."

"What did you use as the bargaining chip?"

"My body."

"The Dracule asked to be taken to your bed?"

"Yes, how did you—"

"That is what Pantaleone did to me. I was newly reborn when Pantaleone appeared in my room late one night. I had been struggling with controlling my freshly awakened hungers. Pantaleone propositioned me. If I would offer him my bed, he would teach me to control all my hungers."

"Did the Queen not teach you to control your hungers?"

"The Queen can only teach one so much," he said. "You became her pet when she brought you over, Epiphany. She taught you to control your hungers more intimately than the rest of us."

I nodded, for it made sense. "So Pantaleone taught you how to control your thirst?"

"As well as other things that I think you would rather not hear about."

"Probably not," I said, eyeing him. "When did Pantaleone give you his mark?"

"Not until some time had passed," he said. "The Dracule do not give their marks lightly."

I glanced down at the curving black lines on my wrist. "Are you so sure about that?"

"I am sure, colombina. If the Dracule gave you her mark, she did not do such a thing on a whim."

"I can understand that. What I don't understand is why she felt I was worthy of her mark. The mark itself seems like a big deal. She said I pleased her and yet, she didn't seem entirely pleased with our people to begin with."

"What did she tell you her reasoning was?"

"That of an alliance," I said.

"That is dangerous for her."

"I know, that's why I don't understand why she chose to give it to me in the first place."

"Perhaps," he said, "after your years with Renata the Dracule was impressed with your...skills?"

"I am not so skilled as that."

"You would be surprised, colombina. The Dracule are a dominant lot. They like lovers that are willing to submit to them."

"I have offered Renata my loyalty and my submission. The Dracule has not earned such a gift from me, not yet."

Vasco gave me a surprised look. "You do not think she senses your innate nature? Our Queen did."

"Are you saying that the Queen brought me over just because she thought I would be her submissive plaything? She brought me over because I was dying, Vasco. She gave me life when life itself offered death."

"I am not saying that is the whole of it, only a sum of the reasoning. She saw in you what she desired, and perhaps, so too does the Dracule."

I wondered then if perhaps my innate nature was sensed by all. Is that why Lucrezia had begun tormenting me as soon as Renata cast me from her bed? Surely, Lucrezia understood the difference between consensual and nonconsensual pain. As soon as I thought it, I knew she didn't. I sensed very strongly that the lines had completely blurred for her many years ago, if they hadn't already been blurry. I told Vasco then about my confrontation with Lucrezia. I told him of the surprise and flicker of fear that I'd sensed from her when she had seen the Dracule's mark on my wrist.

"She is afraid of the Dracule?" He started sliding out of bed and I was glad to see that he didn't die in the nude. A pair of silky blue boxers clung to his Greek statue of a body.

"I believe so, yes." I watched as he disappeared into his closet and reemerged tugging on a pair of black pants. I told him about how I had thought Lucrezia innocent until her comment about Renata and I being wary.

He stopped me while pulling on one of his black boots. "Wait, you threatened Lucrezia?"

I thought about my reply and said carefully, "In a way, yes."

"What did you say to her?"

"I told her to be wary of what powers she chases, for some powers have a way of returning chase."

He sat on the floor lacing his knee high boots. "I do not know whether to be proud of you or afraid for you. I would not say that threatening Lucrezia is exactly a wise thing to do."

"It doesn't matter if it's wise or not, Vasco. If I pass the trials and become an Elder and she keeps trying to torment me, she'll be challenging my status within the clan."

"You're not the only one she enjoys trying to torture, colombina."

"I know there are other Elders that Lucrezia verbally toys with, but she manages not to overstep any boundaries with them."

"She's perfected the art of being an irritant while remaining outwardly courteous."

I nodded. "Precisely. She will insult the Elders in such a way they cannot always take outright offense. I do not think she will spare me the outward appearance of courtesy if I rise in status."

"You are probably right," he said, sitting at a vanity table in front of a large mirror. He began practically trying to rip the bindings out of his hair, tugging at them vehemently enough that I knew he was ripping strands of hair out with the force of his efforts. I placed the sword on the bed and went to him, shooing his hand away from his hair.

"Let me do it, Vasco. You're going to rip your hair out doing it yourself."

He met my reflection in the mirror. "I do not have the patience for it."

"I noticed," I said, carefully undoing the first black binding. I tossed it on the table and used my fingers to unravel the braid. The silver strands were a bit more difficult to unknot, as they had been carefully laced at the base of each braid.

"Who braided your hair for you?"

"One of the younger ones," he said. "She took a fancy to what she said was my pretty long mane."

"And so you let her play with it?"

"Why not?" he said and his eyes started closing like a lazy cat's. "I don't mind the pampering."

The corner of my mouth twitched. "Sometimes I think you were supposed to be a girl, Vasco."

He grinned at me wide enough to flash fang. "With a body like this?" he asked, touching the middle of his chest with one hand.

I thumped him hard on the back of the shoulder. He awarded me with a masculine laugh.

I was on the last braid, trying to untangle the silver tinsel when he asked me, "You think Lucrezia is involved?"

"The Dracule said it was a male that summoned her." I loosened the tinsel, freeing it of the long black strand. "I do feel that somehow, Lucrezia is involved."

"The matter is figuring out how she's involved," he said, "and what she has to gain, considering."

"Yes, I've noticed there's a fair amount of tension between our kinds." I leaned over to retrieve the brush from the table. I started brushing out the untamed waves of his hair, pulling it back so that I could braid it.

Vasco laughed. "Fair amount. That's an understatement. It's been an ongoing animosity for too many years to keep track of. I do not understand why a Dracule would side with a vampire."

"Because they hate us?"

"Or love us," he said. I wasn't sure what to say to that and so we ended up sitting in silence. Finally, I changed the subject.

"When did you get the piercings? I've never seen you wear them."

"I've had them," he said, "since Pantaleone."

I nodded, procuring a black band to secure at the end of the braid. The braid fell to the middle of his back.

"You should finish getting dressed. We need to find Renata and meet with the others."

Vasco stood and I suddenly found myself wrapped in the circle of his arms. I hugged him back, resting my cheek against his bare chest.

"It'll be okay, Epiphany."

"I hope so, Vasco. I truly do."

"We'll figure it out, mia sorella. It's not the first treacherous conspiracy we've had to unravel within the clan and it won't be the last."

Hate and love. Love and hate. I wondered if Vasco had a point. If so, which was it? Or was it something else entirely?

CHAPTER TWENTY

I learned that the vampire the Dracule had taken was named Karsten. I had never spoken to him and did not know him, but he was one of the Underlings and in his years of servitude. Once Renata refreshed my memory, I knew he was the one who had been turned by the Elder Rosabella.

The turning of a mortal to vampire is not a common thing and only happens when the Queen herself decides or grants permission to bring someone over. In my years among the Rosso Lussuria, Karsten was the only mortal I had known chosen by one of the Elders to become a vampire. Like me, Karsten had been taken by the Cacciatori.

Unlike Renata, I do not think it was a matter of pity with Rosabella. Karsten had been healthy when she had taken a fancy to him. She was a creature of whim. She desired Karsten and so sought Renata's permission to turn him some thirty years ago. Renata gave it, allowing Rosabella to give him the kiss of death and rebirth.

Rosabella had taken the news surprisingly well. She had seemed disappointed when Renata told her of Karsten's fate, but other than that, she showed no outward signs of grief. Nor did I empathically sense any from her.

Renata had called upon only the Elders that she knew without a doubt were loyal to her. I was surprised to find that the list was not as short as I had thought it would be. Out of the twelve Elders, eight of them were in attendance. We met in the sitting room connected to Renata's chambers. I sat on the floor next to Renata in her high backed chair. Even if she had been seated on one of the couches, I would not have sat next to her. She was the Queen of the Rosso Lussuria, and so had her throne. Vasco sat on the end of the couch closest to me. Since I was not yet an Elder, I did not sit beside him, as I was not yet in status equal to him.

Nirena, with her long white-blond hair and pale face, sat next to him. Vittoria and Vito sat beside her. They were twins. Both had clear blue eyes, narrow chins, and hair the color of dark coal.

Alessandra and Lorrenzo were seated on the smaller couch. Alessandra's slim face was blank and youthful. Her brown hair that was several shades darker than Lorrenzo's cupid-like curls fell loose around her shoulders. They were lovers and had been since before I was introduced to the clan.

My gaze flicked from them to Severiano. His hair was pulled away from his face, showing the severity of his sharp features. It was the same reddish brown of hawk feathers. He had never threatened me, but the way he watched everyone as if he were the bird of prey that his features mimicked had always been a bit unnerving.

Rosabella shifted in her seat at his side and I turned to look at Vasco, who was watching the two very intently.

"So it is true," Severiano said, "Epiphany is indeed your pet again?"

"Whether she is or is not my pet is none of your concern, Severiano. Does Epiphany being my pet hinder my ability to rule as your Queen?" She fixed him with a look of cool disinterest.

Severiano inclined his head. "I meant no offense, Padrona. I was only curious to find out if the rumors were true or not."

"You did not answer my question, Severiano." Her words were spoken very carefully, very slowly. The warning in them was something tangible, like a match near the tip of my tongue. "Does Epiphany being my pet hinder my ability to rule as your Queen?"

"You know it does not, Padrona."

"How is it a matter of such importance to so many of you when it does not concern any of you?"

Nirena gave a short laugh. "There are those that feel spurned, Padrona. Those that would gladly give you their affection were you to offer your attention and make them feel special."

Renata looked at her. "And are you children squabbling over a mother's doting affection?" Her dark brows arched splendidly with the question. "No," she said, "you are vampires. You are the Elders of the Rosso Lussuria. It is time you start acting like it. The last concern any of you should have is whether or not I have taken Epiphany to my bed again." She fell silent for a few seconds before turning to Vasco, giving them her profile. "What is your concern?"

"I am concerned with finding the traitor that summoned one of the Great Sires to kill us while we slept," Vasco said, and I knew he'd said "slept" for a more politic term.

I looked at each of the Elders. Despite the fact that most of them had enough practice at keeping a face blank from emotion, I knew more than what was readily seen. I opened myself, and like stretching out a hand to feel the folds of different fabrics, touched their emotions, drew that material into myself.

Rosabella was shocked at the mentioning of the Great Sire, as Renata had not told her that Karsten had been taken by one of the Dracule. It was the first true sputter of emotion I'd sensed from her since she'd walked into the room.

When I had asked Renata how the Dracule killed, she would not tell me. The only wisdom I gleaned was that they do not leave a mess. I stopped questioning at that point.

Lorrenzo was filled with disbelief. Alessandra's emotions changed, at first disbelief and then settling on a reserved fear and hope that it was not true.

Vittoria and Vito were somewhat appalled, but at the same time their emotions seemed calmer, steadier, and more certain than any of the other Elders. I knew then that they believed Vasco's words and did not doubt. I sensed Severiano's curiosity, which did not surprise me. After all, he led the Cacciatori.

From Nirena, I sensed uncertainty, as if she were not quite sure how she felt.

Vittoria spoke then, in a voice that was low and clear. "If what you say is true, then we are in grave danger."

"That is why finding the traitor responsible for summoning one of the Great Sires is of utmost importance," Renata said. "That is what you should each be concerned about."

"How do we even begin to figure out who is the summoner?" Vito asked his sister. "It could be any number of us, any one of us sitting here in this room right now."

"He's right," Vittoria said, watching Renata. "It could be any of us or any one of the vampires in the Sotto, lesser and Elders alike."

"It's a suicide mission for an Underling to summon one of the Great Sires," Nirena said. "Not to mention the fact that none of them know who the Great Sires are or what they once were. The Donatore have no power to use to make a summons—"

"The Dracule said that the summoner was a man," I said softly.

They looked at me then, every one of them, and I fought years of court instincts not to turn away. I returned their stares, forcing myself to face them. In order to become one of them, I first had to think of myself as equal to them.

It was not an easy thing, after so many years.

Vittoria and Vito shared a glance with each other.

"You spoke with it?"

"Yes. I spoke with *her*."

"How do we know you did not summon it?" Alessandra asked and I turned to meet her light golden eyes.

"I did not summon her, Alessandra."

"You could have," Lorrenzo said. "You have been close to the Queen, close enough to learn things you wouldn't normally have known if you had not been her pet. You came into your powers long before your two-hundredth year of rebirth."

"As loathe as I am to agree with him," Nirena said, "he is right. She has been your pet. Perhaps she summoned the Great Sire to gain revenge on us?" She sounded more thoughtful than accusatory. "Or simply to gain revenge on you for casting her aside those years ago."

"How do we know you are not saying it is a man merely to rule yourself out as a potential suspect?" Rosabella asked.

I shook my head. So far, Renata was not stepping in. I had to handle their accusations myself. I raised my face and smiled, but not like I meant it.

"If that was my plan, Rosabella, it didn't work out very well, now did it? In fact, why would I speak up at all if I knew it would only attract your attention? I could have simply kept my mouth shut and none of you would be aiming accusations at me."

A heavy silence fell over the room.

Renata laughed.

"Very well reasoned." She touched my hair briefly. "If it were not for Epiphany, many of you might not have risen this night."

Severiano leaned forward. "What exactly do you mean, Padrona?"

"Epiphany," she said, "show the Elders of the Rosso Lussuria what I mean."

I raised my sleeve and bared Iliaria's sigil at my wrist.

For some, it erased doubts. For others, it only added to them. I had wondered if those Renata had called upon were worthy enough to be trusted. I tried to read them while they gazed at the sigil and did not sense anything that gave me a clue as to who the traitor was. There were only four Elders that were not in attendance, and the ones before me were not giving anything away.

"You are bound to the monster that took Karsten?" Rosabella asked. I might've thought that the horrified sound in her voice was over her lost Karsten but knew it was not. She emphasized the word *monster*, and I knew by looking at her that her horror was at the fact that I bore the sigil of one of those *monsters*, not that the monster had taken someone she allegedly loved.

"Yes. I would not call her a monster, Rosabella, as she was kind enough to spare your life."

"What did it cost you?" Nirena asked and I respected her for the fact that she knew enough about the Dracule to know that I had given something for the Dracule's favor. I hesitated to call it a price, though it had been. An enjoyable price, but still a price, nonetheless. I wasn't exactly sure how to answer Nirena's question without feeling like my privacy was being assaulted.

Renata answered for me. "Epiphany and the Dracule struck a bargain."

"What kind of bargain?" Vito asked, seeming more curious than intentionally invasive.

"That is for Epiphany to tell, if she wishes."

"If she wishes us to believe her, then she should tell us," Severiano said.

I narrowed my eyes. "I took the Dracule to my bed, Severiano. I gave the Dracule my body in exchange that she would harm no more of the Rosso Lussuria."

After a few moments, Severiano leaned back in his seat. It was a white flag of sorts.

"You must not scare very easily," Vittoria said, scrutinizing me with her icy gaze.

"Is that a question?" I asked.

Her slim shoulders rose in a shrug.

"How do we know that your sick perversion for this monstrous creature has not clouded your wits and caused you to turn on your Queen, your Siren?" Rosabella scrunched up her nose, looking positively disgusted. "How do we know you haven't met many times in secret with the demon?"

The look Renata turned and pinned her with would've made me sink from the couch and to my knees. As it was, Rosabella flinched.

"I once had several alliances amongst the Dracule, Rosabella. A couple of those allies I would have considered almost friends."

"You are the Queen," Rosabella said, "and within your rights to have alliances."

"How do we know that Epiphany has not been meeting with the Great Sire in secret?" Alessandra seemed a little paler than usual, but her voice was steady enough.

"When Epiphany first met the Dracule I was there, Alessandra. When Epiphany took the Dracule to her bed, I was there. Do you have any more questions that are a waste of my time?"

"Vasco said that the Dracule was summoned to kill us?" Nirena asked. Out of all the Elders, I was noticing that very little slipped past her studious attention. She was observant, which was a powerful tool but potentially a dangerous weapon, depending on how she wielded it.

"Yes," Renata said.

"How is that possible?" Nirena asked, brows furrowing. Her eyes widened slightly. "They have a stone."

We had already spoken with Renata of the Stone of Shadows. She had already suspected that whoever had summoned the Dracule was using one. After all, it was one of the few relics that kept a vampire alive and safe during the daylight hours.

"So it would seem," Renata said. "Whoever summoned the Dracule is working with one of them, I suspect."

"That's the only way they could get the stone," Vittoria said.

"One of the stones, at least," Vito said.

"How many stones are there in existence?" I asked.

He shrugged much as his sister had earlier. "All of the Great Sires are capable of creating them."

"Ah, but they are not so easily made," Nirena added.

"No," Vito answered, "not easy, but not impossible either."

"I will give you that," she said smiling coyly.

"What do you want us to do?" Vittoria asked Renata.

"I have called upon only those of you I trust without a thread of doubt," Renata said and I resisted the urge to glance at Rosabella and Allesandra. Rosabella might not have liked the Dracule, but it did seem she was strangely loyal to Renata. Alessandra, I sensed, was too afraid of the Queen to go against her. Renata turned to Lorrenzo and it wasn't until I saw his Adam's apple bob and felt the wash of fear from him that I knew he too was afraid of her.

"I want you to be Elders," she said. "I want you to protect your people. I want you to offer your aid in finding the traitor who summoned the Great Sire."

"Why not just ask Epiphany if she'll summon her and offer her something in exchange for the name of the traitor?" Severiano asked.

"When the Dracule are summoned a vampire is not required to give their name, Severiano. If Epiphany could have found the traitor for us, she would have already done so."

"Point taken, Padrona."

CHAPTER TWENTY-ONE

The Elders that Renata trusted implicitly had agreed to help. She'd given them the option of refusing to offer their aid, but most of them were politically savvy and clever enough to discern that refusing to help would make them look terribly guilty. When the rest of them left the room I moved to the couch to sit beside Vasco.

Renata remained seated, slumping forward and looking tired in a way that her immortal body would never truly feel.

I went to her.

"Renata," I said.

Her hand touched my wrist and I crawled onto her lap, burying my face in the bend of her neck. She snaked her arms around my waist, holding me close.

"What if what Severiano said had some merit to it?" I said.

"What do you mean, Epiphany?"

"What if I summoned the Dracule and asked her to point out the vampire that summoned her?"

I felt Renata tense.

"I could not do it." I turned to find Iliaria standing in the middle of the room, in the more human of her forms. The glossy cloak of her hair tumbled down the front of her body to her knees. Black leathery wings arched from her back. I was surprised to see that she was fully clothed; surprised because dressing a body with the equivalent of large bat wings didn't seem an easy task.

She moved, bringing my attention to the full-length coat she wore. The coat had been altered so that her wings could fit through wide-stitched openings. The black panne velvet jacket was accented by highlights of gold silk, a reflection of her gold eyes with their veins of black lightning. The sleeves of the coat widened at the wrists. The coat was fastened between her neck and waist, and where it draped open there was a slit of shadowy gold silk underneath. Beneath the clothes, I did not see her tail.

Renata cleared her throat, making me aware that I was staring. Dressed so exquisitely, the Dracule was worth a stare or two…or three.

"Why could you not tell us who summoned you?" Renata asked, breaking the silence that followed my obvious appreciation of Iliaria's presentation.

Iliaria raised her chin. "The vampire who summoned me kept his face shrouded. I could tell you his height, his build, would it help any."

"That may help some," Vasco said, looking Iliaria curiously up and down, "as it is more than what we presently know."

Iliaria moved gracefully and predatorily between the two couches, taking a seat on the smaller one.

"I would put his height at about five-seven," she said. "He was of slim build, not muscular."

"Could you smell him?" Renata asked.

"No," Iliaria said, "he used sage to mask his true smell." What she meant was that, like us, she could smell things mortals could not. We could smell one another's scent. The vampire had used sage to overpower his own scent, so that all she could smell was the sage. He had kept his face shrouded and disguised his scent, obviously not wanting Iliaria to be able to recognize him by it.

"I am fairly certain that whoever he is, he is working with one of my kind."

"We suspected as much," Renata said. "Would you know if he had been marked by one of your kind?"

"If I tried, I would have known," she said. "I did not consider the possibility that he was working with another Dracule until long after I had been summoned. He was very persuasive. He convinced me that the entirety of your clan had turned against us. He played on my dislike of you. I was a fool."

It sounded like the closest thing to an apology we would get from one of the Great Sires.

"You did not know," I said.

She shook her head lightly. "I was a fool. I came so close to believing what the others have said about your kind, Epiphany. If it were not for you, I would most likely still believe many of those lies. I see now how such fallacy has been used as a means to turn us against you."

"What fallacy?" Vasco sat back, crossing his long legs.

She tilted her head. "That all of the vampires are ungrateful, have turned against us, and think us the demons and monsters from biblical stories. Some go so far as to say that the vampires will eventually become greater in number than we the Dracule."

"They're afraid," I said, remembering Rosabella's reaction when she had found out that I wore Iliaria's mark. "It is easy to fear that which you do not understand."

She met my gaze. "Indeed, but you as well, little one, feared me when first you saw me. If you feared me, why did you accept my bargain?"

She was right. I had feared her. I'd even thought her a demon, though I'd hesitated to believe it and say it.

"You are correct. I feared you. I feared because I did not know what you were. I feared because I did not understand."

"Yet still, you took me to your bed. You accepted my offer. Why? Was it only to keep your people safe? Am I mistaken that there was some sincere interest on your behalf, Epiphany?"

"You are not mistaken," I said, carefully perceiving the vulnerability behind her words. How did I explain to her that I was different than most? How did I explain that a little fear was like a heady wine to me? I finally settled for, "A little fear, for me, can be somewhat of an aphrodisiac."

She gave me a long and deep look, but there was something distant in her gaze, as if she were looking through me. Finally, a smile played at the corner of her mouth.

"Only somewhat?"

A little more than that, Cuinn added.

Renata's hand played up my back. It was a comforting gesture, but it caught Iliaria's attention. The look Iliaria gave Renata wasn't necessarily malicious, but it wasn't exactly friendly either. I think it bothered her that I wore her mark, yet, I sat in Renata's lap, with her hand tracing the line of my spine over the lightweight tunic.

I wanted to go to Iliaria. At least, a part of me did. I wanted to go to her and erase that unfriendly look from her eyes.

As if Renata had heard my thoughts, she stopped stroking my back.

Go to her.

I slipped to my feet and began moving toward the Dracule.

Iliaria watched me, her features drawn. "Do not come to me only because your Queen thinks it a good idea. I do not enjoy being toyed with."

"I'm not toying with you, Iliaria, and I'm not coming to you because Renata bid me do so."

"Then why?" she asked, searching my face.

"Because I want to," I said. "Because I know the unfriendly look you gave Renata is only a mask to hide the pain and longing that you feel."

"Then you come to me out of pity."

I bit back a sound of frustration. "This is a delicate dance," I said, "trying to please you as well as my Queen. You are only making this more difficult for me. Iliaria, I love Renata. I've been in love with her for two hundred years. You can't make that go away. It's not going to go away. A mark does not erase it. But just because I love her does not mean that I will overlook you. It does not mean that I do not care about how you feel."

She directed her attention to some vague point in the room. I went to her, touching her cheek with the tips of my fingers.

"Will you one day love me as you do your Queen?" she asked.

"I do not know," I said, for it was true. Who can say who we will love and who we will not love when love itself is often not a conscious decision? "If I told you I would, it would be a lie, for I cannot know, nor can I foresee the future. But I can tell you that I care and I will always try to be considerate."

"And how many others do you care for?" she asked.

"I care for those sitting in this room."

"Epiphany is not casual with her affection," Vasco said, "if that's what you're trying to understand."

Iliaria looked past me to him. What she thought, I could not say. Her eyes flicked back to me. "I would not have you come to my lap like a pet dog."

I was about to reply when Renata's laughter spilled like slow honey into the room.

"If you think I leash her and parade her about the Sotto, you are mistaken," she said, and I did not have to turn to look at her to know the humor in her voice made her eyes lighter. "She came to me willingly, as willingly as she stands before you, Dracule."

"I do not understand that," Iliaria said.

"Epiphany is an empathic vampire," Vasco said. "When she sees pain in another she feels it and tries to soothe it."

"She uses her attention and her love as a balm, Dracule," Renata said. "It is her nature."

"Is this true?" she asked me. I thought about what Vasco and Renata had said and realized that they had spoken truth. I had never seen myself in such a way, but once voiced aloud, the realization slid rightly into place.

"It is."

"Still," she said, "I would not have you come to me in such a way. If you wish to show me you care, stand at my side. I do not ask you to kneel at it."

I moved to sit next to her and she caught my wrist, stopping me and sending the tingling sensation in the mark to buzzing.

"Not now," she said. "If you offer comfort now I will not be able to turn it away and I will forget the very reason I came."

I nodded, stepping back when she let me go.

"What reason is that?" I asked.

She stood. "I came to give you this," she said, reaching into her long coat and retrieving a small scarlet satchel. She took my wrist again, the one with her mark on it, and placed the velvet bag in my hand. She folded my fingers around it. "It is for you and you alone. I cannot take back my misdeed"—her eyes dropped to her hand still cradling mine—"but I can do this. I can offer you my aid in catching the vampire that tried to destroy your kin."

"What is it?" I asked.

"Open and see," she said, letting go of my hand. Her fingers slid across my knuckles and I fought not to shudder at the sweet brush of her skin. She sat back on the couch, watching me.

I opened the bag and guided the contents gently into my open palm. A ring dropped out. It was elegant and appeared to be made of white gold. I raised the ring between my thumb and index finger, examining the smoky black teardrop that caught the light. At its center was a tiny dot of crimson.

"A ring?" I asked.

It was Vasco who spoke, as he moved to the far edge of the couch to see. "That is not just any ring, colombina. *That* is a Stone of Shadows."

I stared at the slender ring. It wasn't large or even impressive in size. On the contrary, it was rather dainty.

I didn't know what to say. If I said it didn't look like something powerful enough to keep a vampire alive during the day, I would've only succeeded in insulting Iliaria's kind gift.

Vasco stood, peering over my right shoulder. "Do you see the spot of red in the center?" he asked.

"Yes."

"That is her blood."

I searched her blank expression. "You didn't have to do this."

"If we are to find your traitor, then yes, I did."

"Thank you."

She tilted her head and dipped it forward ever so slightly.

"You sound like one who knows my kind personally," she said.

He gave her a charming smile that belied the pain I knew he felt. "Knew," he said, "I knew one of your kind very well."

"Who was she?" Iliaria asked.

"He," Vasco said. "His name was Pantaleone."

"The name does not sound familiar," she said.

"It was a long time ago."

"Dare I ask more?"

"Another time, perhaps."

I looked down at the ring. "How does it work?"

"You wear it," Iliaria said. "That is how."

"Just like that?"

"Yes, just like that."

"Does it matter which finger?" Iliaria shook her head.

I slid the ring onto the middle finger of my left hand. I expected to feel some spark of magic, to feel some charge of power, and was taken aback when I felt nothing.

"I don't feel anything," I said.

"A Stone of Shadows does not work that way, Epiphany," Renata spoke from her seat. "You will sense the magic at work once the sun rises. As it is, it lies dormant until you need it."

"You have used one of the stones before?" Iliaria asked.

"No," Renata said, "I merely know of them."

I held up my hand. "Why give me this, Iliaria? How will this help us catch the traitor that summoned you?"

Renata answered before Iliaria could. "She means you to use the stone to stay awake and catch the traitor. No doubt, he will try again?"

"I think so, yes," Iliaria said, "and I plan on staying with Epiphany."

"You said you offered your aid," Renata said.

"Couldn't Cuinn keep me awake?" I asked.

I cannot keep ye awake, he said, *I can only wake ye if there be danger. 'T is not the same type of magic that the Stone bestows upon its wearer.*

Distantly, I heard Iliaria ask who Cuinn was and Renata's smooth reply explaining that Cuinn was the spirit in the fox blade.

I blinked finally, coming back to myself.

"What did he say?" Vasco propped his chin on his fist. I didn't doubt that he'd known I'd been listening to Cuinn's voice inside my head. I still wasn't used to it and would need to work on controlling my facial expressions.

"He can only wake me if there's danger. It's not the same thing as the ring, apparently."

"Of course it isn't," Iliaria said. "Why am I under the impression that you don't want my gift?"

"It's not that I don't want your gift, Iliaria."

"It's that she feels bad you went out of your way to give her something." Vasco grinned and I directed a disapproving look at him.

"You do not like gifts?" she asked, blinking at me as if she really didn't understand.

I wasn't sure how to answer her. I didn't mind the gift, but the fact that she had gone out of her way to create something as powerful as the Stones of Shadows did catch me a little off-guard. I wasn't exactly sure what it required for her to make it. Though, obviously, it required a bit of blood.

Then again, as she'd fed Renata and me earlier, she didn't seem to mind sharing that.

"It is a wondrous gift, Iliaria, and I do appreciate it, but Vasco is right about me. I do not know what it took for you to make this."

"Do you think there are strings attached to this gift?" she asked.

I lifted my shoulders.

"There are," she said and the corner of her mouth curled slyly.

"And what strings are those?"

"It is to aid us in finding your traitor," she said. "However, that is not all. If we succeed in finding your traitor, I expect you to use the ring for me."

"What do you mean use it for you?"

"You bear my mark, Epiphany. We have a bargain. I will give you your nights with your Queen. I will share kindly, but there will be days when I do not want to share you."

A tremble of desire shuddered down my spine.

"I'm fairly certain I can live with that," I said in a voice that was almost a whisper.

She sat back, smiling and looking pleased. "Good. I'd hoped that would be your answer."

"Does my opinion not matter?" Renata asked and her voice was low yet strangely commanding.

"Do you not agree?" Iliaria asked. "Would you prefer to share her bed with me every night?"

Renata's face was a blank porcelain mask. "Not every night, no."

"Some nights?" Iliaria asked.

"Some nights, yes," Renata said, "but not every."

"Then," Iliaria said, "those nights which you do not feel like sharing I will spend my time with Epiphany during the day."

Renata's eyes sparkled with amusement. "I did not say I disagreed, Dracule. I was merely asking if my opinion mattered or not."

"You know it matters," I said, glancing at her.

Renata addressed Iliaria. "I agree, as we have more important matters to discuss, such as your plans for catching this traitor. I imagine you've some idea?"

"I do," Iliaria said.

"And?"

"I will stay with Epiphany and help her find the traitor."

Renata gave a slow shake of her head. "No."

Iliaria narrowed her eyes. "I have gone out of my way for you and yours, and yet you trust me so little?"

"It is not a matter of distrust, Dracule. It is a matter of Epiphany's safety."

"You do not trust me to keep her safe."

"That is not what I said," Renata said in a voice that was dangerously slow.

"It is what you implied," Iliaria continued to glare at my Queen, my lover.

Before Renata could open her mouth and say whatever she was going to say, I interceded. "Then what is the reason, Renata?"

"If this traitor is working with another Dracule and perhaps more than one vampire, you and the Dracule alone will not be enough."

"I wouldn't be so quick to jump to conclusions, Iliaria," I said gently, not wanting to offend her.

Iliaria did not apologize, but she stopped glaring. "Ah," she said. "If we are outnumbered it is true that I will not be enough to protect her," she said. "I cannot make another Stone of Shadows."

"I know," Renata said, watching me.

"But," I said, "I could use the sword."

"That might work," Vasco said. "Cuinn told you he cannot keep you awake? You used the sword today to wake the Queen."

"And you could use it again to wake the others," Renata said.

"The question is," I said, "which others would we wake?"

"Well, to start," she said, crossing her long legs and tilting her head, "Vasco and I."

"That's a given." I smiled softly.

"Who would you wake?" she asked.

I almost responded without thinking it through, but decided that thinking very carefully about whom I would wake was a good idea.

"Not Rosabella," I said.

Renata offered an encouraging nod. "And?"

"I would not wake Lorrenzo or Alessandra."

"Why? Alessandra fears me."

"That fear can turn against you," I said. "I wouldn't give her the opportunity of having my back in a fight, just for caution's sake. Lorrenzo didn't believe what we told him. I don't trust him for the reason that he doesn't seem to take this seriously."

"What about Severiano?"

"He's secure in his power," I said. "That's a point for him. I don't think he'd hesitate to use it. I am uncertain as to whether he would use it for the right reasons, though."

"What do you mean?" she asked.

"Would he use it for his advantage, his gain?"

"Many of us use our powers for advantage and gain, colombina," Vasco said.

"But is it for the right reasons? Would Severiano use his power to help his people or himself?"

"You do not think much like a vampire," Iliaria noted.

"How not?" I asked.

"Oh, she thinks like a vampire," Renata said with a tendril of amusement. "She simply does not think like most vampires."

"She does not think like a majority of the Elders," Vasco said.

"It has never seemed to me like you think like the other Elders either, Vasco."

"I have my moments, bellezza. You will too. As you are learning, in order to survive you have to secure and defend."

"It is so with the Dracule," Iliaria said. "We have that much in common."

Renata steered the conversation back to the previous topic. "Who else would you wake, Epiphany? Would you wake Severiano?"

I turned to Vasco and asked, "Would you?"

Vasco raised his hands, indicating his retreat in answering. "This is your question to answer, colombina, not mine."

I licked my lips, thinking. "Fair enough," I said. "No, I would not wake him."

"Why?" Renata asked, searching my face.

"I have my doubts. If I have doubts about him, then he is not someone I want to offer trust. There is no proof that I should trust him, so I will not."

"The others have not offered you proof of their trust," she added.

"No," I said, "they haven't, but I have more doubts about Severiano's motives than most."

"Then who would you wake? Would you wake Vittoria and Vito?"

"Yes."

"Why?"

"They believed," I said. "Vittoria herself said that if it is true, then we are all in grave danger. They seem to care about the Rosso Lussuria as a whole and not just themselves."

She nodded and seemed pleased with my answer. I was beginning to think the line of questions was a test of sorts.

"What about Nirena?"

"Yes," I said, remembering the look of understanding and the knowledge that Nirena had when she'd realized I'd bargained with the Dracule. "Yes, because she is knowledgeable. She too is secure in her power, but she does not have that dangerous curiosity I've seen present in others."

"Out of twelve Elders, you would wake four, Epiphany?"

"Dante and Dominique. I would wake them."

Vasco grinned at me. "That was well reasoned."

I grinned back. "It just occurred to me."

"I can wake Dante and Dominique," Renata said, "for I made them and they are my guard. Once I am awake, I will be capable of calling to them. The others you will have to wake with the sword."

"Will you be able to wake four Elder vampires with the sword?" Vasco asked.

I sensed Cuinn's ears swivel and flatten against the back of his skull. I didn't need to hear him to know what the gesture meant.

"I'm fairly certain you just insulted Cuinn."

"I did not mean to insult him. I am only checking to make certain."

Aye, Cuinn thought, *ye can wake four. I'd not advise trying to wake the whole clan, but four is cake and as ye've seen, requires little blood.*

"We can do it," I said.

"So we shall," Renata said.

Vasco nodded his agreement.

All three of us turned to Iliaria.

She smiled and there was a hint of danger lurking in her eyes. As far as agreements went, it looked an awful lot like one.

Chapter Twenty-two

D ante was posted just outside the door to the sitting room. Dominique was posted on the opposite door that connected to Renata's boudoir.

Renata went to the double doors leading to one of the lesser hallways, opening it and making a gesture with her head, indicating that Dante should enter. Vasco, having determined the wishes of his queen, opened the other door and told Dominique, "The Queen wishes to speak with you."

Dante wore a black coachman's coat that had a metal clasp at the throat. The coat was reasonably modern. If he wasn't a vampire I might've accused him of trying to look like one.

Dominique, as usual, was the more modest of the two. His hair that was a brown so dark it was almost black was pulled back into its usual low ponytail. He wore a pair of black denim pants with a long sleeved black T-shirt. Generally, it was the younger vampires that embraced the more modern fashion trends of the outside world. We were aware of the trends of the outside world, though very few of us embraced them. There was a great library within the Sotto that held many number of texts, both old and new. The Cacciatori hunted primarily for food, but if they had to go into the city, only those adept at concealing themselves were sent forth to retrieve supplies.

I'd slowly grown an appreciation for slacks and long-sleeved tops, but I would never in my undead life embrace denim. I hadn't even begun wearing pants until I was no longer Renata's pet. I did eventually learn that pants provided a certain protection that a gown did not, and within the Sotto a woman liked to retain some decency.

Renata told them of our plan. However, she did not tell them we would be waking Vittoria, Vito, and Nirena. She trusted her guards more than the Elders, of that I knew for a surety, but I also knew that Renata would only tell as much as was necessary. I learned some years ago that there was always more going on inside her head than she let on.

Dante looked ready to pounce on the prospect, eyes eager as his mouth curled like a cat up to no good.

Dominique bowed. "I understand, my Queen."

"Good," Renata said. "You are dismissed."

I didn't have to see a clock to know that it was some hours until dawn.

The two left to return to their separate posts outside the doors. I sat on the small couch next to Iliaria.

"What of the third challenge?" I asked, meeting Renata's gaze as she returned to her seat in the high-backed armchair. "The others will grow suspicious, will they not?"

"No doubt one of the Elders has already informed the others of the meeting and its significance," she said.

"I thought you called upon those you trusted?"

It was Iliaria that said, "You're fishing them out."

Renata grinned. It wasn't the bright and good-natured grin Vasco often gave. It was slyer, more cunning, and cutting. "In a way."

"I understand what fishing them out means," I said, "but I do not comprehend why you would willingly place your trust in those that you doubt."

"To see who will break it," Vasco said from his perch on the opposite couch.

"Appunto," she said, inclining her head in his direction. "It is a risk I must take to see who is loyal to me."

I understood then. "How will you know who breaks your trust by spreading the word?"

"I have my ways," she said.

"What your Queen means, Epiphany, is that she has her spies," Iliaria said.

Renata raised her brows. "You think so?"

Iliaria smiled wickedly. "I would, were I you."

"And who do you think my spies are, Dracule?"

I caught the flicker in Vasco's features and said, "Vasco knows."

He gave me a surprised look. "You caught that?"

"Yes."

"Once, you would not have."

"I've learned to play closer attention."

"How would I know who your spies are?" Iliaria said.

I remembered Renata's words about hearing talk of her death. Why hadn't I concluded then that she'd had her spies? I tried to figure out the question that she had directed at Iliaria. If I were Queen, who would I appoint as my spies? Vasco was an obvious choice. At least, from my position. I remembered the Underling that had held the doors to the banquet hall open for us. I remembered the girl and the boy that had helped prepare for the dream trial. They too had kept their faces hidden behind their hair, eyes studiously averted.

There were always Underlings. Anytime a mortal was reborn a vampire, they became an Underling within whatever clan they belong to. It was the way our society worked.

Of course, there were Underlings that let their newfound powers go to their head. There were also Underlings that never came into their power and those who chose not to embrace it even when they did. The Underlings that sought to ascend rank sooner than allowed were punished by the clan's head, if not the Elders. Those Underlings that conformed and served their Queen or King, that offered utmost loyalty, they would have made the perfect spies.

The Elders in a clan did one of two things with Underlings. As Lucrezia had done to me, they tormented and taunted, but as some of the other Elders had done, like Vittoria and Vito, they ignored the Underlings in such a way that it seemed almost as if they were pretending they did not exist.

If you were not important enough to be acknowledged, were you important enough for someone to censor his or her words and actions around you?

"The Underlings," I said.

Renata turned to Vasco. "My, my, Vasco. What have you been teaching her?"

Vasco practically beamed with pride. "My lady, I have learned that if you offer Epiphany a grain of sand she will eventually find the ocean."

"Well said, Vasco, but that does not tell me what you have been teaching her."

"I have taught her little in comparison to what she has figured out on her own."

"Again," she said to me, "you surprise me, Epiphany."

I didn't know what to say to that and so I said nothing at all.

"How does she surprise you?" Iliaria asked.

Renata turned to look at her. "You have not known Epiphany these past two hundred years," she said, as if that explained everything.

"No," Iliaria said, "but I too have seen what you must have at one time seen."

"And what is that?" Renata asked in a tone that was almost defensive.

Iliaria looked at me then, her expression most thoughtful.

"She is small and gentle," she said, "and careful not to insult, like a mouse trying to slip quietly through a house full of cats. But you are a clever mouse, aren't you, Epiphany?"

"I don't know."

"Even mice acquire skills to confuse the cat."

She laid her hand over mine, tracing a circle on my skin with the tip of her finger. "And now, those around you are beginning to see your skills. They are beginning to see that you have grown from a scared thing into something more secure." Her fingers trailed up my wrist, brushing across the sigil in my skin. The sigil tingled, itching like mad biting insects. "Perhaps you were never a mouse. Perhaps you are only a kitten learning how to use her very sharp claws." Her voice was a breathy whisper. I shuddered, feeling her touch call to my blood, turning it to fire in my veins.

"The problem with cats," Renata said in a voice gone cold, "is that they are easily distracted."

At Renata's words, I caught the Dracule's wrist. Her pulse thudded between my fingers. The mark at my wrist burned hot.

"I am a vampire," I said. "I am not a cat or a dog or any other manner of pet." I looked at Renata. "Unless I choose to be."

Renata inclined her head in acknowledgement.

The Dracule watched me intently. "And how often do you choose to play the role of the pet? How often, for another's sense of satisfaction, do you choose to appear weaker than you really are? How often do you sheath your claws for the sake of avoiding confrontation?"

I let go of the Dracule's wrist. I did not know how she was able to read me so well, but it was unnerving, as if she read the Braille of my soul. "I do not pretend to appear weak, nor am I weak, Iliaria. I simply am what I am."

"And what are you?" Iliaria asked.

"She is Epiphany," Renata said.

Epiphany. I was not so sure I understood what that meant anymore. When I was a human child I once asked my father why my mother had chosen my name. I never knew her, for she had died not too long after I was born. Most of the memories of my mortal life were shrouded in darkness, which was fairly typical for one who had died and lived.

One memory that remained unaffected was that of my father's reply. I was some seven or eight years of age, eternally curious as most children are.

"To understand why your mother named you Epiphany, you need to know what it means," my father had said. "You know those puzzles you enjoy so much? Well, you know that feeling you get when you find the last piece and put it down and get to see the picture all of the pieces make?"

I had understood that much.

"When you were born your mother saw the picture. You were the piece that made her life whole, dear one."

I had asked what picture my mother had seen.

"Love," my father said. "Your mother saw love."

Iliaria was perceptive, for sure, but she did not know and understand me. Renata knew me, knew my nature. The thought made me turn to look at her.

She did not seek to outwardly understand or explain it. She embraced it. She accepted it.

In her, I saw love. I saw the last piece of the puzzle that made my heart whole.

She held out her hand, her expression gentle, and said softly, "Epiphany."

I went to her, letting her stroke my cheek with the back of her hand. The look she gave me was one of tender affection.

You are my Epiphany, her voice flowed through my mind. *You are my missing piece.*

CHAPTER TWENTY-THREE

T he others waited for sunrise in the sitting room. I lay in Renata's great bed, enfolded within the circle of her arms. We were both silent.

Soon, we would go and try to catch the traitor that had summoned Iliaria. Until then, we would spend what time we had together.

Renata toyed with a strand of my hair, teasing a lock and wrapping it around her finger. I relaxed under her touch, content with the attention.

We had not informed the three Elders that we would be waking them. They had given their aid; we would simply take them up on their offers.

You're awfully quiet, Cuinn whispered through my mind.

You're awfully fond of shattering that.

He made a disgruntled noise.

Cuinn...

The both of you, stop it.

"You heard us?" I said. "I thought you couldn't hear Cuinn?"

"I cannot. I can hear you," Renata whispered against my temple.

"Oh." I felt a gentle smile tug at my lips. "So now it is I that has ruined your quiet moment."

Renata slid her palm down my back, placing her hand flat against the base of my spine. She drew me closer to her.

"Yes," she said, brushing my knee with her thigh. I raised my leg and she nestled her thigh against me.

Sorrow like soft feathers touched my mind.

"What happens when all this is done?" I asked.

"When we execute the traitor?"

"I still have the challenges…"

"Unless you influence a number of Elders to vote in your favor."

I sat up. "You never told me the Elders could vote someone in."

"It is an unusual way, Epiphany. I do not allow them to cast votes lightly, as they more often than not bicker and squabble and try to swing one another's votes in support of their own wills."

"What I am doing does not prove anything to them, you think?"

"It proves everything to me, but if the Elders were to cast a vote you would have to sway them, not I." She searched my gaze. "Is that a path you would like to consider?"

"It is an option," I said, "that's all. Even if I sway enough of them to vote in my favor, there are those that still would not respect me."

"Even if you pass the challenges there will be those that do not respect you. Such is the life of our kind." She leaned forward and I closed my eyes. Her lips followed the line of my jaw to my neck, nibbling lightly and sending desire like wine coursing through my veins.

"What about us?"

Her mouth found my neck and I tilted my head to the side, offering it to her.

"What do you mean?" Her lips framed the words dangerously close to my ear.

"What happens to us after we execute the traitor? What happens to us if I become an Elder? What happens if I fail the challenges?"

She drew back, frowning at me. "Given your position, you are thinking entirely too much."

She leaned in as if to kiss me and I stopped her by placing a hand high up on her chest.

"If you kiss me, I won't be able to think."

"That is the point, cara mia."

"Your sweet Italian nothings will not distract me," I said. "I've been overexposed these past some years and the effect it once had has diminished."

She caught the edge of my earlobe between her teeth, tugging until I made another sound.

"Renata," I said in a breathy voice.

"I want to make love to you."

Italian, English, it didn't matter coming from Renata. I shuddered and tried to focus.

Renata let me push her thigh out from between my legs. I started wiggling toward the edge of the bed.

"Epiphany, what are you doing?"

"Presently trying to remember what I was talking about."

"My sweet Italian nothings will not distract you." She grinned slyly.

I gave her an impatient look. "Before that."

"I do not know," she said, getting to her hands and knees and crawling toward me. "I seem to have forgotten."

I slid from the bed to my feet. Renata crawled across the mattress, following. Her midnight hair cascaded around her like a cloak of dark silk as she moved to the edge of the bed.

"You forget?" I asked. "I don't believe it, my lady."

"Suit yourself." She gave a reserved smile, eyes glistening deviously by candlelight.

I glanced at the plum colored curtain that hid the doorway leading to the other room.

Renata tsked softly, the corners of her mouth curving seductively, predatorily. "We have played this game before, cara mia."

It made me want to run.

It made me want to get caught by her.

It always had.

Renata smiled darkly, as if she knew and was remembering the same thing.

"You forget I can read your thoughts, Epiphany. If you run, I will catch you."

I moved as I had seen Vasco move, as I had seen Renata move. I ran, not for the door, but further into the room. Renata caught me and a sound very much like a squeal came out of my mouth. She snaked her arm around my waist, and with her other hand clutching the arm she had caught, swung me around in a dance-like move to face her.

She laughed, pulling me close.

"I told you I would catch you." Her arms locked like shackles around my torso. I touched those arms, running my hands up the length of them.

"Perhaps I wanted to be caught."

Someone cleared their throat and I turned to see Vasco holding the purple curtain aside. He looked to the opposite side of the room. Dominique stood in the other doorway.

"I heard a noise," Dominique said, looking somewhat foolish as there was obviously no threat. "I beg your pardon, my Queen."

"You are pardoned," she said, looking highly amused.

Dominique stepped out and shut the door behind him.

Vasco grinned at me. "I did not think you were in trouble," he said. "I just could not believe such a noise actually came from you."

I narrowed my eyes at him and he grinned even wider, raising his hands in mock surrender.

"We do not have much longer, my lady."

Renata acknowledged him with a nod. "I am aware, Vasco."

When the door clicked shut and the curtain fell back into place, I looked at her.

"It has been a long time since I have heard you make a sound quite like that," she said.

I knew the expression I gave her was a serious one. "What happens to us, Renata?"

"You are persistent."

"And you are evasive."

"I am not being evasive."

"No, now you are being elusive." I sighed, slightly frustrated.

She took my hand and I followed her back to the bed. Renata pulled me down into the circle of her arms and I tried to relax, but found it hard to because she would not answer my question and I could not understand why she would not answer it.

"I have already decided what I will do whether you succeed to pass the challenges or no."

"And what is that?" I asked, not meeting her eyes, afraid of what she would say.

She cupped the side of my face in her hand and turned me to look at her.

I will declare you Inamorata, she whispered through my mind. *I will inform the Rosso Lussuria that you are my lover and my consort.*

I knew her well enough to know that she had told me telepathically and had been evasive because she was Renata. She was the Queen and once again my lover, but being Renata, she did not want anyone to know until she chose the right moment. She told me because I had asked.

It was a great risk for her and not one I expected her to take.

It is a risk I am willing to take, but you must understand, Piph, that it does not solely put me at risk. It will put you at risk as well.

"I understand," I said. "It is a risk I too am willing to take."

"Good. That pleases me." Her tranquil expression turned quizzically amused as I moved down her body. "Epiphany," she said, imbuing my name with a thread of amusement, "what are you doing?"

My fingers brushed the hem of her dress. I turned my head, hiding behind my hair.

"You were not satisfied earlier."

"What do you propose to do?"

I bowed my head even more, still hiding. It was a demure gesture and a subservient one that I knew would please her.

"I endeavor to please you, my lady."

She touched my chin with cool fingers, turning my face to hers. "If you would please me," she mused, rising and catching the edge of my knee-length tunic in her hands, "take off your clothes."

I undressed quickly, but she did not remove her own attire. Renata merely raised the black velvet of her skirt and allowed me to draw the undergarments hidden beneath the heavy material from her porcelain skin. I situated myself between her legs, kissing her thighs with half-parted lips.

We did not have long until the sun rose. But what time we had left, I would use wisely.

It would not be a quick and passionate outburst. There would be no bloodlust to fan the fire or exquisite force to bend the will. If there had been more time, I would have requested that she disrobe. I would have taken great pleasure in running my lips over every inch of her body. As it was, there was not the time for such languid lovemaking. I kissed her thighs, tracing an invisible path with my lips to the hollow near her groin. The smell of her arousal hung in the air like something sweet and honeyed. With closed eyes, I stroked her cleft with the tip of my tongue, teasing her open.

I kissed her, burying my mouth between her legs. Renata moaned, hips rising to meet my face. I licked her, once, twice, a sensuous glide of tongue, searching and exploring her inner folds.

"Epiphany," she said, voice caught somewhere between a whisper and a moan.

I stopped my prolonged investigation and rose, taking her clit into my mouth with lips and tongue. I sucked her gently, tracing her with lazy circles.

Her hips jerked and she ground herself against my face. I felt her frustration but did not lose my deliberately leisurely pace.

"Epiphany," she said again, and this time there was enough command in her tone that a shiver of excitement prickled down my spine.

She slid from between my lips as I drew back, watching the shudder tremble through her limbs.

"Yes, my lady?"

Her look hardened in a way that promised penalty.

Steady desire like quiet waves murmured through me.

I bowed my head. "As you will."

I took her between my lips, licking and sucking, ceding my mouth to her pleasure without restraint. I drowned in her. The taste of her filled my mouth like honeyed wine, subtle yet no less intoxicating.

She moaned, muscles going rigid as she spent herself against my lips.

I did not resign until I felt her hand stroke down the back of my head. Then I licked her, catching the last of her honey upon my tongue.

"Come here," she said, offering her hand.

Taking it, I let her lead me to her.

She reached between my legs, fingers gliding through the sea she called from my body.

"We don't have time," I breathed the words. Need and want of her made my stomach clench tight.

She slid her fingers inside me, forcing my body to shudder in eternal pleasure. "I say we do."

My hips danced against her coaxing hand.

"Yes," I said.

"Good girl," she said, picking up her rhythm and forcing my hips to move faster to echo the song her fingers played. "Now come for me, Epiphany."

❖

There was a light knock on the door behind the curtained tapestry.

Renata called out, "Enter," and the door opened as Iliaria stepped into the room.

"Vasco has died."

Renata closed her eyes, whispering, "Soon." When she opened them she looked at me. "Go and wake him, Epiphany."

I did not feel any different. In fact, I had not even known the sun had risen, which is something I should have sensed like a great weight pressing against my mind and skin.

The sun had risen and Vasco had died. Soon, Renata would die as the sun made its ascent, spreading its golden fingers out over the land and the world above.

I wondered if the ring gave the wearer the capability of walking in sunlight, but it was not the time for those kinds of questions.

"I will stay here until I can use the sword to wake you, then I will wake Vasco." I turned to Iliaria. "Will you stay with him until I am done here?"

"Yes," she said, nodding, "I will stay and keep watch."

"Did Dominique and Dante make it to the room before the sun rose?" Renata asked.

If Dominique had gone to the sitting room he must've taken the long way to get there, as he had not come through the room. The long way involved navigating a labyrinth of hallways to get to the back hallway and secret corridor.

"They did," she said.

This time, it was Renata who nodded.

The Dracule left, leaving the purple tapestry swinging.

"You waste time, Epiphany."

"Not to me, I don't," I said.

She looked at me through a slit of her dark lashes. "You are being stubborn."

"About this?" I asked. "Yes, but only because I want to make sure you are safe."

"Epifania," she said and I felt her light touch on my arm and turned to her.

Renata's chest rose as she drew a sharp breath, and when her eyes closed I knew that dawn's curse had taken her.

I stood, picking up the fox blade and pressing the tip of my finger against it until a drop of blood welled at the tip. I crawled over Renata's still form and used my other hand to pry her jaw open. I slipped my finger between her teeth and held my other hand above her mouth, squeezing to encourage the blood to flow before the cut healed.

The drop fell, hitting the back of her mouth. The sword in my hand felt warm.

I slid from the bed and stood.

Renata gasped, turning to look at me. Her eyes were swallowed by the black night skies of her pupils. "Go. Wake Vasco now."

I went and as I entered the sitting room Iliaria stood from the small couch. Vasco lay across the other. I went wide around Dante and Dominique, who were both sprawled on the floor. As I had with Renata, I woke Vasco, feeling the pommel of the sword grow warm like a small flame between my hands.

Renata had entered the room when I was waking Vasco and had woken Dominique. She closed her eyes where she knelt above Dante, tracing the line above his brows with her fingers. I felt her power unfurl like a cool wind, tickling my arms and tangling in strands of my hair. Dante jerked upright, waking violently. She put a hand on his shoulder and her energy changed, from a haunting wind to the still peace of a reflective pool.

Dominique reached behind his back, checking his weapons. Dante opened his coat and withdrew two large blades that were nearly longer than my forearms.

I took the hand Vasco offered and stood, going to the doorway.

Dominique moved past us, checking the way as the guards were supposed to do. He gazed back into the bedroom and said, "It's clear."

Renata inclined her head and we went, walking silently through the halls and to the Elders' Quarters to wake the others.

CHAPTER TWENTY-FOUR

Nirena's pale violet eyes flew open and a look of startled curiosity swam to the surface.

"What passes?" she asked, taking in Vasco and Renata standing at the side of her bed.

"You offered your aid, Nirena," Renata said.

"We're holding you to that offer," I said, sitting back on my heels where I knelt beside her.

She sat up slowly.

"What would you have of me?"

Renata turned to me and said, "Go with Iliaria and wake Vittoria and Vito. I will be there in a moment."

I nodded.

"Dante," she said, "take Epiphany to their quarters."

"Yes, my lady."

I followed him to a door next to Vasco's room. Dante used a different key on the ring at his waist to open the door and let me in. Iliaria was close behind as I approached the large canopy. Drawing aside the white gauzy material, I crawled into the bed, setting the tip of my finger against the sword. Iliaria opened Vittoria's mouth for me.

When the blood dripped past her lips, she woke, catching my wrist and wrenching my arm painfully behind my back.

Iliaria was a blur of onyx hair. She grabbed a handful of Vittoria's dark locks and jerked her head back at an awkward angle, as if she would snap her neck.

In a blink, Vittoria had gone for my throat. If Iliaria had not been there to stop her she probably would've ripped it out. I would have healed, but that didn't take away the pain factor or having to feed again to regain the blood I'd have lost.

The blackness of Vittoria's pupils fluctuated. I should have taken better care waking her, for she and her brother were both trained in the art of battle.

"Epiphany?" she asked in a voice that was at once fierce and uncertain. "What are you doing?" I didn't have to sense her accusation and distrust. It was a tangible thing.

"I told her to wake you," Renata said, entering the room.

"We're being recruited," Nirena said. "Get up. Don your armor. I'll explain while they wake your brother."

Vittoria nodded toward a corner of the room that was veiled off by a sea of black hanging material.

"Vito is in his coffin."

I hadn't understood until then that the two shared a room. And from what I knew, there were very few vampires within the Rosso Lussuria that slept in coffins. She drew back the veils of netted material and approached the coffin that was on a slightly raised dais. She hefted the oblong wooden lid. His hands were clasped loosely over his stomach.

"I'll need to be here when you wake him."

"That is fine," I said. "You can hold his mouth open."

She went to the head of the coffin, out of my way but close enough to participate and interfere if need be. She opened Vito's mouth with delicate tapered fingers.

I raised the sword and reopened the wound on my stained finger.

Vito tried to bolt upright and Vittoria placed her hands on his shoulders keeping him from reaching me, even though I'd thought to step back as soon as the blood fell.

"My brother," she said. "My brother, do you hear me?"

The bloodlust and panic receded as recognition began to fill him. He looked at me and there was a flicker of fear, a fear that I had betrayed him. Vito's attention slid from me to that of the Queen and the fear ebbed back into the ocean from whence it had sprung.

"I do not understand," he said. "The sun is high. Why?"

"The Queen calls us, my brother," Vittoria said.

He turned the question to Renata.

"Why, my Queen?"

"You said I had your aid, Vito…unless you wish to revoke your word?"

"I do not," Vito said, looking a little more stubborn.

When Vittoria said nothing, Nirena stepped forward and started to explain in a quiet voice what was going on.

I went to Iliaria and said, "Thank you."

She gracefully inclined her head.

"Do you remember where you were summoned?" I asked.

"Yes."

"Will you take us there?"

"Returning to the same place in which I was summoned may not be the safest option, Epiphany, and the vampire that summoned me will more than likely have changed location to avoid being found."

It made sense.

"Then how will we know when another Dracule has been summoned?"

"I will know," she said.

I sat on the edge of the bed.

I will also know, Cuinn said in a soft tone.

I shook my head. "But there is no guarantee the vampire who summoned you will try again."

"He will," Iliaria said. "He'll keep trying until he succeeds."

And so, we waited.

Vasco sat next to me. "Patience, sorella."

The only response I gave was a slight nod.

Renata pulled a chair from a dressing table into the center of the room and sat.

I felt someone's eyes on me and turned to find Vittoria staring.

"So it is true?" she asked. "The Queen and the Dracule are your lovers?"

I met Iliaria's placid look. "That is for the Queen to say."

"She is my Inamorata, Vittoria."

"Will you claim as such before the entire clan?" she asked, sounding more curious than rude.

"I will make a declaration when the time comes." From Renata, that was answer enough.

"What of you, Dracule?" Nirena asked. "Do you claim love of this one?"

Iliaria fixed Nirena with her unwavering stare.

"She is my dragă."

"I see," Nirena said.

"Dragă?" I asked.

Iliaria's lips parted as if she was about to say something, but she closed her mouth and shook her head, sending the long onyx tresses dancing in a serpentine manner about her body. "I do not know how to explain it in a way that you will fathom."

"Dragă is the Dracule's way of saying that you are someone she cares about," Nirena said.

Vasco nodded his agreement beside me. "It is what they call those they mark but are not in love with."

Vittoria looked like she was going to add to the conversation when Iliaria distracted us all by turning her face toward the door. Her nostrils flared slightly.

Cuinn's voice rang like a clear whistle inside my skull. *Time to go!*

"It is here," Iliaria said.

"Can you track it?" Vasco asked.

Iliaria's only response was a predatory smile. She settled the leathery wings around her body like a cloak and went for the door. As if someone had clapped their hands, all of us that were not standing spilled to our feet.

❖

"Anatharic," Iliaria said. "Halt!"

The Dracule turned at the sound of Iliaria's voice, its long bat-like ears swiveled in our direction where we stood in the great hall just outside the throne room. I kept the fox blade's point down, holding it against the line of my thigh.

Like Iliaria's, the Great Sire's eyes were dark and bottomless in its Draculian form. The coal black of its fur was sprinkled with dustings of smoke and ash.

"Iliaria?"

"Before you commit yourself to a wrongly impulsive decision, let me speak with you. Where is the vampire who summoned you?"

He did not answer.

Iliaria moved toward him. The tip of her spaded tail twitched in irritation.

"Anatharic, you know me. Tell me where he is."

"Why ssshould I?" He looked at me, for I stood closest to Iliaria. Vasco and Nirena stood next to me. Vittoria and Vito stood on either side of Renata, while Dante and Dominique had taken up the rear of our little execution party. "They would kill usss if they could."

"Lies," Iliaria hissed. "Epiphany, show him."

"Ssshow me what?" Anatharic's ears flattened in a smooth flap to his skull.

I raised the sleeve of my tunic, baring her sigil.

"Does it look like we're here to kill you?" she asked.

I think he frowned, but it was not exactly easy to read the Dracule's expressions in such an animalistic face. "No. I do not undersssstand."

"Your summoner," she said, "he asked you to kill for him, did he not?"

"Yesss."

"He told you the vampires hate you. That they would eventually grow in numbers and power and overthrow our kind. How ungrateful they are for the gift of immortality that descends from us?"

"Yesss," he said.

"He is playing you, Anatharic. The Rosso Lussuria and their Queen stand before you and none lift hand or weapon. I ask again, where is your summoner?"

"Why would the vampire play me?"

"The vampire who summoned you plays you in a gambit for my throne." Renata, once again, respectfully lowered her gaze instead of looking him in the eye.

Anatharic moved forward and tension rippled between Iliaria's winged shoulders.

I knew without a doubt that if she had to fight him, she would. She would not hesitate. I moved forward, reaching out and touching the wing folded around her body. I laid my hand flat against that wing. I did not tell him of the alliance between us. I showed with my actions that I stood with her.

"You are either with us or against us, Great Sire. I would hope that you stand with us, for it is true, you are being used as a pawn in a gambit for my Queen's throne."

He knew we were not lying. I could taste it. He knew and that knowledge made him angry. He did not like to think of himself as a pawn.

He turned toward the two great doors that led to the throne room.

"There."

He stated his alliance. He chose a side for which to play. As a group, we stepped through the door he indicated.

A hooded figure knelt in the middle of the throne room in a cloak of white velvet that pooled around him like a circle of snow. The figure kept his head down so that I could not see his face, but as soon as we entered the throne room I knew he had been waiting for us. It was too dramatic and posed a position to be otherwise.

A familiar unstrung laugh trickled throughout the room, and the hair at the back of my neck prickled.

The figure raised his head, dramatically tossing back the hood of the cloak with a pale hand.

No male, was she. Her crimson hair spilled like bloody strokes against the white cloak. A measure of triumph lit her bright green eyes.

"Lucrezia," Renata said. A wave of anger surged from her like an ocean wave crashing violently against a rocky shore.

She stepped forward and a flash of silver spiraled in the torchlight.

"No!" The word burst from my lips.

I heard the sound of metal hitting flesh and bone.

The two Dracule moved like shadows around me.

Iliaria's wings clapped open like a slap of thunder. The sound reverberated off the stone walls. Another heavy clap echoed hers and I knew that Anatharic had also taken a defensive stance.

Iliaria pulled me in against her body, using her wings as a shield.

A blow sent the front of her body slamming against the back of mine, knocking us forward. I had a moment to fear for her safety when something metallic clattered on the stone floor.

"Renata," I whispered, struggling to free myself of Iliara's grip.

Iliaria moved enough that I was able to see Anatharic using his massive form to shield Vasco's body as much as she shielded mine. Vasco struggled with Anatharic, trying to get away, trying to get to Renata as I was.

As if in a nightmare, the sounds of fighting poured over my ears, steel against steel, fist against fist, the meaty sound of a punch, the sound of a blade cutting and singing through the air, the spattering of blood like rain, the sound of daggers whirring like tiny fans.

Vasco turned in Anatharic's grip, breaking the Dracule's hold. He was suddenly on his feet and moving toward the sounds of fighting.

I wrapped my fingers tightly around the pommel of the fox blade.

"Iliaria," I whispered, "let me go."

"Not yet."

There were footsteps behind her. I opened my mouth to warn her when her arms tightened around me. Iliaria's body tensed and jerked, something thick hit flesh. A man screamed like a wounded animal. A wet sucking sound came from behind before her tail swung forward, hitting the stone floor like a discarded whip. Crimson drops fell from the barbed point of her tail.

"Idiot," she mumbled. I felt her smile against my hair and fought to stifle the shudder that wriggled down my spine. If I had ever feared any of the Elders, I had feared them not knowing the Great Sires.

"Iliaria," I tried again. "Let me stand, please."

Someone was hurt. The dagger had hit someone.

I prayed to the Divine it wasn't Renata.

"Stop!" Lucrezia's voice carried over the fighting, above the ringing din of steel. "Fools stop! The Queen is dead!"

Gradually, the sounds of fighting began to fade, replaced by a great silence.

I wasn't sure I'd heard Lucrezia's words correctly. Renata couldn't be dead...

Iliaria moved so that I could see.

Renata's moonlit form lay pale and motionless on the stone floor, bright pool of crimson blossoming out around her body.

The rage burned like something scalding in my veins. I could taste metal and copper on my tongue. I had never known madness, nor thought that I would ever taste it, but in that moment when I caught sight of Lucrezia standing near the dais, standing straight and tall as if she were a Queen amidst the chaos, I knew something akin to it.

I screamed, lunging without thinking.

Iliaria caught me by the shoulders and jerked me back into the safety of her arms. I screamed again, angry and wild, throwing my elbows back into her body in struggle to get free.

Hearing my rage howling her name, Lucrezia turned to face me with a smile.

She moved, stepping close to Renata's still form.

"Well," she said, smiling, "not much of a Queen, after all. I told you to be wary, Epiphany." She pouted. "Now do you see what you have done?"

I drew my lips back and hissed.

I'd kill her. If Iliaria let me go, I was going to claw the skin of her face off with my bare hands.

A blur of silver moved too fast for me to follow.

"I've been dead a lot longer than you, Lucrezia."

Lucrezia went to her knees, eyes wide with pain. Her hands clutched at the dagger Renata had buried hilt-deep in her ribcage. Blood stained her white cloak, pouring down the front of her body.

I saw it, saw Lucrezia try to catch Renata's mouth with hers and knew she sought to use her power. Before I could warn Renata, Renata caught her throat, holding her back with sheer strength. I'd seen Renata move like some liquid phantom in the night, but I'd never seen her pit her strength against another. The hand holding the dagger disappeared into the cavity of Lucrezia's chest.

Lucrezia had sought Renata's mouth, but Renata sought her heart. A bit poetic, that.

Lucrezia glared at Renata. I did not understand why, aside from trying to kiss Renata, she did not fight back. As soon as I thought it, I felt it, the crashing wave of Renata's power.

Lucrezia was fighting back, but it was a useless battle. I felt Renata's power and trembled, the intensity of it paralyzing, but she did not direct her power at me. All of that power was focused on the traitor in front of her.

She may not have been Lucrezia's Siren, but Lucrezia was bound to her and the Rosso Lussuria. Renata was her Queen in more than name.

Lucrezia's eyes blazed like uranium glass. I did not have to see Renata's to know that hers were alight with the radiance of a darkened sky and moonlit waters.

Renata gave one last push, her arm nearly elbow-deep in Lucrezia's chest, and yanked.

Lucrezia fell to her knees and before she could scream, Renata caught her head in her hands.

I turned, burying my face against Iliaria's body, unable to watch.

"Baldavino," Renata said darkly. "So glad you could join us. Is this a friend of yours?"

Something heavy hit the floor and rolled.

A man's ragged scream tore through the throne room.

And then all hell broke loose.

I caught a glimpse of Vito and Vittoria moving back to back.

Epiphany! Cuinn yelled. The fox blade burst into white light and I was suddenly on my feet, moving in front of Renata with the sword held in a two-handed grip.

Baldavino's golden hair like a lion's mane was spattered with blood.

"Baldavino," I said, warning.

"Epiphany," he practically growled. "Get out of my way."

"No."

"Then you will die for her. You think you are the only one capable of wielding a death blade?"

In my mind, I saw Cuinn give a vicious little snap.

The short sword in Baldavino's hands began to glow, burning soft gold.

"I will tell you one more time, Underling. Get out of my way."

"No."

"So be it!"

Cuinn gave a little bark of laughter. *Nothing but an overgrown chicken—*

His words were interrupted as Baldavino chose to take a two-handed swing at my head. The fox and eagle blade met in a clash of white and golden sparks. The impact sang up my arms and to my shoulders.

Baldavino gritted his teeth, glaring at me over our crossed swords. Before he could shove me away, I set my feet and pushed first. Distantly, in some part of myself, I was aware of the orange glow standing beside me, as if I could see Cuinn's fox form in my peripheral vision.

The piercing cry of an eagle sliced through the room. Golden light hit orange and our fight broke out in earnest.

As Gaspare had done, Baldavino took the offensive. He put me on the defensive, making me parry, sidestep, and use the sword to sweep his blows away from my midsection. I used Vasco's memory of footwork along with Cuinn's powers to guide my hands. The two skills together made us fairly well-matched. But I was not like Baldavino or Gaspare, who anxiously sought an opening, who rashly went on the offensive and tried to beat his opponent down with the might of his weapon and ego.

A deep calm settled over my mind and body.

Your greatest weapon is your mind, Renata's honeyed voice whispered, calm and steady, like an anchor securing my body against thrashing waves. She was my Siren and my lover. I drew on the calm she offered. I let my own abilities absorb her quiet reserve, her steady and unflinching calculations.

Baldavino went for my leg. I leapt as the sword sang inches in front of me, barely missing.

He gave a growl of frustration and his pupils shrank to tiny points, swallowed by the color of dark evergreen.

His power was like something scratchy and rough against my skin as he focused it on me.

Which is why he never saw Vasco coming. Baldavino raised his sword and was about to rush me when his mouth opened but no sound came out. Baldavino gaped like a fish.

The point of Vasco's blade protruded from his tunic, skewering him.

Vasco grabbed him by the neck and leaned in close enough to whisper, "I haven't killed you yet, Baldavino, but if you don't drop your blade, I will."

The sword slipped from Baldavino's hand and clattered to the ground.

I moved forward, kicking the eagle blade, sending it spinning away from us.

Renata approached, flanked by Iliaria and Anatharic. Anatharic was taller than Renata, but Iliaria, in her more human form was near the same height, perhaps an inch shorter. Renata met my gaze and reached out to touch my hair. I resisted the urge to throw myself at her, to wrap my arms around her and cling to her as if she were the last solid thing in the world. Instead, I focused on Baldavino.

"Baldavino," she said, giving him a look that was as cold as an arctic winter. "You?"

He gave a sly smile that I certainly would've never given were the situation reversed. "Yes," he said. "Are you surprised, Renata?"

She did not answer his question. "Why?"

He coughed, sending blood and spittle down his chin. "You had something I wanted."

"What would that be, Baldavino, the throne?"

"What else would it be?"

"And what about Lucrezia?" she asked. "How did you sway her from her oath to me?"

"With not much difficulty," he said. "I promised her a crown and vampires to rule. I promised her power." For some reason, he looked at me briefly before turning back to the Queen. "I would not have given it to her. It would have been mine in the end."

"If you could have," I said. "I am certain Lucrezia was thinking to do the same to you, Baldavino. She would not have hesitated to kill you, given the chance."

He smiled and there was rage in it. "I know."

"And yet," I said, "you loved her. You loved her enough to try and avenge her death."

He turned away from me then. Renata laughed and said, "Iliaria, ask your questions."

Iliaria slipped between Renata and me to kneel in front of Baldavino. He tried to move back and Vasco twisted the blade, forcing a cry of pain from his lips.

"Who is the Dracule you are working with?"

When Baldavino did not answer, Vittoria and Vito stepped up. They were both carrying long swords anointed with blood. Vittoria grabbed one of Baldavino's arms and Vito grabbed the other. They pushed the sleeves of his tunic up, exposing his wrists.

Iliaria grabbed two handfuls of his shirt and ripped the tunic open wide, exposing his pale and muscled chest. Blood was smeared across his skin.

There, on the clean skin of his pectoral muscle, was a mark of flowing black lines.

"Damokles," she said.

Anatharic took a step forward, casting his glance at the sigil. I thought he was going to say something, when a serpentine hiss rode the currents of air, echoing throughout the throne room.

"Traitoresss ssspawn."

Iliaria whipped around, searching for the body that went with the voice. I followed the line of her sight to the double doors that spilled into the greater hallway. Beneath the archway stood a tall figure, cloaked in a pair of leathery wings.

Iliaria's spaded tail thumped against the floor behind me, an inhuman growl rumbling in her chest. When she spoke, her words were clear and carrying despite the growl. "I should have guessed it was you, murderer of your own sister."

The figure's ears swiveled, tail twitching. The tension in the air was thick enough it felt as if I could reach out and touch it. I sensed more than saw Anatharic lower himself to his clawed-hands and move up beside me like some great guardian beast from the depths of Hades.

"Ssshe wasss a traitor like you and traitorsss mussst die."

Anatharic's long ears flattened smoothly against his skull, a rumbling growl pouring from his Draculian lips.

Iliaria stood perfectly still, and even her tail slowed its fidgeting motion. I felt it as she put a steady hand over her emotions, going to some cold and dark place inside herself.

Baldavino's voice was thin, holding a thread of pleading excitement and hope. "Master!" he said, and the figure ignored him. "Master, please!"

Renata brought the back of her hand down across Baldavino's face. Blood flew in an arc from his mouth.

"Hold your tongue, dead man. The Great Sire will not save you from your fate."

"They are all dead!" Damokles' face contorted with a ferocious hiss.

"I think not." Iliaria's voice was an angry growl, and then she was moving in a black blur, as if darkness traveled faster than light.

A high-pitched screech, the sound of blade slicing flesh, a cloud of black smoke...

Iliaria stood beneath the archway, holding weapons in both hands. One of the crescent shaped blades dripped with blood.

"Damn you, Damokles! You coward!"

Anatharic was crawling on all fours toward her, long tail held slightly above the stone floor. "Figuresss," he grumbled. "He did murder hisss sssissster while ssshe sssslept."

Her eyes met mine, briefly. She growled again, not at me, simply at her own frustration. Her wings snapped open and she turned, ducking down as if in a dance.

There was a cloud of smoke with flashes of lightning in it and she was gone. Anatharic followed, but before he too vanished, he said to me, "We will find him." Then he was gone, swallowed by the smoke of his own power.

"Epiphany," Renata said, calling me back to myself. "We have a certain matter to which we must attend." She lowered her face to Baldavino.

CHAPTER TWENTY-FIVE

Iliaria and Anatharic returned some hours later to inform us that they had not found Damokles. They would continue to search, albeit quietly. At my insistence, Iliaria agreed to be cautious and discreet.

Before Baldavino had been executed, we learned that they had indeed been waiting for us. Baldavino had not only convinced Lucrezia to join him in his treachery, but some of the Underlings as well. The Underlings that had managed to survive the battle were executed at the hands of Vittoria, Vito, and Nirena.

When Lucrezia had seen Iliaria's sigil on my wrist she had warned Baldavino. They and their Underlings meant to ambush us. But they had not succeeded in killing Renata. Damokles, as Renata had predicted, was not willing to spare Baldavino of his fate, whose ambition made him an easily used pawn.

When we finished interrogating him, Renata moved up behind me, her hand trailing down my arm. She folded her hand over mine where it gripped the fox blade. As if she had given him orders, Vasco moved, withdrawing his blade.

I followed the line of Renata's body against mine and with her hand wrapped around mine, guiding the sword, we buried the blade in Baldavino's heart.

I must say, it was much quicker and a great deal less messy than Lucrezia's execution had been, as the fox blade worked on intent and our intention to kill was most effective. But such an execution had brought me to my own personal realization: I did not enjoy killing.

The eagle blade was destroyed. Vasco had pried the amber stone out with his bare hands and said, "He craved power and wanted more than this."

"Vasco?" I asked. "Did the sword or the spirit in the sword shape Baldavino's ambitions?"

He seemed thoughtful. In the end, he shrugged and said, "I do not know, colombina." He smiled. "I do not think we have to worry about your little fox corrupting you, if that is what you are asking."

Cuinn had chosen that moment to offer his opinion on the matter. *Methinks your Queen does enough corrupting for the both of us.* There was a playful lilt to his tone that implied he was teasing, but still, it did not allay my fears. I was not so certain what repercussions the bond between my little fox and I would have, if any. Had Baldavino slowly taken on personality traits of the eagle spirit? Were eagles ambitious?

At court that night, Renata asked the nobles to cast a vote as to whether I was to become an Elder or not, without me going through any further challenges. I do not think any of us really trusted my safety during the trials. And so, the Elders had voted. Those that had voted in my favor had been Vasco, Vittoria and her brother Vito, Nirena, and Sognare. Yet, the vote that had surprised me the most had been Severiano. Severiano, my captor, who had ridden at the head of the Cacciatori and taken me from my human world so long ago.

Alessandra, Lorenzo, Rosabella, and Gaspare had unsurprisingly voted against me.

Of course, I paid careful attention to my empathy to discern why. The wound in Gaspare's pride was far too big. Rosabella discriminated against me for the simple fact that I had taken a Draculian lover. Lorenzo merely did not like me, for whatever reason, and Alessandra strangely seemed to fear me.

I became the eleventh Elder within the Rosso Lussuria. Renata made the Elders cast a vote by a show of hands. Since she had put them on the spot, she gave them no time to argue or quibble or scheme about the matter. After it was decided and declared, she offered me her hand and announced before the Rosso Lussuria, the Underlings, and the Donatore that I was her Inamorata, her consort, her beloved.

To harm me was a death sentence.

It was quite a change from being the Queen's beloved pet and a quiet Underling.

Elder and Inamorata, I wore the title as proudly as the mark upon my wrist. At long last, I was finally embracing my strengths as well as my weaknesses. I had made Vasco proud, so very proud. I saw it in his eyes every time he looked at me, the brother of my heart.

I gave the Stone of Shadows back to Iliaria for safekeeping. The sword never left my side and Cuinn never left my head, but as I had begun to embrace both my strengths and weaknesses, so Cuinn was learning to embrace that little thing called silence. Well, occasionally, when it suited him.

We talked, of course. I enjoyed getting to know the honorable, clever, and feisty little fox. I learned that he had once been one of the Fatas, a type of fairy creature or nature spirit. He had fallen in love with a druid's son and the druid had grown angry with him, for he feared losing his only son to Cuinn. I had not learned how he had the ability to wake me.

Cuinn had been trapped and bound to the sword by the earth, by the air, by the fire, and by the sea, a powerful and unbreakable spell.

When I had asked if there was any way I could set him free, he had told me, *I am free, Epiphany, though I do not live in your world. I am free, and for the first time in a thousand years, I am happy.*

Oddly, for the first time in what seemed a thousand years, I too, was happy.

Iliaria visited often, though the nights were dedicated to Renata. When Iliaria wished to see me, she appeared with the Stone of Shadows and consulted with Renata out of courtesy and respect.

I was growing fond of my Draculian lover, very fond. It was not yet love, but something akin to it. There were nights when Renata shared me, reveling in my reaction to being trapped, aching and trembling between the two of them. Truth be told, she certainly was not the only one reveling.

Tonight was Renata's night and as such, I knelt in the middle of her room while she set about tying a sash over my eyes. The long tails of the sash trailed down my back, mingling with the fall of my hair. I heard her go to the corner of the room and open the armoire.

The currents of air shifted. Her footsteps sounded again, light and soft. I heard her place a chair not too far from where I knelt.

"Epiphany," she said, her voice sweet and cruel, promising tender pain and excruciating pleasure. "There are two items on the floor in front of you. Choose one."

I knew what she wanted.

In some part of me, I had always known.

I folded my hands behind my back and leaned forward. My cheek brushed an item that was long and thin. I caressed the item, turning my face and feeling the wood of the rattan cane glide between my half-parted lips.

I moved to the next item. The leather was as smooth as suede against my cheek. I followed the line of rich cowhide tassels. I knew by the feel of the leather against my cheek that it was a versatile flogger, capable of producing either a sharp, stinging slap or a light, erotic tickle. It all depended on how Renata chose to wield it.

I trailed my face to the base and opened my mouth, catching it between my teeth. Only then, only when I had selected the flogger, did I place my hands on the floor and crawl to her.

The edge of her skirts brushed the tops of my hands and I raised, letting the flogger fall from my lips into her lap.

She laughed and I knew she had retrieved it. "Ti amo," she said, caressing my face. "Ti amo, cara mia."

Those fingers tickled down my cheek, sweeping lower to the line of my throat.

There are those Elders that thought less of me because I had been the Queen's beloved pet, because they believed that love and submission were for the weak of heart and faint of will. On the contrary, I had learned that to love, one must carry a reservoir of great strength. Their judgments and frowns did not trouble me overmuch. Behind the doors to Renata's bedchambers, she allowed me to be all that I am and more.

She accepted the whole of my being without question, without doubt, and most importantly, without judgment. She did not ask that I restrain any aspect of myself, both the strong and the weak.

I was simply her Epiphany.

About the Author

Winter Pennington is an author, poet, artist, and closeted musician. She is an avid practitioner of nature-based spirituality and enjoys spending her spare time studying mythology from around the world. The Celtic path is very close to her heart. She has an uncanny fascination with swords and daggers, and a fondness for feeding loud and obnoxious corvids. In the shadow of her writing, she has experience working with a plethora of animals as a pet care specialist and veterinary assistant.

Winter currently resides in Oklahoma with her partner and their ever-growing family of furry kids, also known as, The Felines Extraordinaire.

Books Available from Bold Strokes Books

Darkness Embraced by Winter Pennington. Surrounded by harsh vampire politics and secret ambitions, Epiphany learns that an old enemy is plotting treason against the woman she once loved, and to save all she holds dear, she must embrace and form an alliance with the dark. (978-1-60282-221-4)

78 Keys by Kristin Marra. When the cosmic powers choose Devorah Rosten to be their next gladiator, she must use her unique skills to try to save her lover, herself, and even humankind. (978-1-60282-222-1)

Playing Passion's Game by Lesley Davis. Trent Williams's only passion in life is gaming until Juliet Sullivan makes her realize that love can be a whole different game to play. (978-1-60282-223-8)

Retirement Plan by Martha Miller. A modern morality tale of justice, retribution, and women who refuse to be politely invisible. (978-1-60282-224-5)

Who Dat Whodunnit by Greg Herren. Popular New Orleans detective Scotty Bradley investigates the murder of a dethroned beauty queen to clear the name of his pro football playing cousin. (978-1-60282-225-2)

The Company He Keeps: Victorian Gentlemen's Erotica by Dale Chase. A riotously erotic collection of stories set in the sexually repressed and therefore sexually rampant Victorian era. (978-1-60282-226-9)

Cursebusters! by Julie Smith. Teen psychic Reeno and her gay best friend must time travel to an ancient Mayan city to break an ancient curse and save Reeno's sister. (978-1-60282-559-8)

Blood Hunt by L.L. Raand. In the second Midnight Hunters Novel, Detective Jody Gates, heir to a powerful Vampire clan, forges an uneasy alliance with Sylvan, the wolf Were Alpha, to battle a shadow army of humans and rogue Weres, while fighting her growing hunger for a human reporter, Becca Land. (978-1-60282-505-5)

Loving Liz by Bobbi Marolt. When theater actor Marty Jamison turns diva and Liz Chandler walks out on her, Marty must confront a cheating lover from the past to understand why life is crumbling around her. (978-1-60282-210-8)

Kiss the Rain by Larkin Rose. How will successful fashion designer Eve Harris react when she discovers the new woman in her life, Jodi, and her secret fantasy phone date, Lexi, are one and the same? (978-1-60282-211-5)

Sarah, Son of God by Justine Saracen. In a story within a story within a story, a transgendered beauty takes us through Stonewall-rioting New York, Venice under the Inquisition, and Nero's Rome. (978-1-60282-212-2)

Sleeping Angel by Greg Herren. Eric Matthews survives a terrible car accident only to find out everyone in town thinks he's a murderer—and he has to clear his name even though he has no memories of what happened. (978-1-60282-214-6)

Dying to Live by Kim Baldwin & Xenia Alexiou. British socialite Zoe Anderson-Howe's pampered life is abruptly shattered when she's taken hostage by FARC guerrillas while on a business trip to Bogota and Elite Operative Fetch must rescue her to complete her own harrowing mission. (978-1-60282-200-9)

Indigo Moon by Gill McKnight. Hope Glassy and Godfrey Meyers are on a mercy mission to save their friend Isabelle after she is attacked by a rogue werewolf, but does Isabelle want to be saved from the sexy wolf who claimed her as a mate? (978-1-60282-201-6)

Parties in Congress by Colette Moody. Bijal Rao, Indian-American moderate Independent, gets the break of her career when she's hired to work on the congressional campaign of Janet Denton—until she meets the remarkably attractive and charismatic opponent, Colleen O'Bannon. (978-1-60282-202-3)

Black Fire: Gay African-American Erotica edited by Shane Allison. Best-selling African-American gay erotic authors create the stories of sex and desire modern readers crave. (978-1-60282-206-1)

The Collectors by Leslie Gowan. Laura owns what might be the world's most extensive collection of BDSM lesbian erotica, but that's as close as she's gotten to the world of her fantasies. Until, that is, her friend Adele introduces her to Adele's mistress Jeanne—art collector, heiress, and experienced dominant. With Jeanne's first command, Laura's life changes forever. (978-1-60282-208-5)

Breathless edited by Radclyffe and Stacia Seaman. Bold Strokes Books romance authors give readers a glimpse into the lives of favorite couples celebrating special moments "after the honeymoon ends." Enjoy a new look at lesbians in love or revisit favorite characters from some of BSB's best-selling romances. (978-1-60282-207-8)

Breaker's Passion by Julie Cannon. Leaving a trail of broken hearts scattered across the Hawaiian Islands, surf instructor Colby Taylor is running full speed away from her selfish actions years earlier until she collides with Elizabeth Collins, a stuffy, judgmental college professor who changes everything. (978-1-60282-196-5)

Justifiable Risk by V.K. Powell. Work is the only thing that interests homicide detective Greer Ellis until internationally renowned journalist Eva Saldana comes to town looking for answers in her brother's death—then attraction threatens to override duty. (978-1-60282-197-2)

Nothing But the Truth by Carsen Taite. Sparks fly when two top-notch attorneys battle each other in the high-risk arena of the courtroom, but when a strange turn of events turns one of them from advocate to witness, prosecutor Ryan Foster and defense attorney Brett Logan join forces in their search for the truth. (978-1-60282-198-9)

Maye's Request by Clifford Henderson. When Brianna Bell promises her ailing mother she'll heal the rift between her "other two" parents, she discovers how little she knows about those closest to her and the impact family has on the fabric of our lives. (978-1-60282-199-6)